I0669373

BLOOD PACT

COURTNEY MAGUIRE

CITY OWL
PRESS

This book is a work of fiction. Names, characters, places, and incidents either are products of the author's imagination or are used fictitiously. Any resemblance to actual events or locales or persons, living or dead, is entirely coincidental and not intended by the author.

BLOOD PACT
Youkai Bloodlines, Book 2

CITY OWL PRESS
www.cityowlpress.com

Cover Design by Mibl Art. All stock photos licensed appropriately.

Edited by Heather McCorkle.

For information on subsidiary rights, please contact the publisher at info@cityowlpress.com.

Print Edition ISBN: 978-1-64898-083-1

Digital Edition ISBN: 978-1-64898-084-8

Printed in the United States of America

For all the monsters just trying to be good.

ONE

River of Flowers

THIS WAS TRUE SUFFERING.

I rolled my shoulders and struggled to maintain my seiza sitting posture. My thighs ached, and my feet had long gone numb to the scrape of the tatami beneath them. Oil lamps burned in every corner, making the air sharp and bright as the day. Yamaguchi Tojirou, a regular guest at the okiya, lounged beside me on a cushion. He leaned back on one arm, flushed with drink, long, spiderlike legs splayed. I stifled a groan as he scratched himself and let out a wet belch.

What did I do to deserve this?

Our okiya was one of the finest in Shimabara, our oiran one of the most beautiful and respected courtesans in all of Kyoto. Rich merchants, samurai, and even the occasional daimyo were happy to spend their money here, in no small part due to the etiquette both practiced and expected by our staff. A visit to the okiya was akin to a visit to a noble house. Yamaguchi, on the other hand, treated us like a brothel. Under normal circumstances, a man like him wouldn't get past the front gate.

Unless, of course, his name was Yamaguchi.

The smell of natto and cheap whiskey made my eyes burn, and I pressed a discreet finger against the corner of my eye. Yamaguchi laughed a deep, hoarse laugh, head thrown back and mouth open wide, at a pair of taikomochi acting out a raucous sexual pantomime, their lower halves hidden behind a paper screen. An extravagantly dressed lord conducting an illicit affair with a palace mistress or something like that. I'd long lost track.

I wondered if the taikomochi felt as I did. Bored, lost, perhaps even a bit degraded. They once served real nobility as both attendants and advisors to the daimyo. They were skilled musicians and entertainers who had performed for generals as well as marched beside them in battles, beating their drums to awaken the soldiers' fighting spirits. They called themselves geisha, men of arts. Now with no wars to fight, they'd been reduced to minstrels, donning elaborate costumes and entertaining guests with crude performances filled with toilet humor and dirty jokes as they awaited the services of the oiran.

I had never worked in a noble's house or fought in battle, but I, too, was geisha. I played shamisen and shakuhachi, and I had made quite a name for myself in Kyoto as a singer. Men requested me by name and were often so captivated by my songs, that they would forget their appointments or stay long after they were done just to hear my voice. I'd earned so many drunken confessions of love at the end of a song, I'd begun to wonder if the words ever really meant anything at all.

A gong sounded, signaling the fictional lord's ill-timed climax, and I pretended to laugh, hiding my face behind my sleeve to muffle a yawn. My part in this particular spectacle was long over, my sole purpose now to keep Yamaguchi company and attend to the level of his saké glass. As if on cue, he lifted the ceramic cup and leaned in my direction.

"This is quite the performance, ne, Hiro-kun?" he said in a guttural slur as I filled his cup from a white carafe.

I gave a polite nod. "I'm happy you're pleased, Yamaguchi-han."

"And your voice." He leaned closer and licked his thin lips. "Exquisite as always."

"You flatter me, Yamaguchi-han. I'm just an ordinary singer."

"Nonsense." He leaned even closer, blowing his stinking breath into my ear. "If only we could have some time alone together, I could make you really sing. Why don't we send these fools away—"

"As pleasant as that would be, Yamaguchi-han," I said, turning my face away and blinking back reflexive tears, "it is not permitted."

He grunted. "Don't tell me you don't service men."

"I don't service anyone." I kept my voice even, matter of fact, while disgust writhed in my insides. "If you'd prefer the company of men, there's a brothel—"

"I could take you away from here." He grabbed my elbow, his voice harsh and tinged with desperation. "Give you a new life."

"Thank you for your kindness, Yamaguchi-han," I said from between clenched teeth as I pried my sleeve loose from his hand "but I'm quite satisfied with the life I have." The tatami bit into my legs as I tried to scoot away.

"Please, Hiro-kun." His grip tightened. "If I don't have you, I will die."

The door slid open, and I melted with relief at the sight of the oiran, decked out in all her finery. The sweet scent of plums made us lift our heads, and even Yamaguchi's interest was momentarily swayed. She entered silently, bare feet floating across the tatami beneath the hem of her elaborate kimono. She was called Hanagawa, meaning river of flowers, and she drifted into the room like petals on a current. Layers of pink silk painted with bright-white flowers and falling leaves pooled around her. She held her hands tucked beneath the knot of her thick obi, a wide band of red that wrapped her from breast to hips held together by an intricate bow at her chest. Bright-red flowers spilled from her sculpted hair, vibrant rivers of color against a sea of black. Kanzashi tinkled lightly as she bowed, the silver hairpins catching the lamplight, and smiled with crimson lips.

"I'm sorry to hear that, Yamaguchi-han," I said in a hushed voice so as to not break the spell. "Feel free to think of me while your lady rides you to oblivion."

With a small bow, I extracted myself from his grip and followed the taikomochi out the door. I shot Hanagawa a sympathetic look as I passed and didn't miss the subtle roll of her eyes. Biting back a smile, I —not for the first time—found it hard to reconcile the goddess with the fiery girl who used to drop bugs in my teacups and took bets on which of our guests would last the longest. I admired her poise but didn't envy what she had to do, yet I knew she would handle it with grace.

"Hiro-chan, otsukaresama deshita." The house mother shuffled down the hall toward me, a knowing gleam in her eye. She was an oiran once, and though time had done its work on her appearance, she moved with the same airy grace. Take away the deep wrinkles around her eyes and the creases in her fine lips, and one could almost see the beauty she once was. Though she was much more modestly dressed in a deep-blue kimono, her back bent and shoulders sagged as if still carrying the weight of the oiran's finery.

"Good evening, Okaasan." I bowed, warmth spreading through my chest and a smile tugging on my lips. All the muscles in my back unknotted, her mere presence enough to chase away the discomfort.

"Yamaguchi-han is comfortable, I assume."

"Yes, Okaasan." I lifted my collar to my nose and cringed. "Though I fear I may need a wash after so long in a room with him."

Okaasan smiled sympathetically, patting me on the arm.

"Can someone else wait on him next time?" I pleaded.

"You know he favors you." Her eyes flashed mischievously. "I heard him offer to steal you away. Should I be worried? What if you fall in love?"

The terror on my face had her nearly doubled over in hysterics.

"Please, Okan," I drawled, leaning my head on her shoulder and putting on an exaggerated pout. It worked when I was ten. I hoped it would work now. "If I have to listen to one more story about gutting pigs, I might throw myself into the river."

"And what should I do when all of Yamaguchi-gumi shows up at my door to avenge my insult?"

A tendril of fear slithered across my heart. I had to suffer Yamaguchi Tojirou's presence not because of his station, but because of his associations. Yamaguchi was the head of the local tekiya, a group touting itself as a chivalrous union of street peddlers aiming to keep the streets of Kyoto safe for commerce. In reality, they were thugs, charging high rent for dirt stalls and extorting the local businesses for protection money. His wiry frame might not have cut an imposing figure, but the invisible army behind him was enough to make even the bravest man pull out his purse.

I let loose a dramatic sigh. "All right, but only because I love you so much."

"That's a good boy, Hiro." She gave my cheek a pinch. "Now, get some rest. Tomorrow's a big day."

"Is it?" I quirked an eyebrow in her direction.

"It's our anniversary. You didn't forget did you?"

Of course. The anniversary of the opening of the okiya thirty years ago. How could I forget? It was the biggest day of our year and the only time we were truly open to the public. Okaasan threw a grand party, opening the house up to anyone who'd like to come and getting everyone properly drunk. It served as both a publicity opportunity and a much-needed day off for the oiran, as most left too inebriated to manage anything more than a stumble into a futon.

"I need you at your most charming, Hiro-chan. I don't care if half the room falls in love with you as long as they return with full purses."

I bowed, my cheeks hot, and she left me in the hands of the house attendants who would strip me of my kimono. It doubled as our anniversary too. The day Okaasan found me as a baby, abandoned in a fruit crate in the alley behind the okiya on their tenth anniversary. She said my screams woke her from a dead sleep and she had no choice but to bring me in or never sleep again.

Twenty years later, I was still searching for a way to thank her.

While my kimono was nowhere near as fancy as the oiran, it still took two people to get me in and out of it. The best part of my day was when they loosened the obi with their deft hands and the heavy silk dropped from my shoulders. Free of my bright confines, I lowered to my knees in front of a mirror and loosed my hair from its knot. It fell around my shoulders in thick waves. Some found its natural curl along with the flecks of green in my eyes exotic, others evidence of mixed heritage. I wondered if it was true. If it was what made me so disposable in the first place.

A sound separate from the usual revelries of the house caught my attention. A sad smile tugging at my lips, I slipped out of my room toward the back garden, stopping to grab a steamed bun from the kitchen. I followed the rustling to the back corner of the yard where an ornamental bush shivered from within. It could have been a rabbit or a fox, but I suspected it was something else.

"Hello, there."

The shivering stopped, replaced by tense silence.

"Come on out. I won't hurt you."

More silence followed by the slow separation of leaves and branches as a small face emerged from the dark. Dirtied cheeks sat beneath deep-set eyes and tangled hair. A little boy, no more than seven years old, appeared from behind the bush, muscles bunched like a scared mouse ready to flee. I'd seen him before, picking through our kitchen garbage for scraps. My heart hurt, but I forced a smile.

"Don't be afraid." I squatted down an arm's length away and held out the bun I'd snagged from the kitchen. "Hungry?"

Wary eyes bounced from me to the bun, and he licked his lips. He snatched it from my hand quick as a snake and darted away.

TWO

Sakurai Hideyoshi

"Hiro-chan!"

I had just drifted off to sleep when the door to my room slid open. The taikomochi I shared it with snorted and burrowed deeper into their beds to evade the invading light of her lamp.

"Okaasan. Is everything all right?"

"We have a guest. You've been requested, Hiro-chan." She grabbed me by the wrist and dragged me out of bed and into the dressing room. Kimono boxes lined the wall next to a low vanity topped with a round brass mirror. White powders and brightly colored paints littered the top, along with a variety of hair ornaments. All the affectations that made the oiran glamorous.

"Why must he come so late?" I complained around a roaring yawn.

"He's just arrived from Edo. I don't dare turn him away."

Hanagawa stumbled in after me and collapsed in front of a mirror, her face rumpled and eyes bleary. "He better be handsome," she said with a ferocious pout.

With the help of one foggy-eyed attendant, Okaasan yanked me out of my jinbei and into a nagajuban. I yawned again and scratched at my hair as they draped me in layers of cotton, topped by a fine kimono. Black silk adorned with bright-pink sakura blossoms that made my fair skin shine. Her fingers trembled as she ran them through my long, wavy hair and arranged it into a nest of curls high on my crown, fastening it with glinting silver pins.

"Okaasan, my hair—"

"There's no time, Hiro. This will have to do."

"Who is he?" My heart skittered with anxious excitement as I watched her in the mirror, her small mouth pursed into a tight little knot and eyes wide.

"Just a samurai."

I frowned, exchanging a look with Hanagawa, but didn't press the subject. A lifetime of experience had taught me better. Okaasan was a strong, sometimes severe woman, willing to throw herself in the path of any danger to protect the ones in her care, yet she was shaken. There was something different about this samurai, something she didn't dare say, and it made my skin tingle with apprehension.

Her task done, she squeezed my shoulders, and I turned to face her. "Be beautiful, Hiro," she whispered into my ear, pressing a light kiss to my temple before pushing me out the door. "Make your mother proud."

With a deep breath, I squared my shoulders, picked up my head, and slipped out into the main house. Our guest had already arrived, and a herd of servant girls in their sleeping clothes had gathered around the door to his room, all whispering and peeking through the crack. Saki, a petite girl with a small, round face, straightened and rushed to my side as I approached.

"His name is Sakurai Hideyoshi," she said in a hurried whisper. "They say his katana has killed a thousand men and he drinks the blood of his enemies."

"That's ridiculous," I chided, frowning toward the crack in the door.

"It's true!" chimed in another girl. "I heard he was once struck in the heart by an arrow, pulled it out, and used it to kill the archer!"

"He traded his soul to a demon in exchange for immortality," Saki said. "Now, he's doomed to walk the earth for a thousand years."

I groaned and shooed them all away, swatting them across the shoulders with my fan. They disappeared down the hall in a giggling mass, leaving me alone in front of his door. Surely it wasn't these fantastical stories that had the house in such a stir.

The crack in the door was just wide enough to emit a flickering beam of light. Despite myself, I leaned toward it, my head filled with images of ghosts. When I was a boy, a traveling merchant told me a story of an old battlefield haunted by the headless spirits of fallen soldiers, their consciousness gone, fueled only by spite. I'd spent every night for a week after that in Okaasan's bed. But now I was grown, and the magic had worn off such stories. Yet as I peered through the gap in the shoji, the boy inside me thrilled at what could be behind it.

A shadow passed through the light, and I jumped back. "Just a samurai," I whispered to myself, taking a deep breath before sliding the door open and entering the room.

What I found inside wasn't a ghost, but a man sitting cross-legged on the floor, back straight, sipping saké from a white ceramic cup. He was dark like the night. All the customary lamps had been lit, yet the light pulled away from him like a retreating tide. His simple but elegant black kimono and hakama stood in sharp contrast to the white screen behind him. Extremely long black hair spilled from a high ponytail at his crown and fell in a thick stream over his shoulder, the end grazing his waist. His free hand rested on a short sword on his hip, and his katana lay out on the floor beside him.

The katana that killed a thousand men.

"Hajimemashite, O-Sakurai-han," I said with a low bow.

"You must be Hiro," he said in a deep, soft voice, flicking eyes like razors up at me.

"Yes." Heat crawled up the back of my neck as he raked that gaze over me. I bowed lower. "Please forgive my appearance, Sakurai-han. Your arrival took us a bit by surprise."

He made a low sound in his throat, almost a growl. "You've come to sing for me?"

"Y-Yes, if it pleases you."

With a wave of the hand, he signaled me to begin. I unfurled my fan and found his eyes again, dark as obsidian and just as hard. Something caught in my chest, and for a terrifying moment, I couldn't draw breath, like the shock of sudden cold.

I closed my eyes and held the song in my heart until it warmed again. It was an old song, filled with mystery and romance. One I'd sung a million times, and it never failed to move me. It told the story of a woman who fell in love with the spirit of a lonely mountain, and as my voice swelled with the lamentations of love, of desires just out of reach, my imagination drifted with the words and I was transported.

I walked the base of the mountain in search of my love, felt the cold air on my face and the earth beneath my feet. Real longing, not the empty affections of our patrons, tingled across my skin and warmed my cheeks. I peeked out from under my lashes. Over the years, I'd pasted a thousand different faces into this fantasy, let them fill my heart and mind until they believed I sang only for them. That was my talent, my gift, to bring my patrons into the fantasy with me, and this time it was Sakurai Hideyoshi, his fierce eyes softening, his dark presence warming with every note.

The song drifted to a close, and reality settled around us again. A faint smile crossed his lips, and a thrill went through me as he nodded his approval. He set his empty saké cup on the small wooden table in front of him. Like the dutiful geisha, I knelt beside him, took up the carafe, and refilled his glass.

"You're not like the others, are you, Hiro?" He looked me squarely in the eye, and I shivered. Those eyes. I couldn't escape those eyes.

"H-How do you mean?"

"You're not rough or crude like the other men here."

My cheeks heated as his gaze drifted over my face. I nodded in acknowledgement, flashing a demure smile. He drained his glass and made a small hum of pleasure as I leaned in too close. Our arms touched, and my sakura-perfumed hair brushed across his shoulder.

"What about you?" I asked, a bit of a tease in my voice. "Are you like the other men I meet here?"

He pulled his gaze away from me, and his expression shuttered. I saw him so clearly then, sat atop that high mountain. And like the girl in the song, I felt the desperate urge to reach him, to touch him, to warm the cold that had leached into his heart.

I wanted him to look at me.

I tried to shake off the thought, but it stuck like a burr. When it came to the attentions of my patrons, I was apathetic at best, and the feeling was unfamiliar and disconcerting. My fingers brushed his as I refilled his glass, sending a truly undignified heat racing across my cheeks. His gaze drifted to my exposed wrist and then up my arm. I sweated beneath my kimono as he lifted a hand to my hair and let it curl around his fingers. Normally, such an action would have repulsed me, triggering a string of polite but witty quips to divert his attention, but instead my heart fluttered. As he leaned closer, I told myself it must have been the song, the lingering emotions we'd shared pulling us together, not those eyes so dark they could swallow me whole.

The door slid open, and I jerked back as the Hanagawa appeared, tired-eyed but ethereal as ever. Sakurai-han frowned as I lifted to my feet and gave a deep bow.

"If you'll excuse me, O-Sakurai-han, I'll leave you to enjoy your time—"

His katana rattled as he snatched it up and stomped out of the room without giving the oiran so much as a glance.

THREE

Anniversary

OKAASAN'S BROW PULLED INTO A KNOT AS I RELAYED MY BAFFLING interaction with Sakurai Hideyoshi. She wasn't angry—he'd paid for his time whether he used it or not—but she pursed her lips in disappointment. The patronage of a high-ranking samurai was worth more than gold. Not only did it offer the house some degree of protection, even if in name only, but it could also inflate the reputation of our oiran tenfold. It was the best endorsement an establishment like ours could ask for.

But he'd left.

I could only assume I'd done something to offend him. His reaction to my innocent question suggested I had spoken out of turn. My job was to make him comfortable, and by getting personal, I'd done the opposite. I went down on my knees in front of Okaasan, ready to take any punishment she saw fit to give me, but she only patted me on the head and told me to get some sleep.

I dreamed of Sakurai Hideyoshi.

I couldn't remember the dream, but I woke the next morning with the distinct impression he had been there, as if his dark presence had left an ink blot on the back of my eyes. I spent most of the morning trying to scrub it out as we prepared for the day's festivities. I focused on arranging flower-shaped cakes on porcelain plates and hauling in large jars of saké from our underground storage, but with every lull in activity, I would catch it in the edge of my vision like a specter.

The main body of the okiya consisted of one large, open room with a wing of three guest rooms jutting off the east side and our private residences clumped against the west. We hung the front of the house with colorful streamers and paper lamps. When the sun reached its zenith, we threw open the doors to the main house, and the warm spring air was almost enough to chase that dark feeling away. A pair of taikomochi, decked out in their finest kimono and bearing the flags of our house, marched up and down the street with their drums to beckon people inside. Soon the house was rowdy with drunken laughter. The sharp notes of the shamisen filled the air, and saké flowed like water. I danced. I drank. I even flirted with the regulars, and with the glare of a hundred lamps in my eyes, I almost didn't notice the dark shape in the doorway.

Almost.

The music slowed and voices quieted as if the air thickened with Sakurai Hideyoshi's entrance. Okaasan noticed him too and was at his elbow within seconds, escorting him to a low table and pouring him a glass of saké. His cold glare raked over everyone in the house before stopping on me. Ice slipped down my spine. I was very drunk.

"You're here." I didn't even realize I'd crossed the room until I was standing in front of him.

"Mn."

"Why?" The drink had worn my etiquette down to a nub, and I dropped sloppily to my knees before him, leaning forward with my elbows on his table.

"You're drunk."

I smiled and batted my eyelashes. "We're celebrating."

"I see."

"You should congratulate me." I leaned even farther forward, my nose precariously close to his raised saké glass. His gaze bounced down to my lips for the briefest of moments, sending a burst of heat to my gut. "It's our anniversary."

"Mn."

I rocked back on my heels as he drained his glass and then held it out for me to refill. I couldn't read him, and it set me off-balance. Did he like me or didn't he? Why did I care?

"Have I offended you, Sakurai-han?"

His brows pulled together, but he didn't answer.

"You left so quickly last night." The carafe clinked against his cup as I filled it with unsteady hands. "The oiran…you didn't even—"

"I wasn't here for her."

"Hiro-kun!" A shout from behind me caught my attention before the shock of his words could properly set in. Yamaguchi approached, his face flushed and his kimono rumpled. He flailed his arms as he wobbled toward me and grabbed me by the shoulders. "How dare you neglect me so!"

"I apologize, Yamaguchi-han," I said, straining away from his touch. "I don't mean to neglect you. I was only greeting our guest."

Yamaguchi narrowed bleary eyes at Sakurai-han. His gaze raked over every inch of him, sizing him up, stopping briefly on the two swords he carried.

"Samurai." He spat the word like a curse.

Sakurai-han didn't react.

Yamaguchi's lips twisted before he threw a possessive arm around my shoulders. I flinched as he shouted his command directly into my ear. "Sing for us, Hiro-kun!"

I glanced back at Sakurai Hideyoshi, who looked completely unperturbed, his attention focused on his saké glass, before allowing myself to be pulled away and into the center of the group. The taikomochi struck up a song, lively and joyous, and I wove my voice into it. Soon the whole room was dancing, clapping, and raising their glasses.

All but Sakurai Hideyoshi.

The song ended with a wild cheer. I should have been happy, but I was dizzy, too hot, the walls too bright and too close. I bowed my appreciation to the crowd and slipped away, weaving through the house and out to the back garden. Night had just fallen, and stars poked their way through a deep-blue sky. Wisteria hung in ropey vines from arched trellises, making the air thick and sweet. I dropped off the engawa onto the stone path beneath them and listened to the wind through the leaves until the roar of the party faded into the distance.

"Well, look who's playing coy."

I spun around so fast I nearly toppled over. Yamaguchi Tojirou stood less than an arm's length away, a lewd smile stretching his gaunt face. I jerked backward, hitting the trellis and releasing a shower of wisteria petals.

"I'm doing no such thing." I forced a tight laugh. "I just needed some air. I'm afraid I drank too much."

He stepped closer, his eyes darkening. "Who was that man?"

"What man?"

"The one you were talking to inside."

"Oh." I swallowed hard, pushing tighter against the trellis. "I told you. Just a guest."

"You seemed awfully…friendly."

"It's my job to be friendly."

He took another step closer. "Well, I don't want you to be friendly with him."

A line of sweat trickled down my back. "I'm sorry, Yamaguchi-han, but—"

"There is no *but*." His hand whipped out and caught me by the neck, squeezing hard enough to cut off my cries of alarm. Rank breath poured over my face, and flecks of spit hit my cheek. "I could have your little okiya burned to the ground, the oiran sold to a whorehouse, and your precious Okaasan dumped in the gutter with a word. If I say don't talk to him—"

He was interrupted by the loud *snak* of the shoji being whipped open. Sakurai Hideyoshi stood framed in the bright light of the lanterns, a black spot against a sea of color. His sharp eyes bored into Yamaguchi so hot that for a moment, I almost believed all those stories. Yamaguchi's grip around my neck loosened.

"O-Samurai-han." Yamaguchi dropped his hand as he turned to face him, and I crumpled against the trellis. "I was just having a talk with Hiro-kun."

Sakurai-han didn't respond, but he tightened his hand around his sword. He stepped down from the engawa, his feet making almost no noise against the stone. Yamaguchi stood his ground, but he grayed a little, jaw clenched and throat working. After a long, hair-raising silence, he huffed and moved away from me and back toward the house.

"I think I need more wine," he said with a tense laugh. He cast a glance back over his shoulder as he walked away. "Think about what I said, Hiro-kun."

Yamaguchi disappeared back into the house, giving Sakurai-han a wide berth as he walked past.

"Are you all right?" Sakurai-han's voice was so low, I barely heard him over the din of the party.

"I'm fine. He just gets a little…overzealous when he drinks too much." I tried to shake off the tension, but it coiled in my gut. "I should get back to the party."

Sakurai-han stopped me with a hand on my arm as I slipped past. His touch sent a shiver through me, gentle but firm. His hand drifted up from my elbow to hover over the bruise rising on my neck. For some reason, I found myself fighting back tears.

"I'm all right. Really." I bowed, more to hide my face than anything else. "Thank you."

He nodded, and I shuddered as his hand dropped back to his side.

"Omedetou."

I blinked. "What?"

"You said I should congratulate you."

"Oh." I forced a laugh, but it didn't quite make it past the tightness in my throat. "Thank you."

He took a step forward, and everything else went soft. The wine had taken the edge off everything except him.

"Have you really killed a thousand men?" My gaze dropped to the swords on his hip and the hand draped over them.

He nodded again and took another step forward. He was close now, and the extra few centimeters of height he had on me seemed mountainous. "Does that scare you?"

"No." It surprised me how true it was. Something shifted behind his eyes like a candle lit in the dark, and the corners of his mouth ticked up. "But you do scare me."

Another step forward. The hilt of his sword bumped against my hip, and for some reason I reached out for it. I slid my fingertips over the rough cloth wrapping, and my heart skittered. The sword that killed a thousand men was such an ordinary thing.

We both jumped as a small knot of men exploded out of the back of the house in a burst of laughter, likely looking for a bush to piss in. I snatched my hand away and sidestepped onto the walkway, shuffling as fast as my drunken feet would allow back into the house and away from Sakurai Hideyoshi.

FOUR

Comfort

"GOOD MORNING, HIRO-CHAN."

I groaned, kneading my forehead with the heel of my hand as Hanagawa breezed into the kitchen as if blown by a mischievous wind. I'd spent the whole night tossing and turning and most of the morning in the kitchen restocking the pantry and washing dishes and actively avoiding interacting with anyone else. I hadn't even bothered to tie my hair, and it frizzed in the steam. A headache rolled like a thunderstorm between my ears, made worse by the souring of my stomach. Hanagawa, clean-faced and dressed in a simple yukata, dropped down to her knees beside me and leaned on the edge of the tub. Aside from the elaborate hairstyle meant to last for days, she was practically unrecognizable from the oiran.

"I saw you," she said, voice low and eyes flashing.

"Saw me what?"

"With that samurai."

I froze, a half-washed dish in my hand, and a wide smile stretched her face.

"I knew it!" she proclaimed, grabbing my arm and giving me an excited shake. "You must tell me everything, Hiro-chan."

I swatted her off, fighting a wave of nausea. If our clients knew the oiran was such a gossip, it would cause quite the scandal. "Please, O-nee. Nothing happened. We just talked—"

"Usotsuki."

"I'm not lying." I scrubbed at a piece of food on the plate as if I could make her and her questions go away with it. I loved her. She was my sister in spirit if not by blood, but sometimes her prying made me want to crawl out of my skin.

"It's quite rude, you know," she said on a sigh, draping herself over the edge of the tub and trailing a finger over the soapy surface of the water. "I got all dressed up for him, and he didn't even look at me."

"Hiro-chan." Okaasan stuck her head into the kitchen, cutting off what was sure to be quite a dramatic performance. "You're needed in a guest room."

"Can you find someone else? I don't feel very..."

"He asked for you especially."

Dread slid a cold finger up my spine, and Hanagawa sat up straighter. "Who?"

"Sakurai Hideyoshi." She grinned and gave me a sly wink. "Seems he's really taken with you."

That devilish smile cut across Hanagawa's face again, and I swallowed hard.

"You should get dressed as well, Hana-chan."

Hanagawa released a drawn-out sigh and lifted gracefully to her feet. "I wonder if I should even bother," she said with a knowing glance in my direction.

"What was that about?" Okaasan asked on a laugh.

"Nothing. She's just teasing me."

"About Sakurai-han?"

"What else. She convinced herself we're having some sort of secret, forbidden love affair."

Okaasan laughed. "A hopeless romantic, that girl."

Having finally won against that stubborn speck of food, I set the plate aside. Okaasan knelt beside me, her shrewd eyes studying my expression as she plucked the rag out of my hands. The bruise on my neck throbbed like a warning. "Maybe..." My already dry mouth went absolutely barren. "Maybe I shouldn't..."

Okaasan arched a sparse eyebrow. "Shouldn't?"

"Shouldn't encourage him." The words tumbled out before I could bite down on them.

"You act like this is the first time you've attracted a man's affections," she scoffed.

"This is different."

"How so?"

I paused, rolling the answer over in my mind. "Yamaguchi-han is jealous."

Okaasan's eyes widened.

The interaction I hadn't wanted to explain to Hanagawa spilled out of me. "He confronted me at the party last night."

"Confronted?"

"Threatened." I pulled my collar up a little higher. "He doesn't want me talking to him."

"He can't expect you to—"

"'All of Yamaguchi-gumi,' remember?"

Okaasan sat back on her heels. Her gaze shifted down and away as she put the pieces together, calculated money, calculated risk, and my whole body burned. I loved her as if she were my mother and I knew she loved me, but this part of our relationship always rubbed. The part that saw me as a commodity, as a part of her business and little else. Her lips pursed, and she nodded sharply as if coming to a decision before laying her hand on my arm.

"You know what we sell here, Hiro-chan?"

I swallowed hard. "Fantasy."

"That's right. More than saké, more than sex, even. You sold Yamaguchi-han a fantasy, and now you will sell one to Sakurai Hideyoshi."

"But the things he said...if he—"

"He won't." Her eyes held mine, and they shone bright as polished stone. "Do you have any idea how much protection money we pay him? You think he'll throw that away for a sexual conquest?"

I turned the plate over in my hands. The remembered venom in Yamaguchi's voice made my already temperamental stomach turn. But then there was Sakurai Hideyoshi. His hand on my arm and the strange way it made me feel.

"What about Sakurai Hideyoshi?" I asked.

"What about him?"

"He has no interest in the oiran." My cheeks went hot, and I closed my eyes to calm my racing heart. "I'm afraid he might...have the wrong impression of me."

Okaasan gave a small smile, her eyes softening. "Men come here to forget the troubles of the world and be comforted. Comfort him. Let him have his fantasy. He will either live it out with Hana-chan or come back tomorrow with a full purse longing to see you again."

Something twisted inside me, and I took a deep breath to loosen it. She was right, of course. I had to think beyond myself and my own discomfort and toward the good of the house. We needed his influence. More than that, we needed his money. I could treat him like any other man who'd shown a passing interest in me. Allow him to believe what he wanted to believe while keeping him at a careful distance.

I dropped the plate back into the basin and rose to my feet. "I should change."

Okaasan smiled, sweet and a little sad. "Don't take too long. He's waiting for you."

I ARRIVED AT SAKURAI HIDEYOSHI'S DOOR WITH A FRESH BOTTLE OF saké in hand. I'd changed into a clean black kimono and tugged my hair into a high ponytail. A few curls managed to pull free no matter how hard I tried to tame them, and I batted them out of my face with a frustrated grunt before announcing my entrance.

"I'm sorry to keep you waiting, Sakurai-han."

His gaze lifted, and though his hard expression never changed, I felt every place his eyes stopped. My bare toes. My hip. The neckline of my kimono. They reached my eyes, and I flinched away before dropping to my knees beside him. His saké cup was empty. I moved to refill it, and he snatched the bottle out of my hands.

"Hey, wha—"

"This will help." He filled his glass and pushed it toward me. "With the headache."

"I don't have a…"

He leaned forward and touched a fingertip to the bags under my eyes. A nervous laugh burst out of me, making him frown.

"What's funny?"

"Nothing. I'm just surprised." I lifted the glass and grinned at him over the rim. "Are the stories I heard about you wrong? Are you secretly a good person, Sakurai Hideyoshi?"

His shoulders dropped a tick, and he looked away. The air between us cooled, and I couldn't help but feel as if I'd said something wrong. I quickly downed the drink he'd served me, refilled the glass, and pushed it back toward him.

"I'm sorry."

"For what?"

"I've hurt you somehow."

He released a long breath and sipped from his glass.

"I should apologize for last night too." I picked at the hem of my kimono before smoothing it down over my knees. "For the scene with Yamaguchi-han and…after. I may have behaved inappropriately. I don't want you to misunderstand…"

"Misunderstand what?"

"My role here." His eyes cut back to me. My palms went clammy, and I rubbed them on my thighs. "If you prefer the company of boys—"

"I prefer your company."

My heart seized. "Sakurai-han—"

"Do you believe the things they say about me? That I drink the blood of my enemies?"

"Of course not. That's ridiculous."

"Is it?" he asked around a dry laugh. He finished off his glass and set it upside down on the table. His usually sharp eyes went dull as if focused on something only he could see.

"Why do you really come here?" I swallowed thickly, my ears burning hot. I was taking a risk, but I had to know. "You know I'm not…available to you…in the way I think you want me."

His eyes refocused with a blink. He shifted his weight toward me, reached up, and brushed his fingertip over the bruise on my neck, and my whole world tipped sideways. "The world is full of ugly things, Hiro. Sometimes it helps to be in the presence of something beautiful."

A panicked fluttering started in my chest, followed by warmth that ran all the way down to my toes. Something shifted between us, and it was as if I understood him. My life wasn't perfect, but the okiya had sheltered me from much of the world's ugliness. Sakurai Hideyoshi, on the other hand, stood toe-to-toe with it, held it on the end of a blade. Okaasan's words came back to me. *Comfort him.*

"Would you like me to sing for you?" The words came out rougher than I expected.

He nodded sharply. "Mn."

I took a deep, steadying breath and cleared the gravel from my throat before launching into a sweeping ballad full of romance and tragedy. Normally I would stand and perform at a distance as if to an audience of a hundred, something perfect and unreal. This time I stayed on my knees beside him, close enough to touch. I might have been selling him a fantasy, but I wanted him to see the truth. I let my voice falter and crack. I sang for him and him alone, and with each note, a little more of the tension he carried fell away until he collapsed entirely, his head landing in my lap, a mountain toppled.

His long ponytail draped across my thighs and curled around my hip. As I dragged my fingers through it, I thought of his scratched and dented sword that inspired such legends. Was he the same? An ordinary thing surrounded by extraordinary stories?

By the time my song ended, he'd fallen asleep. Hanagawa poked her head in, and I waved her away. I knew I'd just proved her right and I'd be subjected to her gloating, but I didn't have the heart to wake him. I didn't want him to leave.

FIVE

Off-Limits

I STOOD OUTSIDE OKAASAN'S DOOR, A TRAY HOLDING A TEAPOT AND two glasses balanced in my free hand. We had long closed for the night, and the house was silent save for the occasional snore leaking through the paper walls. I couldn't sleep. I'd spent the better part of an hour staring into the dark before I gave up and found a lamp burning down the hall.

I raised my hand to knock but stopped short at the sound of a familiar male voice. "Do you not value our protection?"

"Of course I do, Yamaguchi-han." Okaasan's voice, strained but patient, as if talking to an unruly child. "But we've already paid—"

"Didn't you hear?" Yamaguchi's voice took on a superior cadence. "My price has just gone up. Ten ryo."

"Ten—" Okaasan gasped.

"A small price to pay for the safety of your house."

"It's more than we bring in in a month. I have mouths to feed here. I can't pay it. I won't."

"You will."

A loud crash sent me bursting through the doors. Okaasan sat on one side of a chabudai, one arm thrown up in front of her. Yamaguchi loomed over her, up on one knee and leaning over the table. He'd slapped its surface with his palm, and tea glasses lay on their sides around it, their spilled contents pooling on the table's surface and dripping off the sides. He turned slightly at my entrance, a slow smile crawling across his face.

"Okaasan—"

"Everything's fine, Hiro-chan," she said quickly, waving me away, eyes bright with panic. "Go back to bed."

I frowned and stayed put, a wary eye on Yamaguchi.

"On second thought, maybe we can come to some other arrangement." His gaze slid over me like eels, and I took a reflexive step back.

Okaasan's face paled. "What kind of arrangement?"

Yamaguchi stood up, so close to me the acrid smell of sweat stung my nose. "I want Hiro-kun to sing for me and me only."

Okaasan shook her head, lips tight. "I'm sorry, Yamaguchi-han, but you must understand. Hiro is one or our biggest assets, second only to Hanagawa herself. People come from all over to hear him sing."

"Making him well worth the difference in my pay." Yamaguchi lifted a hand to touch me, and I shrank away, earning a shriveling look.

"He is not for sale." If her words were scorpions, they would sting.

"Yet he dotes on that samurai." The words came out a hiss, and my mouth went dry.

"I treat all our guests with the same courtesy." I struggled to keep my eyes up and my voice steady. The hair on my neck stood on end, and sweat broke out on my brow. My grip tightened around the tray I carried as he took another step forward.

"You have three days," he said to Okaasan without taking his gaze off me. "I will have what I'm owed one way or the other."

Yamaguchi pushed past me, the door snapping closed behind him. Okaasan let out a loud breath, deflating under the weight of her worries. I knelt across from her, set my tray down, and hurriedly cleared the upended tea glasses from the table and wiped it down. The tea filled the room with its grassy aroma as I refilled the glasses from the pot on my tray. She lifted her glass under her nose and breathed in deep.

"Bakayaro," she cursed under her breath.

"I'm sorry."

"It's not your fault, Hiro-chan."

"I think maybe it is."

Her eyes went wet before lowering to her glass. I'd never seen her as anything but a warrior, but there was a fragility to her now that made my heart ache. The creases around her lips, her yellowed skin stained from years of oiran makeup, the light-blue veins crisscrossing the backs of her hands. I had the sudden urge to stop time before it could do any more damage.

The corners of her mouth curled into a soft smile. "It's been a while since you've sneaked into my room in the middle of the night."

"Has it?"

"Mn." She took a sip of the tea, her gaze drifting a bit. "You used to come in here all the time when you were little, rolling around like a pill bug while I tried to work."

"I remember you threatening to throw me to wild dogs if I couldn't sit still."

She laughed. "You were such a nosy little thing and stuck to me like glue. I couldn't breathe if it didn't involve you."

"Well, you were all I had."

A gentle silence fell over us, along with a warm nostalgia. I felt a million years away from that boy yet exactly the same. I needed her then. I needed her now. No amount of time could change the scared little boy who just needed someone to love him.

"Have you ever been in love?"

She choked on a sudden laugh, nearly spraying a mouthful of tea. "Have I—Hiro, what is this about?"

"Nothing. Forget I said anything." My ears went hot, and I buried my nose in my tea glass.

Okaasan's eyes narrowed. "Is this about Sakurai Hideyoshi?"

Now it was my turn to choke. It wasn't like she didn't know where my tastes lay. I'd been discovered when she'd caught me staring too long at a guard washing himself in the well when I was seventeen. But for two people constantly surrounded by sex, we talked surprisingly little about our own experiences, and the question caught me off guard.

"No! Of course not!"

Okaasan scowled and snatched me by the ear, pinching until I squealed for mercy. "Don't you lie to me, boy. I may not have given birth to you, but I am still your mother."

"Ow! All right! I'm sorry!" She released my ear, and I rubbed the soreness away. "It may be…kind of…a little about Sakurai Hideyoshi."

She crossed her arms and fixed me with a glare that made my teeth ache.

"I'm not in love with him. It's just…he makes me feel…"

She arched her eyebrow.

"Strange."

"Strange?"

"Scared." I clenched my hands together in my lap as my palms started to sweat.

"Did he do something to you?" Her voice rose in pitch, her irritation at me turning to concern.

"No, nothing like that." I shook my head, floundering for the words to make sense of the ache in my gut. "It's as though I'm scared that he…likes me. Scared that he doesn't. Every time he shows up here, my heart pounds and I feel like I'm going to be sick, and I don't know if I should run away or…"

I glanced up to find a mischievous glint in Okaasan's eyes and a smile on her lips.

I cleared my throat and shook my head as if I could rid myself of thoughts of him. "It doesn't matter. Yamaguchi is right. I treat him differently. I should just…stay away."

"You're allowed to be attracted to him, Hiro," she said. "You're a grown man. He's handsome and mysterious."

"He's off-limits," I said firmly. "I won't draw Yamaguchi's jealousy any more than I already have. Besides, if we can't come up with ten ryo in three days…"

"Hiro-chan…"

"I'll make it right, I promise. I'll find a way to get the money. If not…" My stomach rolled, but I kept my face carefully neutral. "I'll give him what he wants."

"No. You will not."

"Okan…"

"I won't allow it." She slapped the surface of the table, her eyes wild and glassy. She took both of my hands in hers, and they shook. "You let me worry about the money. In the meantime, you should take a day away from the house. I'd rather you not be here if he comes around looking for you."

My gaze dropped to our clasped hands. "I won't let him hurt you."

"Look at me, Hiro." She squeezed my hands, pulling my attention back up to her. Her eyes flashed with determination. "Do you think I got to this age by letting thugs like Yamaguchi get the best of me?"

A smile tugged at my lips. "No."

"No," she repeated with a small smile before releasing me. "Now, go to bed. Tomorrow is a new day."

SIX

A Break

I SHOULD HAVE KNOWN OKAASAN WOULDN'T TAKE NO FOR AN answer. By midday, I'd been kicked out of the house, ordered not to come back until the next morning. I spent most of the afternoon just wandering the streets with my stomach in a knot. The sun shone bright and warm overhead, a harbinger of the coming summer. Silk fans flashed their pale colors as ladies struggled to keep cool in the heavy kimono that hadn't quite turned with the season. Sweat gathered along my hairline, as much from nerves as the heat, and I dabbed at it with my sleeve.

Despite Okaasan's orders to not worry about money, it was all I could do. I peered inside shops and teahouses, wondering how much I could make in a day sweeping floors. It wouldn't be nearly enough. Common laborers would be lucky to make a single ryo in a year. I had no real skills other than music, nothing to sell except the clothes on my back, and even that didn't belong to me.

As the sun dipped lower and I'd wearied of the calls of street vendors, my tired legs took me in a direction I had been avoiding. The narrow streets of the Ponto-cho red-light district were dim, the close-packed buildings blocking what was left of the evening light. Glimpses of the Kamogawa river that ran behind them flashed through the alleyways in shards of gold. Red lanterns dangled from the eaves, and painted faces peeked out from slatted windows.

Feminine voices called out in sugary tones from every direction. Someone bumped into me from behind, a stumbling drunk with dark skin and a weathered face. He burped an apology before falling toward one of the windows and hanging on the slats, reaching dirty fingers toward the girls inside.

I shivered and focused my gaze on the road. It was all so barbaric, so carnal.

Ten ryo in three days.

I swallowed hard and told myself it wasn't any different from what we did in the okiya. We classed it up, gave it a pretty face, but the oiran was just a prostitute by a different name. I didn't look down on her. On the contrary, I admired her. And what I found here couldn't be any worse than what Yamaguchi had planned for me. Maybe if we actually managed to pay him off, he would leave me alone. It just had to be the one time.

"Oi."

A deep voice pulled my attention to a building across the street. A man stood in the entryway, dressed in all black. He leaned casually on the doorframe, one ankle crossed over the other, wooden geta dangling from his bare foot. A pair of swords swung from his hip, but they hung wrong, the weight and balance making them sag. A woodcut painting of a samurai.

We sell fantasy.

"Looking for company?" He rolled a toothpick from one corner of his mouth to the other, a slow smile stretching his face.

"I…uhh…"

He stepped down from the entryway and moved toward me. The image of another samurai wavered in my vision like a mirage. The man in front of me wasn't as tall or as broad. His hair wasn't as long. His eyes weren't as dark or as menacing. He held out his hand, and something tightened low in my belly.

"I'm looking for work, actually." I picked my head up and pressed my hands against my sides to keep them from shaking.

The man huffed and arched a thick eyebrow. "Are you?" He pulled his hand back and crossed his arms over his chest. Dark eyes raked coldly over me. "Well, you're certainly pretty enough."

"It would be temporary."

Another huff. "Sure."

"I just need to make some money for..." I cleared my throat and shifted my weight from one foot to the other. "I just need to make some money."

"You ever done this before?"

"I'm not a virgin, if that's what you're asking."

The man sucked on his toothpick, flicking the end with his tongue as his lips stretched into a smile. "All right. Come with me."

He turned and jerked his head back toward the brothel he'd come from. I started to follow when a flash of black and another body appeared between us, so close my nose bounced off his shoulder blades. I reeled backward, rubbing the end of my nose. A familiar broad back now stood between me and the man from the brothel.

"Hey—"

"Not interested." Sakurai Hideyoshi's sharp voice cut off the man's protest.

"Sakurai-han." My voice came out a whimper as shame cut through me like a hot blade.

"We were just talking." The man from the brothel took a step back, his carefree expression never changing.

"Sakurai-han!" I leaped forward as his hand went to his swords and grabbed him by the wrist. "Stop."

His gaze cut down to me, to my hands on his arm, and then back to the man in front of him, his body tense like a drawn bow. The man laughed and plucked the toothpick out from between his lips.

"You have a real jealous one, there," he said, pointing with it to Sakurai Hideyoshi. My face burned. He took another step back before bending into a sarcastic bow. "Shitsureishimasu."

The man disappeared inside his brothel. Neither Sakurai-han nor I moved. The air around us crackled, and with a shock, I realized my hand was still on his arm. I jerked it back.

"What do you think you're doing?" I sputtered.

"You're not at the okiya." His voice was low and flat, glare still pinned on the door of the brothel.

"No, I'm not."

"Why?"

Irritation prickled up my spine. "I needed a break."

"From me."

"From everything." I lowered my head as a bit of guilt dropped on it. "Maybe from you."

His already dark eyes went a shade darker. He pivoted on his toes and marched past me without a word. That fluttering panic seized me once again. I felt pulled toward his retreating back as if on a string.

"I'm sorry, Sakurai-han," I said as I fell into step behind him, "but you have to understand my position."

"What position?" he snarled. "You'd rather sell yourself as a whore than serve me drinks?"

"That's not—it's more complicated than—"

"That is beneath you," he growled, stabbing a finger back toward the brothel without turning his head.

"Beneath me?" I choked on a dry laugh. "I serve tea to horny men who hate their wives. I'm an abandoned child with no status and no name. What exactly is beneath me?"

He didn't answer, just continued his stomping path away from me. My chest squeezed, and my throat constricted. I didn't owe him an explanation. I didn't owe him anything, but the thought of him walking away thinking I was a common whore made me sick.

"He threatened my house."

Sakurai-han stopped but didn't turn. "Yamaguchi Tojirou?"

"He doubled our protection money. Ten ryo in three days."

He turned his head, the sinking sun cutting out the hard lines of his profile. "Why?"

"He's jealous." My eyes burned, and my shoulders sank. "It's my fault. I...showed you favor."

He turned to face me fully. I didn't dare meet his eyes, ducking my head so low my chin rested on my chest.

"He warned me that night at the party, but I didn't listen. Now, it's up to me to fix it."

He took the smallest step toward me, and his hand twitched as if he would touch me. I wanted him to touch me, and the realization poured over me like hot water followed by ice. I pulled back just out of his reach.

"I'm sorry, Sakurai-han," I said, the words barely making it past my throat. "I don't think I can be around you anymore."

SEVEN

Disgrace

SAKURAI HIDEYOSHI DIDN'T COME BACK TO THE OKIYA.

I fell back into my old routine, or rather it fell in around me. I poured saké, I sang songs, but the color had been bleached out like a banner left in the sun for too long. I resented everything about this life I used to be grateful for. The things I merely found boring were now tedious. Mild irritations turned into full-blown annoyances, and even Hanagawa kept her distance, though questions shone in her eyes. Every time the door opened, my heart jerked and I looked up. It was never him. It made me angry, and I didn't know why. I'd told him to stay away, and he had.

I cursed as I tripped over the hem of my kimono, sending the contents of the tray I'd been carrying careening to the floor. I'd told Okaasan about my last interaction with Sakurai-han, going down on my knees once again to apologize for my behavior. I'd underestimated how hard it would be to walk away, to give up all that intensity, and halfway through my confession, I broke. In twenty years, he was the only thing I'd ever wanted for myself, but having it would come at the cost of everything I loved. Sadness filled Okaasan's eyes, and for a moment, she stopped being Okaasan and was just my mother, folding me into her arms and consoling me over my heartbreak while praising me for doing the right thing.

But I couldn't stop thinking about it, about him, about the darkness that surrounded him and how it lifted a little when I sang. I'd witnessed the effects my voice had on people, but none were so profound as him. As much as I didn't want to acknowledge it, it affected me too. When I sang for him, they weren't just empty words meant to fill the time and the silence. When I sang for him, the songs became true.

But it didn't matter. I couldn't put my family at risk, and soon I would belong to someone else.

"Hiro-kun."

A lean shadow accompanied by the familiar smell of whiskey and sweat fell over me as I mopped up spilled saké and broken glass. My heart seized. Our protection money was due to Yamaguchi, and he'd come to collect.

"Yamaguchi-han. Welcome back," I said with a plastered-on smile. "Please, mind your feet—"

"Oh, let me help you." He dropped down beside me despite my protests. His mouth pulled into a lecherous smile, revealing one broken and heavily discolored tooth. "You shouldn't get those pretty hands dirty."

"Really, Yamaguchi-han, it's not nec—" I hissed as he grabbed my hand, causing a sliver of glass to bite into my palm. I tried to pull it back, but he held me tight, his eyes dark and his thin lips twisted.

"Yamaguchi-han." Okaasan's voice rang calm and clear from down the hall.

Yamaguchi dropped my hand and stood as she approached. Blood pooled in my palm and ran down my arm. One of the serving girls handed me a rag, and I quickly wrapped it around the wound.

"I'm here to collect my fee," he said with a pointed look in my direction.

Okaasan smiled sweetly and pulled a packet out of the folds of her kimono. Yamaguchi's smug expression fell as she held it out to him. "Ten ryo as promised."

I nearly melted into the floor with relief. He snatched it out of her hand, ripped it open, and peered inside. The gold plates tossed shards of light across his red face. He'd made a demand he was sure we couldn't meet in order to get what he really wanted. Yamaguchi's nose curled as if smelling something rancid before he huffed and shoved the packet into his collar.

Okaasan watched with her head high, calm and dignified. Only after Yamaguchi had stomped off to his regular room did she drop to her knees beside me, hands shaking and eyes wet with worry. She took my injured hand in hers and slowly peeled back the rag to examine the wound.

"You found the money," I said, breathless.

"No. *You* found the money." She laughed at my bewildered expression. "It arrived by courier this morning. From Sakurai Hideyoshi."

My head swam, and I pressed my free hand against my forehead. "S-Sakurai…why…"

Okaasan shrugged with one shoulder, a knowing smile pulling at her lips. A burst of warmth ran through me that made me both giddy and incredibly sad.

"I should see to Yamaguchi," I said, swallowing the feeling like bad fish. I tried to stand, but my knees wobbled, and I fell against Okaasan's shoulder.

"Nonsense. You will give that monster no more of your time."

"Ignoring him is what got us here in the first place." I took a deep breath and forced myself straight. "He's received his money. If he does anything inappropriate, we are well within our rights to bar him. He has no claim to me, and he knows it. I'll be fine."

Her lips pursed. "Fine. But take care of that hand first. I'll send the taikomochi in to keep him occupied in the meantime."

I nodded and squeezed her arm. Guilt over my earlier behavior sat like a lump of ice behind my breast bone. "Thank you, Okan."

Yamaguchi was guffawing at yet another raunchy pantomime when I returned with a bottle of wine and a freshly bandaged hand. He didn't acknowledge me at first, seemingly engrossed in the antics of the taikomochi as I knelt beside him and poured him a glass.

"I'm impressed."

I froze, the bottle still tilted over the glass.

"She must be very resourceful, your Okaasan." He swiped up the glass and drained its contents in one swallow. He leaned toward me, his arm brushing mine and his lips close to my ear. "The thing is, I still don't want to share you."

My stomach dropped, and I closed my eyes against the burning behind them. Sakurai-han's money, while well-intentioned, would only delay the inevitable. Yamaguchi had set his eyes on me, and he wouldn't stop until he got what he thought he was owed.

"You're still thinking about him, aren't you?" he snarled "Your samurai."

Sell him. Sell him the fantasy.

I turned to face him and smiled sweetly despite the roiling in my gut. "Of course not, Yamaguchi-han. Like I told you before, he was just a guest. A guest that won't be returning."

He blinked, his cheeks a little pink from the wine. "He won't?"

"No." I leaned into him. "He upset you, so he is no longer welcome."

He narrowed his eyes with suspicion, but a smile twitched around his lips. He sneaked his hand under my kimono sleeve and slid it up my forearm to my elbow. "I hope that I misjudged you, Hiro-kun."

"As do I." As an excuse to shake it off, I reached for the wine bottle, poured him another glass, and held it out to him. "The last thing I want is for you to think badly of me."

Two bottles of wine and a few artful dodges later, Yamaguchi was too drunk to notice me slip out of his room. I sagged against the wall just outside as I struggled to catch my breath, shaking all over. I scrubbed at my arm where he had touched me as if I could scrape him off my skin.

You can do this, Hiro. Just think of the house. Think of Okaasan and all she's done for you. You can make this sacrifice for her. You can do this. You can do this. You can do this.

I couldn't do it. With the wine I'd drunk threatening to make an inglorious exit, I ran out to the street. In all my time working in the okiya, no one had made me feel this way. No matter how aggressive their overtures, they were ultimately harmless. Our patrons understood there were some lines that couldn't be crossed. Yamaguchi no longer saw those lines. If he did, he certainly didn't respect them, and with one touch, he'd made me feel dirty and unsafe.

Sakurai Hideyoshi's face flashed behind my eyes, and my ragged breathing evened out. He'd touched me a number of times, small, soft brushes of his fingers that left me feeling light, and I suddenly longed for the touch he'd wanted to give me in Ponto-cho.

A samurai of his reputation didn't come into town without being noticed, and I was able to get directions to his house from the second person I asked. I stumbled through the narrow streets to an estate in the shadow of the Imperial Palace. It looked like a palace itself, with sweeping tile roofs peeking over a high stone wall. A small torii marked the entrance to a shrine no bigger than a closet on the south corner, the smell of burned incense still hanging in the air around it.

Standing in front of his heavy wooden gate, I bunched my hands in the sleeves of my kimono. What was I doing here? I couldn't ask him for help. The problems of a geisha were far beneath him, and he'd already done more than his fair share for me. I told myself I just needed to thank him, maybe apologize for the brush-off I'd given him in Ponto-cho.

I took a deep breath and knocked lightly on the gate. "Sakurai-han?" My voice cracked terribly, and I cringed, clearing my throat before trying again. "Sakurai-han? It's Hiro."

I leaned closer to the gate, ears attuned to movement. I knocked again, more firmly this time, and the gate swung inward a little.

"Ojamashimasu," I called softly as I poked my head through the gap.

Lavish gardens abloom with wisteria and hydrangea stretched out before me. My sandals scraped across the stone path that crossed over a pond teaming with koi and led to the entrance of the sprawling estate. The shoji were all closed except one, which was open just enough to give me a peek inside. Lamplight flickered over screens depicting ink-black birds on a field of gold.

A shadow moved inside. My skin flushed hot and cold at the same time. My heart did a strange little dance over my rib cage. I took another step forward and tried to call out to him, but couldn't squeeze my voice through my clenched throat.

My fluttering heart came to an abrupt stop when I realized he wasn't alone. Another person stood very close to him, his arms wrapped around them, his head lowered into their neck.

I should have stopped. I should have turned around and walked away, but even though my stomach felt full of pins, I stepped closer. The person he was with—a woman—took shape as I drifted onto the engawa. Slender, fair skinned, modestly ornamented hair in a fashionable topknot. Someone befitting a man like Sakurai Hideyoshi. A person who mattered.

Had I read it all wrong? His complete disinterest in the oiran had led me to believe he was disinterested in women altogether, but maybe it was something else. His reaction to me pursuing work in Ponto-cho hinted at a distaste for the profession. A hollow opened up in my chest. Maybe all he'd wanted was to hear me sing, after all.

She made some small sound, and my insides twisted into something ugly. They swayed together like the interlocked branches of a tree caught by the wind. I shrank back but stopped as the hands that had been knotted in the fabric of his kimono relaxed, went limp, and fell to her sides. Her knees buckled, and Sakurai-han went down with her until she was flat on her back. There was something strange about the way she fell, like the air had all gone out of her.

With a groan, he straightened and sat back on his heels, eyes closed, the back of his hand pressed against his mouth. His cheeks were ruddy, his expression loose and serene as if he were drunk or high. When he dropped his hand, something thick and dark clung to his lips, and his tongue swept across them.

Blood.

EIGHT

Mysterious Calamity

I MUST HAVE MADE SOME SOUND. HIS EYES SNAPPED OPEN AND JERKED in my direction, irises white as marble. I fell backward off the engawa, crawling in a panic back toward the gate. My lungs seized. My mind blanked.

"Hiro."

I'd made it as far as the gate and to my feet. I spun around at the sound of my name, low and even and without malice, my back pressed against the stone wall.

"What are you doing here?"

I balked at the sight of him. He'd stopped a little more than arm's length away, posture rigid and expression guarded. Was he always so tall? His cheekbones always so high?

"Hiro?"

"Y-You didn't come to the okiya." The words tumbled out of my mouth before I could stop them.

He blinked. The white had left his eyes, returning them to their usual black, and I wondered if I'd imagined it all. "You told me not to."

"Oh."

He took a step forward, stopping when I flinched and pressed my shoulders into the wall. His gaze dropped to my bandaged hand.

"What happened?"

"Nothing," I stammered. "An accident."

He stepped forward again, slower this time, watching me as if I were a rabbit ready to bolt. Fingers calloused from sword training wrapped around my wrist and lifted my hand out from where I'd tucked it behind me. He cradled it in his, gentle as if it were made of eggshell, and unwound the bandage. Just like every other time he touched me, I felt a wash of warmth.

He drinks the blood of his enemies.

"You saw," he said, voice soft and full of sadness.

"It's true what they say about you, isn't it?" My voice broke around the words.

He nodded, eyes focused on my palm.

"Is she dead?"

He nodded again.

"Who is she?"

"I don't know."

I closed my eyes against the prickling that had started there. My slowed-down mind now ran double time, the reasonable part telling me to run, get as far away from Sakurai Hideyoshi and the murder he'd committed as I could. Some other, deeply physical part wanted me to stay just so he'd keep holding my hand.

He traced the line of the cut on my palm, and it stung, but not in an unpleasant way. I sucked in a breath, and a shiver ran up my arm. I opened my eyes and found him pressing the pad of his thumb against a long, pointed incisor. How had I never noticed that before?

A pearl of blood gathered around the puncture. Still cradling my hand in one of his, he swept his thumb across the wound, leaving a thin layer of blood behind. I gasped as a bright, almost effervescent feeling filled my palm and radiated outward. The edges of the wound shimmered and stretched, pulling together like the seam of a garment. I watched, jaw agape, as it went from an ugly gash to a thin red line to clean, unblemished skin in a matter of moments.

"Youkai." The word dropped from my lips like a lead weight into the silence between us.

Sakurai-han's shoulders sagged a little, eyes still lowered, the groove between them deepening. He wiped the last traces of blood from my hand and allowed it to curl closed.

"Does that scare you?" His voice was scarcely a whisper.

I thought of my song, of the lonely spirit of the mountain. "No."

"But I scare you."

I nodded.

He released a long breath through his nose and let go of my hand, his own falling clenched to his side. His expression closed like a fist. I searched for his eyes, but they never lifted.

"Go home, Hiro." He spun on his heel and stomped back to the house.

"B-But, Sakurai—"

"Don't come back here."

The shoji snapped shut behind him, cutting off any argument. I was left staring at my newly healed hand, still tingling from whatever he'd done to it.

I DRIFTED THROUGH THE STREETS LIKE A GHOST. THE MOON HUNG low and bright in the sky, painting everything with a silvery sheen that made the world dreamlike. I could almost believe that I was asleep, stuck in a surreal nightmare, and when I woke up, there would be no Yamaguchi, no dead girl, and no Sakurai Hideyoshi.

I cradled my hand against my chest. I was afraid of him, just not in the way I should have been. I wasn't afraid of his strange eyes or his sharp teeth or even the murder I'd witnessed him commit. I was afraid precisely because I wasn't afraid. Because when he held my hand, I felt safe. Because when he told me to leave, it hurt like being cut open.

Just like everyone else, I'd grown up on stories of youkai that lived among us, mysterious creatures that were capable of both good deeds and horrific evils. I'd heard old women whisper warnings behind their hands, seen the shrines built to appease them, played children's games where I ran from them. I never really believed in them.

But Sakurai Hideyoshi was real. So real, he made everything else feel like an illusion.

"Hiro!"

I spun around as the sound of my name in a coarse voice cut through the dark. Igarashi Sato, one of the taikomochi, ran toward me at full speed, his body hardly keeping up with his feet. He crashed into me, and I caught him by the shoulders before he could fall.

"Sato-kun? What's the matter?"

"It's Okaasan." He doubled over, hands on his knees, the words coming out a wheeze, face pale and stricken.

My heart jerked. "What do you mean? What happened?"

"That kusogaki, Yamaguchi Tojirou," he snarled, spitting on the ground. "He was blind drunk and looking for you. Crashed through every room in the house waving a knife around like a fool. Scared the life out of the serving girls. He was sure he would find you with that samurai."

I cursed, my mouth sandpaper dry.

"Okaasan tried to stop him."

"Is she…" My throat closed around the question.

"She's alive. But she's hurt. Bad. And we were able to chase Yamaguchi off for now, but—"

I didn't wait for him to finish. I took off in a flat run, not stopping until I reached the okiya. Confused patrons and terrified serving girls milled around on the street outside, whispering behind their hands. I pushed past them through the main house and to the guest rooms. Shoji had been pulled from their frames and lay in piles on the floor. A dark pool ran off the wood panels of the hallway and soaked into the neighboring tatami. I followed a trail of fat drops and smudged footprints to Okaasan's private room.

Just as I laid my hand on the door, a pained wail sounded from behind me. I turned to find Hanagawa, framed by the open door of her room, one of the serving girls with her arms wrapped around her in an effort to calm her. Her fancy kimono was rumpled, her makeup smeared and streaked with tears.

"Where were you?" she cried, her voice broken with despair. Anger flashed in her eyes as she struggled against the girl at her side. "What have you done?"

Igarashi Sato materialized in the hallway and snapped the door shut between us. He turned, back against it, and opened his mouth as if to speak, but no words came. A hot pain seared through my chest.

What had I done?

I shook off the feeling as best I could and turned back toward Okaasan's door. There was no time for that now.

"Okan!" I burst through it and fell to my knees beside her futon where she lay, surrounded by grave-faced taikomochi.

A thick strip of cloth had been tied around her shoulder and across her chest, and it was dark with blood. Her face was pale, sagging, and shone with sweat. The taikomochi made way for me as I scooped up her hand and pressed it to my lips. She felt thin as paper, as if she could blow away in a breath.

"Hiro-chan." Her eyes struggled open.

"I'm here." I lowered my face into her wavering field of vision. "I'm sorry, Okan, I'm so sorry."

She shook her head, brushing her frail fingers across my cheek.

"I shouldn't have left." Tears clouded my vision and streamed down my cheeks. "I should have just given him what he wanted…"

"No, Hiro-chan," she said as firmly as she could manage. "Bad people will do bad things. This is not your fault."

"But—"

She shushed me, pressing her fingertips against my lips before cupping my face in her hand. "You're so beautiful, Hiro-chan. I'm so lucky to have found you."

My skin went cold as her eyelids drooped, and her face went slack. I squeezed her hand between mine and called her name, but she didn't respond. I looked around in a panic. "Where's the doctor?"

"He's on the way," someone answered from beyond my blurred vision.

I laid my head on her chest. Her heart tripped behind her breastbone, her breathing fast and shallow. There was no time. For some reason, I looked down at my palm and the smooth, pink skin without even the lingering ache of a bruise.

Sakurai Hideyoshi.

NINE

Pact

I POUNDED ON SAKURAI-HAN'S GATE UNTIL MY FISTS WERE RED. I tried pushing it open as I had before, but it was locked. I screamed myself hoarse calling his name, but I didn't stop. I wouldn't give up. I couldn't.

"I told you not to come back here."

The gate whipped open, and I fell through it, grabbing onto his collar before he could stop me. He stumbled backward, grasping me by the wrists as the gate slammed closed behind us. He'd changed into a dark-blue jinbei, and his hair hung loose around his shoulders. He looked like a different person, and for a moment, I thought I'd made a grave mistake.

"Is it real?" I asked, the words tumbling over each other in their race to get out. I gripped his shirtfront white-knuckle tight. "Is this real? What I saw, what you did...this..." I turned one hand over, the one that had been cut, exposing my palm.

"What are you talking about?"

"Are you really what I think you are?"

He was silent for a long time, his eyes dark, his jaw clenched. A strange, irrational hope fired in my chest. If what I saw wasn't real, maybe none of this was. This was all just some terrible nightmare I could wake up from.

"Mn."

My eyes flooded, and I dropped my head into his chest. "Help me."

"What?"

"Please. Yamaguchi-han…he…Okaasan…I think she's dying."

"Slow down, Hiro." He peeled me off his chest and forced me to take a step back.

"He attacked the house. He was drunk. He was looking for me." My body shriveled under a wave of guilt and grief. "This is our fault. You have to help me fix it."

"What do you expect me to do?" His voice was flat and without sympathy.

"Save her."

"I can't."

"Heal her." I thrust my hand out between us, palm up. "Like you did me."

His brows lowered over his eyes, and his voice softened. He took a step back from me. "It doesn't work like that, Hiro."

I stepped forward. "Why not?"

"That was a small thing. A trick." He shook his head, speaking as if to a stubborn child. "I can't stop her from dying."

That hot pain curled through my chest again. I'd come all this way for nothing. He couldn't save her. Okaasan was going to die. She was going to die, and there was nothing we could do about it.

"Then avenge her."

We were both taken aback by the venom in my voice, the heat of my conviction. It burned through me like wildfire, consuming everything in its path. It made my hands shake and my back sweat.

He squinted down at me, fists curling at his sides. "No."

"Then give me the power you have so I can do it myself."

For a long time, he just stared at me, his expression unreadable, before turning away and walking back toward the house.

"I know it's possible," I shouted after him. "People make deals with youkai all the time."

"Stories, Hiro," he shot over his shoulder.

"If you're real, then the stories must be too."

"You have no idea what you're asking for," he said, wheeling back around on me, teeth bared and eyes white. "Or what you're asking of me."

"I'm asking you to make me strong."

"You're asking me to destroy you." He squeezed the words through clenched teeth.

"What do you want? I'll give you anything."

"You said it yourself," he said with a bitter laugh. "You are a geisha with no status and no name. What could you possibly have that I want? That would be worth this?"

"Me."

He balked, his angry expression jerking into shock. I moved toward him, my stride loose and hips swinging. His gaze bounced over my face, pupils dilating.

"I see how you look at me." I dropped my voice low and husky. "Do this for me, and I'll be yours. I'll sing only for you."

I slid my hands over his chest as I drew nearer. His cheeks pinked, and his breath grew ragged. Heat radiated off him, from anger or desire or both. Hope flared in my heart again as he leaned toward me. He cupped my elbows in his hands, fingers stiff with restraint, before grabbing my forearms and shoving me roughly away.

"You make me no better than him," he said, voice rough and chastising, "and yourself into a whore."

Panic clenched in my chest as he turned away from me again. "Bakayarou!" I flung the curse at his back like a stone, and he flinched as it struck between his shoulder blades. "You act like you care about me. You treat me gently and help me when it's convenient and easy for you. But when it matters, you're just like the rest of them."

My hurt poured down my face in fat drops. My heart pounded in slow, painful beats as if my blood had turned to sludge. I realized then that I was wrong, that I'd believed my own fantasy and let it blur and mix too much with reality. I'd been waiting, wanting, yearning for the confession I'd heard from so many others and he'd never give me. I was just a geisha, a beautiful thing to push back against the ugliness, and now I was wasting what could be my mother's last moments begging for something that was never mine to have.

Tension rippled through Sakurai-han's back, and he whipped around on me again. He covered the distance between us in two long strides. Before I could react, he took my face in his hands and crashed his lips into mine, hard and possessive. He walked me backward until my back was against the wall, the entire length of his body pressed against mine.

My mind went blank, aware only of the solidness of his chest and the scrape of his teeth. Little fires ignited under my skin. A whine slipped past my lips as he pushed deeper, and I gave in, first in increments and then in one great rush that left me weak and boneless.

He backed away just enough to allow me to breathe, and his eyes filled my vision, those eyes that so enthralled me, pupils blown wide and rimmed in white. Desire spiraled through me, hot and desperate. A few ragged breaths, and I pulled him in again, fingers tangled in his long hair. I drank him down in deep gulps that only left me wanting more. I could have ended there, existing only on his lips and in his arms.

He grabbed my wrists and pressed them against the wall over my head to force some distance. He stared at me, cheeks flushed and lips swollen. Strands of his hair still clung to my fingers like spiderwebs, like we could never come apart no matter how hard we tried.

"There's no going back," he said, face stern though his voice shook. "I will be a part of you."

My eyes burned, and I blinked rapidly to keep the tears at bay. "I have nothing to go back to."

"It feels like dying."

"It's only a matter of time before Yamaguchi comes for me." I swallowed down a sliver of fear, and it caught in my throat like splintered glass. "I'd rather die in your hands than his."

He took a deep breath but didn't move. His heart tapped a fast rhythm against my chest. I leaned forward just enough to brush my lips against his. He made a low sound like a purr, and I strained against his hold as he deepened the kiss, a momentary tease of teeth and tongue before moving down my jaw. My breath caught as he nipped at the tender place just below my ear and flicked his tongue over the vein beneath it.

"Do you want it?" he whispered against my skin.

I could barely get the word out between gasps as he trailed featherlight kisses down the line of my neck. "Yes."

"Tell me again." His voice shook. "Tell me you'll stay with me forever."

"Yes, yes. Please. I want it." His breath against my damp skin sent a spiky heat cascading through my body, and it gathered low in my belly. I arched toward him and dropped my head back. I almost forgot what I was there for. Man or monster didn't matter anymore—I only wanted him. I allowed myself to give into the fantasy, and it bloomed with delirious joy.

He tugged me even closer until there was no space left between us, his lips pressed to the column of my throat. My toes curled as he traced the vein with his tongue, followed by the graze of teeth and a sharp sting. A fiery sensation started at his lips and cut through my very core. Not quite pain, not quite pleasure. My head swam as something was sucked, dragged, pulled out of me.

Another sensation, this one slower, softer, started at his hands and flowed over me like a warm rain. My muscles relaxed. My mind went soft. Any fear I had dissolved and washed away, replaced with peace and complete trust. I would give him everything, my heart, my life, my soul. It didn't matter if I died because I would be with him, a part of him. I wept, not from sadness, but from release.

He let go of my wrists and hooked one arm around my waist as my strength waned and my knees gave out. He cradled my head with his other hand as he lowered me to the ground. It was almost tender, the way he brushed my hair away from my face and wiped the tears from my cheeks. His features blurred as my consciousness wavered. I thought briefly of the girl I'd seen him with earlier, how she crumpled at his feet. Did she feel this, too? This complete and total surrender to his power?

"Drink, Hiro." He teased my lips open with his thumb and sealed his over them. Thick, coppery liquid filled my mouth. Blood. I choked on it at first, my body convulsing reflexively beneath him.

The first swallow was like a burst of light. All the pleasure, all the heat of our passionate embrace returned and redoubled. My vision instantly cleared. My muscles came alive once again, and I wrapped my fingers in his hair, hooked my leg around his waist. My ears rang with the sound of our hearts, and I took in everything he gave me, my tongue fighting his for every last drop.

Finally, he released me, and I lay gasping on the ground. My skin lit up. My body burned as if every cell was turning itself inside out. It wasn't pain or pleasure, but something entirely new. I writhed as my body remade itself, screaming as this new sensation coursed through me. I fell into darkness deep as a well, wondering if I had made a terrible mistake.

TEN

Revenge

I awoke in stages. First, with a gradual and intense awareness of my body, down to the ends of the smallest hair, and all of it buzzed, ached, groaned. I tried to move, but the brush of fabric, even the changing currents of the air, sent a crash of sensation through me that took my breath away. Heart pounding, head reeling, my whole body pulsed, and I gasped when I realized it was my own blood sliding beneath my skin, whispering a secret I couldn't quite grasp.

And then, there was sound, the light, rhythmic ting of metal on metal, not loud, yet each repetition pricked like needles. I groaned, and the sound paused, followed by a distinct rustling that drew steadily closer. Footsteps. Cold fingers slipped around my heart and squeezed the air from my lungs, gradually tightening as the sound grew louder, closer.

"Open your eyes, Hiro."

Something brushed against my cheek, warm and familiar yet completely foreign. I jerked into violent motion, pushing off the floor and slamming my back against the wall. Eyes still squeezed tightly shut, I swiped at the empty air in front of me.

"Stop fighting," he said softly, rough hands clamping around my wrists in an iron grip. "Focus."

"Sa-Sakurai—" I clamped my hands to the sides of my head as my own voice pounded in my ears. Loud. Everything was so loud. The wind in the hallways. The birds in the trees. Sakurai-han's heartbeat. Mattaku, I could hear his heartbeat.

"What—what's happening to me?"

"Look at me, Hiro," he said, low and commanding, taking my face in his hands. "Open your eyes slowly and look at only me."

With a deep, wheezing breath, I cracked one eye open, slamming it shut again as the flickering light of an oil lamp swam into my vision. I groaned and pitched forward as the world tilted under me, and I gripped Sakurai-han's wrists as if it might buck me off. He shifted his hands to my shoulders, and he forced me upright, silently urging me to try again.

His eyes. I lifted my head and found his eyes, black as obsidian and flashing darkly, thin, straight brows pulled low over them. They filled my vision until I could see nothing else, and I fell into their cavernous depths. Before I even realized it, I was touching him, my fingers brushing lightly over his brow, down the wide bridge of his nose, along his high cheekbones. His face glowed from within the shadow of his long hair like the moon in the midnight sky.

"You're…" *Beautiful.* The word seemed so inadequate.

His eyes lost some of their edge, and I swooned. He caught my hand in his and pressed it against his chest. Beneath my palm lay hard, lean muscle and heat and the subtle but quick *thump thump thumping* of his heart.

He mirrored the action against my heart, his hand nearly spanning the width of my chest. "Listen, Hiro," he said in a thick voice. "Not to the world, but to your heart."

As if a switch had been flipped, my ears turned inward, and an overwhelming warmth enveloped me. I heard his heart beating beside mine, within mine, our souls mixing and folding into each other, a strong but gentle presence inside me.

With a whimper in my throat and tears burning behind my eyes, I fell into him. I knew only him, the heat of his skin, the brush of his breath, his arms wrapped protectively around me. I had the feeling he'd done something unspeakable to me, yet with my nose buried in his broad chest, I felt safe.

"What...what did you..." I started, still struggling to catch my breath.

"I've made you." His lips brushed against my hair.

I lifted my head and felt my cheeks flush with an emotion I didn't understand. It was as if I'd died and Sakurai Hideyoshi had taken possession of my soul.

The world closed in again as he rose to his feet. I fell forward into the space where he had been, my hand pressed against the warm spot on the floor. Gold screens flashed in the lamplight, and tatami scraped against my bare legs. He'd brought me inside.

He snatched up his sword from where it lay next to a sheet of rice paper and a little bottle of oil and ran the paper quickly over the blade before snapping it into the saya. He'd changed back into a kimono. How long had I been out?

"Okaasan!" I jumped to my feet, wobbling and falling to my knees. My muscles burned, and my joints felt filled with sand. Every movement sent hot bolts through me that made my breath catch and my head throb.

"What's wrong?" he asked, catching me by the arm and pulling me back up.

"I don't know," I said. "Everything hurts."

"You're hungry." He held me up by my shoulders until I regained my balance. "It's best you take as soon after the change as possible."

"Take...?" I swooned again as my mind tried to make sense of the word. In the course of the change and...that kiss...my kimono had become twisted, and the brush of Sakurai-han's hands against my skin as he straightened my collar made me tingle all over. Pleasure and pain swapped places so fast it made me dizzy. He leaned close, his arms encircling my waist as he tightened my obi, and it was all I could do not to bury my face in his hair.

With a sharp yank, he set the knot on my obi and pulled away, leaving me breathless and flustered. He turned his back and marched out the door, an unspoken command of "follow" hanging in the air between us. He left no opportunity for protest. It was follow or be left alone with the sounds and the textures and my own swirling fears filling my head and my heart and my lungs until I drowned. No matter what new horror he had planned for me, nothing could compare to that.

The outside air hit me like something solid, carrying with it all the sounds and smells of Japanese springtime, the sweet smells of sakura and plum. Cicadas buzzed so loud it sounded like the trees were breathing. Moonlight gilded every surface, turning the rooftops liquid. Real but not real. A Kyoto I'd never seen.

Sakurai-han cleared his throat, and I jumped. I slipped awkwardly into my sandals, shuffled toward him, and caught his sleeve just as he started to walk away. I felt like a child following his father into some unknown world. Every movement fascinated me. Every sound enthralled me. Every step filled with nervous anticipation until I trembled all over. A little startled sound escaped me as a street cat leaped into our path. Without a word, Sakurai-han reached down and took my hand, hooked my arm through his and pulled me close. The heat of his body against mine calmed me, and I closed my eyes and rested my nose against his shoulder, trusting his confident steps to lead us wherever we would go.

We stopped, and when I looked up, Sakurai-han's face had gone hard, predatory eyes fixed on a shadow stumbling up the street ahead of us. I squinted into the dark, focusing all my overblown senses on the familiar, lanky frame.

"Yamaguchi." His name came out a snarl, my new, sharp teeth biting down on it. Something dark coiled inside me and begged to be unleashed. I lurched forward.

Sakurai-han restrained me with an arm wrapped around my torso. "Wait, Hiro."

"But he——" I struggled against his grip as the image of Okaasan lying pale and bleeding filled my vision. Rage cut through me as I was reminded of my true purpose, the revenge I had given myself over for. Yamaguchi lifted a saké bottle to his lips, exposing a splash of blood across the sleeve of his kimono. Did he even realize what he'd done? Did he care?

All Sakurai-han's gentle protectiveness vanished, and he pulled me roughly in front of him, hands gripping my shoulders and mouth pressed against my ear. "Look at him," he whispered, almost growled. "What do you see?"

"I...I don't...see—"

"Look!" he said again, giving me a sharp shake. Panic seized me again, freezing my lungs, and all I could do was stare openmouthed. I saw everything, pebbles in the road, the little black birds chasing insects stirred up by horses, individual grains of dust hanging in the air, but not what he wanted me to see. With a frustrated growl, he released me and pushed me aside.

That strange pain cascaded through me again, and I nearly buckled without Sakurai-han supporting me. His back silhouetted by the moon, he took slow, deliberate steps toward Yamaguchi. Once within arm's reach, he slapped a heavy hand down on his shoulder. Yamaguchi spun drunkenly to face him, his lips curling.

"Samurai," he slurred. He dropped his wine bottle and went for his sword.

Sakurai-han caught him easily. He jerked Yamaguchi's arm up by his wrist. Yamaguchi tried once to pull away before his eyes clouded, and his face went slack as if all volition had drained out of him and pooled at his feet.

Sakurai-han cast a meaningful look over his shoulder at me before disappearing into a nearby storage shed, Yamaguchi in tow. Arms wrapped tight around myself, I stumbled after him. That dark thing inside me stirred with an even greater intensity, and I gritted my teeth as pain slithered through my muscles.

The shed was barely big enough for the three of us. I fell into it to find Yamaguchi on his knees facing me, Sakurai-han standing over him still gripping his wrist. He dropped it at my entrance, and Yamaguchi blinked back into awareness, squinting in the dim light.

"Ah, Hiro-kun." His mouth twisted into a smile both lewd and malicious. "I've been looking for you."

"What is this?" I asked in an unsteady voice.

Sakurai-han had drifted back to my side, and his breath wisped across my cheek. "Your revenge. Take it."

My heart skipped. "How?"

The corner of his mouth ticked up, and the moonlight caught in his white eyes. "However you want."

ELEVEN

First Blood

Yamaguchi's drunken brain finally caught up to what was happening, and he lurched to his feet. He flailed around for his sword and, finding it absent, threw himself at me, teeth bared, fingers curled into claws. His weight slammed me back against the door, cutting off the meager moonlight that filtered through it and dropping us into almost total darkness.

Despite the surprise, I held him off surprisingly easily. Unnatural strength surged through me. He fought blind, but my eyes pierced the dark. With a giddy laugh, I caught his forearms, and he thrashed against me. His blows struck light, his struggle no more than that of a sheet caught in the wind.

"Take him, Hiro."

Pain shot through my limbs, and my vision went hazy, Yamaguchi's outline blurring until he disappeared. And then, I saw it. A light, warm and soft and permeating his every cell. One by one, the physical parts of him fell away until it was all that was left, pulsing and bright. And a smell. Oh, the smell, sharp and spicy, filling my lungs like something sensual, something sexual.

Heart pounding, breathing shallow, I went still inside. Hiro the geisha faded away, and all I knew was the want, the need, to have that light inside me. To feel it sliding through my veins and coating my insides.

I relaxed my hold on him, bringing the light closer. Baring fangs I didn't even know I had, I plunged them into the source of that light. Yamaguchi screamed and thrashed anew as I pressed against him. This wasn't the embrace of a lover but of a python, deadly and inescapable. One hand fisted in his hair, I stretched his neck back so far it strangled his cries. I filled my mouth over and over, pulling hard and swallowing deep, and his light filled me to my very toes. I glowed. I had never smoked opium, but I imagined this must be what it felt like, head in the clouds, body numb to everything but the smoke in my veins.

The body in my arms shuddered and groaned. His fight weakened. The light dimmed. Its flow slowed, and I tore deeper into his flesh to get at it with a greedy, hungry sound. It ran thick down my chin and sprayed my clothes. Yamaguchi released one last gargling cry before going completely limp.

"That's enough, Hiro." Sakurai-han's hand on my shoulder set my already burning veins on fire.

I let Yamaguchi drop with less care than I'd give a bag of rice and latched onto Sakurai-han instead. He let out a bark of surprise, followed by a low moan as my lips connected with his. The same need I felt vibrated through his skin as he licked the light from my lips and chased my tongue. He sucked it from my chin, followed trails of it down my neck, and his breath sent shivers of pleasure across my skin. Every touch, every emotion heightened. My head felt light, my body like gunpowder, and his fingers like sparks. His presence, that mystical presence inside me, burned like a bonfire, high and hot as he pressed my back against the wall, groaning his own desire into the crook of my neck.

Little by little, the high mellowed into an all-over buzz. Gravel crunched under my feet, and rough wood scratched at my back. The dark shadows took shape around me, crouching like beasts and a strange little pile in the middle of it all, broad shoulders, pale skin, legs bent and crumpled underneath him.

"He's dead," I said, breathless.

"Mn."

"I saw…"

"I know."

A shard of panic cut through my euphoria. I shoved away from Sakurai-han and dropped to my knees beside Yamaguchi. There was no more light, only blood painted down his neck and chest. My hands and face were sticky with it.

"I killed him."

"It's what you wanted."

I shook my head, fighting against a riot of conflicting emotions. I wanted justice, I wanted him to hurt the way I hurt, to pay for what he'd done to my mother, but this felt wrong. I crouched over the ugly, twisted thing that didn't even look like a man anymore, doubled over under a wave of cold, sick guilt. My stomach lurched and I retched, hard and painful, but nothing came up. My stomach was empty. I'd devoured his life and made it my own, and there was no going back.

"Get a hold of yourself, Hiro." He grabbed at my arms and tried to pull me away. "He took something from you. You've taken it back."

I swayed as everything suddenly made sense. The word he'd used after I'd woken from the change: *take*. Not drinking, not feeding, but taking. I took his blood, his life, his power. It rushed through me even now, the hot thrill of it making my human mind reel at the contradiction. Yamaguchi was dead. Dead, and I'd killed him. I'd killed him, and it felt good.

"Okaasan…" I pressed the heels of my hands against my eyes hard enough to see sparks. I wanted my mother. A sob burst through my chest as I thought of her kind smile, her soft touch, all the love she'd given to a boy who was nothing to her. What was I now?

I staggered to my feet and pushed blindly out of the shed. Sakurai-han grabbed for me again, but I shook him off. He followed just a couple of steps behind me as I took a wavering path through town toward home, still drunk on what I'd taken.

My insides went cold as we approached the okiya. An eerie quiet lay over the house. The colorful lamps usually left burning outside were extinguished. The earthy smell of incense itched my nose even from the street, and my eyes burned as I realized what it meant.

The shoji were closed, and I hesitated outside, Sakurai-han a dark but steady presence at my back. He didn't speak or try to stop me. He just waited while I wrangled my overloaded emotions into some kind of control.

The shoji slid open silently, as if the house itself didn't want to disturb the quiet. Once inside, I raised my eyes to the kamidana, a small shrine built like a miniature house set high up in the wall. The doors were closed and hung with white paper. I looked back at Sakurai-han, whose eyes were also lifted, his expression solemn. When they fell, they touched mine for the briefest moment, and his shoulders slumped before he retreated outside.

Vision blurry and mouth dry, I drifted deeper into the house. The guest rooms, usually bright and full of energy, were empty and dark. All but a few lamps had been extinguished, the smell of the burning oil acrid against the incense. Igarashi Sato stood outside Okaasan's door, face rumpled and eyes red.

He didn't notice me until I stepped into the light of the single lamp in the hallway. His eyes, full of hurt and sympathy, widened as they took in my appearance, hair mussed and covered in blood. He opened his mouth to speak, but something stopped him when he reached my eyes. I wondered if they were white, like *his*. He backed away as I moved closer and lay my hand on the door.

"I'm so sorry, Hiro."

I swayed as my chest tightened, and I struggled to breathe. Part of me wanted to walk away, to disappear into the night where I could believe that she was all right, that I had slain the monster and her house would be safe.

I slid the door open. The only light came from a single candle next to a burning stick of incense. Okaasan lay on her back on the futon, hands folded against her chest. She'd been cleaned and changed into a white kimono, a dagger placed on her chest to ward off evil spirits.

"Okan..." I whispered her name as if she would answer, and it hung in the silence like a ghost. I dropped down to my knees next to her. Her expression was serene despite the violence that had been wrought on her. Just as beautiful as I remembered. A small bowl of water sat on the table next to her. I dipped my finger into it and leaned over to wipe it across her lips, stopping short at the sight of blood still clinging to my hands.

I couldn't even do this for her.

A violent sob wrenched its way out of me. I fell into a bow, head pressed into the tatami. "I'm so sorry, Okan." Tears dripped down my nose and clogged my sinuses. "I'm sorry for every time I disobeyed you. For every time I lied to you. I'm sorry for falling for a man I shouldn't have. I'm sorry I was such a bad son. I'm sorry I couldn't protect you."

"This isn't your fault, Hiro-chan."

I lifted my head slowly to find Hanagawa standing in the doorway, leaning on the frame as if she could scarcely hold herself up. Her eyes were red and her cheeks raw from the constant stream of tears flowing over them. Even her elaborate hairstyle had been taken down, and her hair hung limp around her face. She was no longer the poised and mysterious oiran, but a girl in mourning, a bird plucked of her feathers.

What have I done?

"You were right. I shouldn't have left." The words came out choked, squeezing past the lump of guilt and shame in my chest.

She shook her head. "I'm sorry. I shouldn't have said those things. I didn't mean—"

"I should have given him what he wanted. I was selfish—"

"No," she said firmly. "No one should have to endure what we did from that man. He's the monster, not you."

She lowered herself down beside me as my body quaked with violent shivers. She draped her arm over my shoulders, stiffening when she noticed the blood on my clothes.

"You killed him…didn't you?"

The shivers stopped. My sobs quieted, engulfing us in a loud silence. "Good."

I released a long breath and sank back into a bow, Hanagawa's hand resting gently between my shoulder blades.

I stayed in that position until my knees burned and my back ached. When I finally made it outside, Sakurai Hideyoshi was waiting for me, back straight and eyes on the sky, a black spot on the night itself. He'd given me what I asked for. He'd given me power and he'd given me my revenge, but it changed nothing. My mother was still gone, my family shattered, my world still empty. The taste of blood on my lips turned sour, and my vision went dark around the edges. Sakurai-han wrapped his arms around me, and I sank into them as the world faded to black.

TWELVE

Price

I came to back in the house where it all started, tucked into a futon, a soft blanket carefully draped over me. Greif pressed in on me from all sides and lurked in the corners of my consciousness like a monster who, once spotted, would pounce and devour me whole. I focused on the idea of Sakurai-han carrying me home bundled up against his chest, his fingers lightly brushing my cheek as he pulled the blanket over my shoulders. I clung to those romantic images, allowing myself to forget what had happened, what I'd done, and what I'd lost.

I stretched my arm up toward the ceiling, fingers splayed. Just a hand, no different than it was before. The painted images of animalistic claws and twisted limbs portrayed in books swam in front of my eyes. I'd been taught that youkai were tormented animals, resentful spirits, abhorrent things that bore no resemblance to men, yet I looked no different. But a nagging itch under my skin reminded me I was different. Little by little, the reality found its way back in, and my chest tightened around it. A hole opened up inside me I didn't know how to fill.

I found a robe folded neatly at the end of my bed, threw it over my shoulders, and forced myself up and into the main room of the house. Sakurai-han sat on the porch, the shape of his back silhouetted in moonlight. A bottle of saké sat next to him. He hunched, as if some invisible presence stood behind him, pressing down on his shoulders. Unsteady fingers reached for the bottle beside him, and I skipped the last few steps toward him to catch it before he knocked it over.

Surprise, concern, and relief all flashed across his face as I settled down next to him, shaking the suspiciously empty bottle and clicking my tongue. He frowned, turning his face away and rolling his empty glass between his fingers. I touched his hand and lifted it toward me, filling his glass before setting the empty bottle next to me.

"I've never killed anyone before," I said after a long silence.

"It gets easier," he replied, raising the glass to his lips.

"I don't want it to get easier," I said, a lump in my throat. "I'm geisha. An artist. I shouldn't be killing people. It shouldn't feel good." I swallowed hard, blinking back tears. "I hate that it feels good."

"It should feel good," he said almost angrily, a slight slur in his voice. "You've rid the world of something terrible."

"But it doesn't change anything, does it?"

Silence sat heavy between us. He sipped at the last of his saké. "I'm sorry," he said finally, his voice rough, "about your mother. And my part in it."

My throat went tight and my sinuses burned as I pushed hard against the grief. "I don't blame you."

"You don't?"

"You think you're the first man to fall for me?" I said with a dry laugh. "You are not unique, Sakurai Hideyoshi."

He scowled, nose curling as if he found the idea of other men trying to win my favor distasteful.

"No. I was the one who…"

Who what? Got carried away? Believed too much in the fantasy? Fell into something like love? I squeezed my eyes shut and dropped my head onto his shoulder. He stiffened but didn't pull away. I didn't need his sympathy. I just needed something solid to lean on.

"I don't blame you," I said in a voice barely loud enough for even me to hear. "I just wish I never met you."

I SPENT THAT NIGHT IN SAKURAI-HAN'S BED. WHETHER FROM HIS blood inside me, or because I had nothing else, I felt a deep, instinctual need to be near him. He didn't comment when I slid beneath his blanket and buried my face in his broad chest. I expected to have nightmares, to spend the night tossing sleeplessly, but wrapped in his arms with his steady, strong heartbeat filling my ears, I slept the hard and dreamless sleep of the exhausted. I woke with the sun painting orange light against my eyelids. I burrowed into the blankets, afraid to open my eyes and face the reality waiting for me and a world that felt a little emptier than it had the day before.

A cacophony of shouts and bangs from the front of the house ultimately roused me from my drowsy haven. Groaning and scrubbing at my eyes with my fists, I reached blindly across the futon to find it empty and cold. Donning a heavy robe to protect me from the morning chill, I found Sakurai-han in the main room, barking orders at a horde of workers loading trunks onto the back of a horse cart.

"What's going on?" I asked, pulling my robe tighter around me.

He didn't turn, his attention focused on the workers. "I've been called back to Edo."

"You're leaving?"

"*We're* leaving."

My mouth went dry. "For how long?"

"What do you mean, for how long?" he asked, arching his eyebrow toward me. "I live there."

"I live here."

"You live with me."

My face flushed hot with a surge of anger. "What about the okiya? I have…responsibilities. I'm just supposed to leave behind my whole life—"

"What life?" He whirled around on me, lips curled into a snarl. "You made a promise to me, Hiro."

"Fuzakeruna, Hideyoshi!"

"'*Hideyoshi?*'" he echoed with a mocking laugh. "Not so polite, now?"

"I *had* a life. I've lost everything. My family, my profession. Now you take my home away from me, too?" The workers had all stopped to watch as I thrust my nose in his face, but I didn't care. "You have no heart in you. You're a monster! A demon!"

"Tell me something I don't know."

"I'm not going."

"The hell you're not. You say you don't blame me, then stand here and count the things you've lost. They're not losses—they're *sacrifices*." He advanced on me, one slow step at a time. Bitterness and hurt flashed in his eyes before he reined them in. "Power. Revenge. You asked for them, and I gave them to you. I *made* you. You're mine. Your home is where I am now!"

I reeled as if he had slapped me. Tears welled in my eyes, but I bit them back, refusing to let him see how he'd stung me. The eyes of the workers burned like hot coals, and I ducked my head to escape them, pushing roughly past Hideyoshi and out the door.

"I leave at noon," he called after me. "I will not wait for you."

I stomped past his gate and onto the road on my bare feet. I didn't know what I was doing, where I was going. All I wanted was away from him and his cold arrogance, but every step I took made it harder to breathe until I was gasping against the corner of a nearby shop. It was as if the tears I'd been holding back poured inside and I was drowning.

I wanted to go home.

With a deep, ragged breath, I pulled upright and stumbled down the dusty streets toward the okiya, my mind reaching for memories of the only home, the only family I'd ever known. I'd had a childhood filled with hard work, but also a host of brothers and sisters who laughed, cried, fought, and even though we didn't share blood, cared for each other. The child inside me ached for his mother, for her warm touch and soft voice telling him everything would be all right.

The house was as quiet as it had been the night before. The doors were shut, its colorful banners taken down and replaced with those of mourning. Normally at this time of day, the house would be busy with preparations for that night's guests, but now it was an empty shell, a cold monument to what used to stand there, the stone on a grave. I wondered if they knew, all those temporary inhabitants who found a home there if even only for a night. The men who professed love with delirious tongues. The more vain part of me wondered if they would miss me or even notice I was gone. Did they mourn with the rest of us, or simply find someplace else to spend their time, some other person to pledge their fickle heart to?

I thought of Hanagawa, Igarashi Sato and the taikomochi, even the orphan boy who picked through our garbage. What would happen to the okiya now that its Okaasan was gone? As her son, I felt a certain responsibility to take care of it, to keep it running and make sure the people who depended on it still had a home. But then I remembered the look in Sato's eyes when he saw me, felt how my veins burned with increasing urgency. If Okaasan was here now, what would she see? Her son? A monster?

I knew Sakurai-han was there without even turning. His dark presence pressed against my back. A lick of bitterness chased away some of the despair, and I swiped at the wetness on my cheeks.

"There's really no going back, is there?" I asked without turning.

"You're not like them anymore," he said, his tone flat. "You can't protect them."

I remembered Hanagawa's reaction to the realization that I'd murdered the man who murdered our mother. "What if I'm the only person who can protect them?"

"Your presence endangers them," he answered with a growl. "With every show of strength, you risk exposing what you are. You would give them the illusion of safety, but you can only take. That's the price of the choice you—we—made."

"*We* made?"

"Mn."

"And what price did you pay?" I asked, voice shaking.

Silence stretched long and heavy between us and then, "You wish you never met me."

Guilt slid coldly beneath my skin. I turned to face him. He stood stiff, every muscle tense as if tied in a knot. I'd begged him, goaded him. How many times did he warn me? How many chances did he give me to change my mind? Hazy memories of the change and the fiery kiss that preceded it made my skin flush—a kiss both passionate and desperate, something longed for that he might never be allowed again. I'd been standing here treating him as if he'd done this horrible thing to me. When all the while, maybe I was the one who did it to him.

There was another truth to his words, what he was saying but not saying, and it fell on my back like a stone. I was dangerous. It didn't matter how much I loved them or needed them, there was no place for me in their world anymore. But it didn't change the responsibility I felt. I couldn't leave. Not yet.

"There's something I have to do first," I said after a long breath. "Can you just…give me a little time?"

His brows lowered and his lips tightened, but he nodded in agreement.

I FOUND THE BOY SLEEPING BEHIND A FORMATION OF PRODUCE crates, curled up like an alley cat on a pile of torn fabric. He woke the instant my shadow fell over him, his whole body charged with the hypervigilance that comes from living on the street. He popped up out of the mound of rags, eyes wide and jerking around in search of an escape, dirty cheeks flushed.

"It's okay. I'm not here to hurt you." I held up my empty hands and went down on one knee, making myself small. "I'm here to help you."

He blinked at me warily, his little nose scrunching up, but he didn't run.

"What's your name?"

He knotted his fingers in his tattered kimono. "Hiro."

I released a surprised laugh. "Hiro? My name's Hiro, too!"

The boy's eyes brightened a bit, the corners of his mouth pulling upward. "You live in a castle." His voice, though still small and cautious, held a note of wonder.

"It's far from a castle. But it does have a lot of rooms," I said, sweeping my gaze over his makeshift dwelling and back to him. A soft, familiar warmth radiated through me, and I almost looked up to see if Okaasan was there, standing beside me. "Would you like one?"

The boy pulled back, hope and suspicion warring in his eyes. I simply offered my hand and waited until little by little, the hope won, and he slid his small hand into mine. Warmth flooded through me again, and I swallowed back the push of tears.

"Let's go home."

A STREAM OF SMOKE ROSE FROM THE ROOF OF THE OKIYA WHEN WE returned, a small sign of life coming back. I led the boy up the engawa, and he hesitated at the door, fear creeping into his eyes again. I squeezed his hand in reassurance, and he did his best to wipe his bare feet before stepping inside.

The front of the house was still dark, but lamps had been lit in the hallway, and the smell of roasting fish drifted in from the kitchen. Pulling the boy along with me, I followed the sounds of subdued voices and tried my best not to look in the direction of Okaasan's bedroom. Hanagawa and a couple of the taikomochi sat around the fire, Hanagawa poking listlessly at the coals while the others cooked. Sorrow hung around them thicker than the smoke.

"Hiro-chan." Hanagawa lifted to her feet when she saw me, breathing my name like a sigh of relief. The taikomochi paused their cooking and bowed low, the added deference making my throat tight. "Where have you been? Who's this?"

Her gaze dropped to the boy beside me, her thin brows bunching over her eyes. I pulled him in front of me, my hands on his shoulders. "This is Hiro."

"Hiro?" Hanagawa echoed, a question in her eyes.

"Imagine that," I said with a shrug and a laugh. "He needs a place to live."

Her eyes widened and jaw dropped. "I don't think this is really the time…"

"Okaasan took me in off the street. Saved me when I was helpless just like him. Maybe this is…" My voice cracked, and I took a deep breath to steady myself. "Maybe this is how I repay her."

Hanagawa's eyes welled. She bent at the waist to address the boy, who leaned toward the smell of food, licking his lips. "Why don't you get something to eat?"

Without hesitation, the boy dashed toward the taikomochi and what must have looked to him like a grand feast. Hanagawa hooked her arm through mine and tugged me out into the hall.

"Your heart is in the right place, Hiro-chan, but how are we supposed to take care of a little boy?" she whisper-yelled into my ear as she dragged me back toward the front room. "You know we'll be closed for mourning with nothing coming in—"

"Anything you can spare him is better than what he has."

"And where is he going to sleep?" She faced me now, hands on hips.

I hesitated for half a beat. "He can sleep in my bed."

"Your…" Her shoulders sagged, and her arms dropped limp to her sides as the truth settled over her. She shook her head violently, and even though she wore none of the ornament, I could still see her silver hairpins rattling around her head. "No. You can't. If this is about what I said—no one here blames you, Hiro. You don't have to leave."

Tears poured down both our cheeks. "It's not about blame. I wish I could explain…"

"But without Okaasan…" She wrapped her delicate hands around mine. "The house is yours now. You can't abandon it."

"I'm not," I said, squeezing her hands against my chest. "I'm entrusting it to you."

Her eyes flew open wide, and she took a step back. "I don't want it."

"O-nee…"

"What about Yamaguchi-gumi?" she asked. "It's only a matter of time before they come around looking for revenge for Tojirou."

"They won't be a problem."

We both spun around at the sound of another voice from the doorway. Sakurai-han's dark form materialized in the room, a square wooden box in his hands. Though he carried it easily, it made a solid sound when he set it down between us, making the floorboards rattle. Hanagawa and I stared dumbly until he made an exasperated sound and flipped the box open.

Inside lay more money than I'd ever seen in my life, stacks of gold plates and coins on strings, paper envelopes bursting from the weight of what was inside. Hanagawa gasped behind her hand, and I dropped to one knee beside it, reaching a finger inside only to draw it back.

"It's everything they've ever stolen from you," he said flatly.

My stomach twisted. "Not everything."

"Consider it reparations," he said gently, "for the things that can't be replaced."

"They just gave it to you?" I arched an eyebrow in his direction, and the corner of his mouth quirked upward.

"Not exactly."

Something bloomed inside me, softening the sharp edges of my resentment. I closed the lid of the box as he turned and walked quietly out the door, leaving Hanagawa and I alone again.

"He scares me," she said after a long silence.

"Me too."

"You're going with him?"

I nodded, and as soon as I stood, she threw her arms around me.

"Make sure he takes care of you, Hiro-chan."

My eyes spilled over again, and I held her tighter. I missed her already, with all her grace and secret fire. Letting her go felt like cutting off a limb, and my heart raged against it even though I knew Sakurai-han was right. I hated that he was right.

I found Sakurai-han waiting for me outside, his back to the house and silhouetted by the morning sun, like a heavy brush stroke with too much ink. He turned slightly toward me as I approached. I couldn't look at him.

"Let's go."

THIRTEEN

A Long Ride

ACCORDING TO SAKURAI-HAN, THE TRIP TO EDO NORMALLY TOOK about a week, but with our physical advantages—greater stamina meaning fewer stops, fewer necessary provisions meaning a lighter horse —and a change of horses midway, we could cut it down to three or four days. As far as I was concerned, it might as well have been on the moon. All I knew of Edo came from stories told by my patrons. The home of the shogun, Tokugawa Ieharu, a fortified city protected by moats and high walls. I'd never dared dream of ever going there.

We walked most of the first day in silence, Sakurai-han brooding, me sulking, our horse, a rather large Kisouma, twitching and snorting between us. My grief had been temporarily overrun by anger, though not as much at him as at myself. What he'd said wasn't wrong. I couldn't go back. My human life was over the second I banged on his gate. But being forced to leave without being able to see my mother off made my chest ache as if being squeezed from the inside, and regrets piled up so high I couldn't see past them anymore.

I expected to see Sakurai Hideyoshi among them, standing somewhere near the top with his fangs bared, but he wasn't. When I'd told him I wished I'd never met him, it wasn't entirely true. As much as I loved Okaasan and everyone in the okiya, I was bound by that place, indentured even if only in my own perception, grinding out a pointless existence and biding my time until the inevitable day my beauty faded and my voice gave out. Sakurai-han materialized into my life like a specter, bringing with him a world of possibilities I didn't even know I wanted. He had, in his own way, liberated me, and though I wasn't sure what this life was, at least it was a life beyond pouring saké.

Yet every time I looked at him, my blood boiled. His face was relaxed, easy but alert, yet all I could see was that hard, cold look in his eyes when he said *"You are mine,"* the complete lack of empathy for what I'd just been through. My whole world had turned upside down, and he didn't care. All the rose-colored moments, all those momentary warm inclinations toward love, now seemed so childish. I'd offered myself to him, thinking that somewhere beneath all that darkness he cared about me. But he didn't want a companion or even a lover—he wanted a pet, a dog to follow at his heels, to sit, stay, and heel at his command. I'd made him a promise, traded my life away for my revenge, and he would take his due.

"What!" he barked. I'd been glaring at him without realizing it.

"I'm not talking to you." I frowned and turned my eyes back onto the road.

"Fine," he said with a shrug.

"Fine."

We fell into silence once again, and the sounds of the forest felt amplified. Birds screamed in the trees. Gravel popped like fireworks under our feet. Everything felt tense and fragile, and I gritted my teeth as if the very air might explode.

"Why?" The word burst from my mouth before I could stop it.

"Excuse me?"

"Why me?" I clenched my fists at my sides. "You could have gone anywhere, could have gone to Ponto-cho and had your pick of any number of boys far prettier than me."

He scoffed, his ears going a little red.

"But instead you show up to my okiya. Ask for me by name. Pay an absurd amount of money for the attention of an oiran you have no interest in using to spend time with someone you can't touch."

"If this is you not talking to me, this is going to be a long trip."

"Answer me!"

"Because I wanted you," he answered with an exasperated growl.

"It's an okiya, not a brothel," I scoffed.

"What do you want me to say?" he shouted angrily under the horse's neck, making him jerk and whinny.

"I don't know. Something!" I said desperately. "Something that tells me you're not a monster."

He inhaled sharply as if preparing to fling an insult, but his jaw snapped shut around it, trapping it in his throat. He ducked his head back behind the horse again and released his held breath in a long, slow stream. All I could see of him was his hand on the reins, clenching and releasing, clenching and releasing.

"My daimyo," he started slowly. "I was escorting him to Kyoto from Edo. On the way, he told me about an okiya in Shimabara boasting the finest oiran in the city. He spoke at length, of course, about the oiran, her beauty and her...skill, but what struck him most of all was a boy, a geisha, with a beauty to rival their finest women and a voice that could melt men's hearts."

"He meant me." I ducked my head again, just catching the line of his profile around the horse's neck.

"Mn. Call it curiosity or *loneliness*"—he said the word with a roll of his eyes and curl of his lips—"call it whatever you want, but I couldn't stop thinking about it. We arrived in Kyoto, he released me of my duties, and even though it was the middle of the night..."

I swallowed around the memory of being roused out of my bed and the strange, fluttery feeling of our first meeting.

"Are you saying," I asked, feigning sarcasm though my heart was in my throat, "that I melted your heart?"

"No." His fist clenched around the reins again. "But I felt the possibility. And that's more than I've felt in a long time."

I blinked, shocked into silence by the honesty of his confession. Not exactly a profession of love, but it made my heart beat faster all the same.

"I could ask you the same question," he said, a touch of mirth in his voice. I peeked beneath the horse's head to catch him leering at me, eyebrow arched mischievously. "Why?"

"Why what?"

"You're scared of me."

"With good reason, I think."

He rolled his eyes. "You tell me to stay away from you, then show up at my house. One would wonder at your intention."

My face heated, and he chuckled.

"As you said, I'm not the first to show an…inappropriate interest in you. I'd bet they made you all sorts of high promises." I groaned, and it only made him smile wider. "Why did you follow me home and not the others?"

"Who says I didn't?"

His eyes widened, and his jaw clenched the same way it had when he stood between me and that man in Ponto-cho.

"Because promises are just that: promises," I conceded with a groan. "If I showed up at their door looking like this, you think they'd want me?" I gestured to my simple, if not ragged, appearance. "No. They wanted the fantasy. The beautiful, mysterious, and ultimately untouchable. But you…" I drew in a long breath as if it would give me courage to continue. "You made the fantasy feel real. Like I could be that person, or at least it didn't matter if I wasn't. I was scared of you, but also felt…*feel*…safe."

The horse snorted as Sakurai-han yanked it to a stop, pushing past his head to stand in front of me.

"I…I don't know," I stammered, cheeks growing hot under his piercing gaze. "Maybe…maybe I felt the possibility too."

Once again, my heart skipped as he released a long breath, and a little, just a little, of the hardness leaked out of his eyes. Out of wild, reckless impulse, I took a step forward, halving the distance between us. He lifted a hand to brush a wayward lock of hair out of my face, allowing his knuckles to graze my cheek, and I leaned into them. He traced my jaw, lifted my chin.

And stopped.

"Sakurai-han…?" Eyes that had been pinned on me now focused on the tree line, and the hand on my face dropped slowly to rest on his sword. Soft rustling and a twig snapped, and with a flash of steel, it was drawn.

"Get on the horse," he said softly, placing his body between me and the forest.

"Sakurai-han, what's going on?"

"Just get on the horse!" Before I could protest, his free hand went around my waist, and he threw me over the horse's back.

"But I don't know how to—"

Bandits. Two of them rushed out of the woods, swords drawn. Sakurai-han gave the horse's rump a sharp slap, and with a jolt, it bolted into the trees and away from the fray. The forest rang with the sound of steel on steel as I struggled to grab hold of reins, mane, saddle, anything to help me gain control of the panicked beast beneath me. Each hoofbeat, each metallic clang behind me, drove all rational thought from my mind until there was only one thing left.

I have to go back. I have to help him. I have to do something.

Finally, I managed to grab hold of the bridle just below the stallion's right ear and give it a hard yank. The horse screamed and bucked, nearly tossing me off, before coming to a shuffling, nervous stop. I righted myself in the saddle and, trying to emulate the posture of every horse-riding nobleman I'd ever encountered, gathered up the reins in both hands and dug my heels into the horse's side. With a stomp and snort of protest, he started back the way we came, nearly throwing me again as he bounced and surged beneath me.

We reached the battleground in time to see the last bandit fall under Sakurai-han's blade, and my heart froze as he sank to the ground beside him, clutching a wide bloodstain on his middle. I jumped from the horse before he even stopped, landed hard, and something in my leg snapped, sending a razor of pain all the way up to my hip. Ignoring it, I dragged myself along the ground to Sakurai-han's side. I looped my arms around his shoulders and pulled him into my lap just as he took one ragged, shuddering breath and then—

"No..." I breathed, my skin going cold as his pupils dilated and lost focus. I pressed my hand to his wound, gave him a hard shake, but he was limp. My chest burned, and he didn't even twitch as tears I didn't know I was crying fell on his face. It didn't make sense. He was youkai, immortal, but as sure as I was living, he was dead.

Shaking my head in disbelief, I pulled him closer, pressed my forehead against his, clinging to him as if I could hold him tight enough to keep him with me. First Okaasan, now him. That pit in my heart grew so wide I thought it would swallow me.

"Please, don't leave me alone," I pleaded through a haze of sobs. "Please. Stay with me."

As I withered under the weight of my grief, the body in my arms leaped back to life. With a jerk and a gasping cough, Sakurai-han's eyes snapped back into focus, his face twisting and back curling around the pain in his abdomen. Immobilized by shock and disbelief, I stared dumbly as he groaned into my collar, clutching at my sleeve. Little by little, his body relaxed as the pain eased, and his eyes slowly rolled up to meet mine.

"Oh…Hiro," he said, still catching his breath. "Are you all right?"

"Am I…*all right?*" I echoed, shock giving way to irritation. "You were dead."

"I know." He groaned as he pulled himself up into a seated position, face pale, movements stiff, and scrubbed at his ruined kimono. He scowled at the bandit lying dead just a few feet away. "I can't believe that kusogaki got a piece of me."

"Hideyoshi!" I said sharply, drawing his attention back to me.

"Why is it you only call my name when you're angry?"

"You didn't tell me you could come back from the dead."

"I thought it was obvious—Ow!" He flinched and jumped to his feet as I punched him hard right between the shoulder blades.

All my fear and grief morphing into a hot ball of anger, I stood up and tried to storm away, but a sharp pain in my leg sent me immediately back to the ground. Uttering a long string of curses, I tried again, stubbornly making it a few steps before crashing into a frustrated heap.

"What's wrong with you?" Sakurai-han asked coldly.

"Nothing." I pouted, turning my face away, but I could feel him staring me down. "I fell off the horse."

"Is it broken?" he asked, squatting beside me.

"I don't know—" I hissed as he took my leg in his hands, probing the bones of my ankle with his thumb. Wrapping one hand around my ankle, the other around my calf, he gave my foot a wicked yank, sending white-hot pain shooting from my hip to the tip of my toes.

"Iiitatatatataiiii! Chikushou!"

"I like you when you're vulgar." He laughed.

"Damare!"

"Just give it a minute," he said, his hands resting gently around the offending bone. Gradually, the pain faded, replaced by a tingling warmth, and then nothing. Blinking, I wiggled my toes, flexed my foot.

"You fixed it."

"No," he said, pushing himself onto his feet. "All I did was align the bones. You did the rest."

"That's incredible."

He gave a little snort before offering me his hand. I took it and gradually eased up, gingerly testing my weight on my once-injured leg. I felt no pain, not even the bruised soreness of old injuries. Like my cut palm, it was as if it never happened. My head spun with a rush of euphoria. I felt impervious, like I could race through the woods and nothing could stop me. That thing, that dark thing I'd felt during my first kill, grinned with long fangs.

"You should carry this," Sakurai-han said, breaking me out of my fantasy by thrusting a short sword he'd taken from the bandits into my hands.

"What? Why?" I asked, bewildered.

"For protection," he answered. "I may not be around next time."

"What does it matter?" I said with an arrogant grin. "It's not like they can hurt me."

"Don't allow this power to make you overconfident, Hiro," he warned, pinning me with a stern look. "You're not invincible, or even immortal. Don't misunderstand what just happened here."

"I watched you come back from the dead," I said. "What is there to misunderstand?"

"Every time we come back from death, it's a choice," he said, his face going hard and immobile as stone. "A fight. Sometimes, it's easy. Sometimes it's hard, and if you don't have something to anchor you here, you will lose." He took a deep breath, releasing it slowly, and his expression softened just a bit around his eyes. "Don't be careless with your life, Hiro. Death is a powerful force, and though we may have been given a tool to fight it, in the end it always wins."

My face paled as my naïve arrogance melted away. I gripped the blade in my hand, slipping it just an inch out of the saya. I'd never held a sword before, and it felt heavy and inappropriate in my hands.

"What did you come back for?"

Sakurai-han's eyes flickered before he turned them away with a snort. "You think I'd leave you alone here in the woods?" he asked with a dry laugh. "You can't even ride a—"

Sakurai-han leaped forward as a third bandit burst from the woods behind me, filling the clearing once again with the smell of blood and the snap of a broken blade.

FOURTEEN

That Look

THE BANDIT SANK TO THE FOREST FLOOR, BLADE SHATTERED AND ARM severed cleanly at the elbow. He was silent at first, wide eyes shifting from the limb laying in the leaves to the stump at his side as if it belonged to someone else. Then with a mournful cry, he grasped at it with his remaining hand, clutching it to his chest as if having it nearby would make him whole again.

My stomach turned as Hideyoshi stood calmly over him, white bleeding into his dark irises like ink dropped on paper. He went down on one knee, and the bandit's screams raised in pitch as Sakurai-han caught him by the neck and pulled him forward.

"You have good timing," he said hoarsely.

The screams cut off as Sakurai-han plunged his fangs into the bandit. All I could see of him were his legs, kicking and scrabbling at the dirt and leaves until they couldn't anymore. A tingling sensation ran up my back and over my scalp when Sakurai-han dropped him and sat back, blood still clinging to his lips. My heart beat like battle drums, and it made me dizzy.

"Are you all right?" Sakurai-han asked as he drew himself to his feet, tugging an already bloody rag out of his sleeve to wipe down his sword.

I swallowed hard and nodded. "We should get out of here. Go fetch the horse, would you?"

I scrambled to my feet, still breathless. The tingling had traveled down to my fingers, and I shook them out, ignoring how badly I wanted to lick the blood from Sakurai Hideyoshi's lips.

The horse's crunching hoofbeats sounded from just beyond the tree line. I grasped the sword Sakurai-han had given me and, tucking it clumsily into my obi, jogged off toward the creature. He shivered with tension but seemed otherwise unaffected, all our gear still securely stowed on his back. With a few gentle words, I was able to calm him enough to lead him back to the road.

When I returned, I found Sakurai-han glaring at a piece of the final bandit's broken blade. There was something different about it. The light bounced off it like ball bearings, making it shine and flash in the narrow beams of the setting sun. Something in Sakurai-han's demeanor unnerved me as he looked at it, brow furrowed, jaw clenched as if barely containing a tyrannical rage.

"What is it?" I asked, touching his elbow.

"Silver."

"Only his?" I asked, gaze bouncing over the other swords strewn around our feet. "Who makes a sword out of silver?"

"A fool," he said simply, wrapping the piece in a bit of cloth and tucking it into a saddlebag. "It's too soft. That's why it broke when it met my steel."

"Then, why would he—"

"Doesn't matter," he said, pulling himself into the horse's saddle and holding his hand down to me. "He's dead, and we have time to make up."

I eyed the horse suspiciously, and Sakurai-han rolled his eyes.

"He's stronger than he looks."

With a deep breath and one last look at the carnage around us, I took Sakurai-han's hand, and he lifted me into the saddle in front of him. The horse huffed and stamped under my weight but didn't crumple beneath us as I would have expected, and I relaxed back into the saddle. With Sakurai-han's broad chest pressed against my back and his arms around me, he felt so strong, yet I couldn't stop thinking about him lying seemingly dead in my arms. In that moment, the bitterness I held against him seemed irrelevant. There was only the emptiness of a world without him. In the few days since we met, my heart had tied itself to his, welcome or not, his blood in me only making the bond stronger. No matter what he did or how we fought, he had become necessary as the clothes on my back and the blood in my veins.

I caught his bloodstained sleeve in my fingers and started to shake. He didn't say a word, but for a moment, he held me a little tighter, pressing his nose into my hair and breathing deep as if he could pull me into his lungs.

And then, with a click of his tongue and a kick, we were on the move again.

I hadn't realized I'd fallen asleep until I woke with Sakurai-han's weight on my back. He'd dozed off as well, his forehead resting on my shoulder and his hands lying lightly on my thighs. Our horse dutifully trudged on, following the road with heavy steps and punctuating the silence with weary huffs.

I rubbed my face and squinted into the darkness, trying to make sense of my surroundings. Long, slim shadows of bamboo trees stabbed at an ink-black sky, the rasp of their thin leaves giving voice to the wind. Dark pressed in on us from all sides, broken only by the dim lights of a farming village winking in the distance. The path broke off into a narrow dirt road lined with a few squat buildings. With their torn shoji and sagging roofs, I would have thought them abandoned if it weren't for the modest but well-kept fields that surrounded them.

I turned my head so that my lips pressed against his ear. "Sakurai-han," I whispered. "Sakurai-han, wake up. There's a village." He groaned, his weight shifting behind me as he stirred and stretched. "We should stop."

"No," he said groggily. "We need to make up time."

"Come on, I know you're tired."

"I'm fine."

"Well, I'm not." I huffed. "And unless you plan to carry all our things to Edo on your back, I suggest we rest the horse before it drops. We're too heavy as it is." He scowled and growled stubbornly under his breath. "Please. We've been through enough. What is there in Edo that can't wait a day?"

His lips curled, but finally he relented, urging the horse's head in the direction of the village. The horse chuffed as his hooves hit the hard-packed road as if he too were happy to see some form of civilization. It was late and the street deserted, but luckily we found a building with a lamp still flickering in the window.

A smart-looking middle-aged woman appeared at the door, plain but still rather pretty in her own way, with pink cheeks and a small mouth that curved like a bow. Her simple kimono was a bit threadbare at the elbows, her hair neat and ornamented with dark wooden pins.

"Good evening, Oneesan," I said, dropping from the horse's back and giving her a polite bow. She bowed deeply in return, balking slightly at the blood on Sakurai-han's clothes. "We ran into some trouble on the road," I explained, flashing my most endearing smile. "We're looking for a place to rest. Would you have a room for rent?"

She returned my smile with a tight one of her own and bowed again before gesturing us inside. Like everything else in this town, the home was modest with a rather abused-looking tatami floor. She led us to a room in the back corner, hardly more than a closet, with a rolled-up flat futon and a pitcher and basin in the corner. Sakurai-han curled his nose snobbishly, and I quickly thanked her, dumping a handful of coins in her hand and sending her on her way.

"Well, it's better than sleeping on the road," I said with a good-natured grin.

"Hardly."

"Stop it," I said, giving him a slap on the arm. "At least here, we can get you cleaned up. Take off your kimono." He arched an eyebrow at me, and I laughed as I tugged on his obi. "It's a little late for modesty, don't you think—?"

I stopped short as his collar fell loose, exposing his chest and abdomen. His nagajuban was stained a dark red. Dried blood covered his entire middle from breastbone to hips, running in thick, crusted rivulets down his thighs, evidence of the horrible wound that had once been there. Somehow during the ride, I'd managed to push the whole thing out of my mind, but here it was again, sticky under my fingers and sharp enough to take my breath away.

"I'm all right," he said gently, taking my shaking hands in one of his and tipping my face upward with the other.

"I know," I said with a shaky voice and weak smile. I pushed his kimono down off his shoulders, leaving it gathered at his waist before fetching the pitcher and basin from the corner. I filled the basin with water from the pitcher, dipped in a clean rag, and dabbed at the blood and dirt caked to his chest. I followed the hard lines of his muscles and found them crisscrossed by scars, thin white ones, hard pink ones. The marks of a soldier. My eyes burned as I traced them with my fingers. From the time I'd met him, I'd thought him something magical. Something fantastical. For some reason, I'd never considered that he was human once too.

A tear threatened to drop from my lashes, and before he could catch it on his finger, I moved around behind him and pushed him down to the floor. Falling to my knees, I loosed his hair from its binding and let it cascade down his back. I picked up the pitcher, and he let his head fall back as I carefully poured a little stream of water through it. He sighed as I pulled the water through his long black locks with my fingers, brushing out the dust and oils until it shone.

I picked up a wide-toothed comb and, humming quietly, worked my way through the knots and tangles. His shoulders relaxed a little more with each note, slowly unwinding like coiled serpents under his skin. My mind drifted on the song's gentle current, and I remembered what he'd said before. *A voice that could melt men's hearts.* I remembered the way he looked at me when I sang for him in the okiya, when he was my patron and nothing more. I remembered the feeling, that electric feeling, when he touched me the first time.

My voice trembled and grew thick, and I had to stop and clear my throat to rid myself of the knot that had formed there. Once again, I felt like I had more than one consciousness. One resented him, hated him even, for ripping me out of my comfortable, boring life. Another desperately wanted him to look at me like that again.

Heart fluttering, I pressed my lips against his ear, and he leaned into my touch. I let my hands slip out of his hair and wrap around his shoulders, slide down his chest. He curled his fingers around mine as he pivoted on his hip to face me. My song trailed off on a long, breathy note as he lifted his hand to my face and knotted it in my hair, his lips drawing closer and closer to mine.

And then, he stopped.

"W-What...?" I stammered as I noticed his attention drawn to something just over my shoulder.

"Look." He pulled back and pointed toward the door with his nose. The girl, the pretty but plain innkeeper, had returned with an armload of linens. She stood in the doorway staring, eyes glassy, expression blank. Even her arms had gone slack, her load of linens dropping to the floor.

"Did you..." I remembered Yamaguchi. How he'd taken on the same attitude when Sakurai-han grabbed his arm.

"I'm not touching her. Besides, she's looking at you," he answered with a smile in his voice. As if to illustrate his point, he rose to his feet and stepped away from me. Her eyes never moved, dilated and fixed on me. I stood, and they followed as if transfixed.

"But how?" I asked. "I didn't do anything."

"It's your voice," he answered, voice breathy as if in awe. "Of course, it's in your voice."

My gaze swung between him and the girl, eyes wide in utter bafflement. What was in my voice? Was he telling me there was some kind of mind-control magic in my voice? That I had unwittingly drawn this poor girl into my spell, a spell I didn't want or understand? I took a step closer to her, reached out, and touched her arm, and she didn't react except to follow me with her doe eyes, shining with blank adoration.

"Take her."

"No," I said, pulling back from her as if she might bite.

"Take her, Hiro," he repeated, eyes wide and trembling with excitement. A little white had seeped into his irises, turning them a milky, swirling brown. "She wants you to."

"But I don't need to," I insisted, but it was a lie. The dull ache I'd been ignoring since I woke on the back of the horse now made itself painfully known. My skin itched with the need. Already my vision was blurring, my awareness splitting, that thing inside slowly pushing itself to the surface.

"Take her," he said again, this time in my ear, chest pressed against my back and hands on my shoulders urging me forward.

The image of Yamaguchi lying in the dirt, his throat torn open, flashed behind my eyes, and I resisted. "No. I don't want to do that to her."

"So be gentle," he said, his voice almost a whisper. "If you do it right, she won't even feel it. It'll be like a lover's embrace."

I hardly heard him. All I heard was the beating of her heart, the light inside her calling to me. My resistance drained away like water from a leaking bucket, and I slipped my hand around her waist. Her body melded to mine as I pulled her to me. Intoxicated by the smell of her, I traced her vein with my finger and felt it pulse beneath it. She tipped her head back. I kissed her neck, whispered into her skin.

"I'm sorry."

Her delicate skin gave with a subtle pop under my fangs, spilling the light inside her in a great gush over my tongue. She gasped and stiffened in my arms as I sealed my lips over the wound and pulled hard. This was completely different from the first time, yet so much the same. Just as before, that first bright burst felt euphoric, sending my head immediately into the clouds, but unlike Yamaguchi, she didn't fight. She gave it up willingly, pulling me into her like a suckling babe. There was no fear or rage, only a gentle openness as her life flowed into mine. Through it all, Sakurai-han's steady hand lay on my back.

"Take her slowly," he said in a husky voice, "and it will be as pleasurable for her as it is for you."

With a whine, I eased the pressure on her veins, coaxing the blood out of her with the rhythm of her heart. Her body relaxed, shuddering as she released a long, breathy moan. Her arms came up to encircle me, and I swooned, swaying with her as if in a dance. Her breath turned quick and ragged, her body arching slightly into mine, but already she was weakening. Her fingers, curled in the sleeves of my kimono, loosened, slipping little by little until they fell limp.

The flow stopped, and I released her. My body ringing, so blinded by pleasure I could feel nothing else, I sank to the floor with her, my nose still buried in her neck. Those twin feelings of pleasure and despair curled through me. She was part of me now, and it was both a tragedy and a dreadful, intoxicating power. I wanted to cry. I wanted to scream. I held her until she went cold. Sakurai-han knelt next to us, silent, waiting for me to lift my head.

"How do you feel?" he asked gently.

"I feel...on fire," I answered breathlessly. I looked down at her, fighting the sadness that threatened to well up inside me. "I can feel her, pulsing in every one of my cells. I feel drunk and high all at once. I want to run the streets, draining the lives out of every member of this town just so I can feel it again. I feel dangerous. Like a monster."

"You are not a monster," he said, taking my face in his hands and forcing my gaze away from the dead girl in my arms. "You're beautiful."

There it was. That look.

FIFTEEN

An Unbreakable Chain

YOU'RE BEAUTIFUL.

His words reached down through the fog of blood and into my heart, ripping free a surge of emotions so strong they burst out of me in fat, ragged tears. Beautiful. I certainly didn't feel beautiful. Not now, maybe not really ever. No matter how many men and women sang my praises, I always felt they were mistaken. They praised a sculpture, something fanciful, not me. I would smile and bow and accept, all the while the plain, disheveled boy behind the costume quivered in jealousy and self-doubt.

But not him. He looked at me. *Me.* He saw the knots in my hair and the dirt under my nails, my too-long nose and slightly crooked teeth. He heard my voice crack and still, *still* he called me beautiful.

He reached out to brush the tears from my cheeks, and I latched onto him, pulling myself into his lap and wrapping my arms tight around him. He made a small sound of protest, which I ignored, before he sighed in resignation and returned my embrace. I mourned. I mourned the loss of my mother and my humanity. I mourned for the dead girl lying next to me. I mourned for every life I would inevitably take, praying for some sort of forgiveness, for some way to make it all worthwhile.

Sakurai-han slowly combed his fingers through my hair, and I lifted my head. His hard eyes softened only slightly with concern, he traced the path of my tears with his thumb. My hiccuping sobs gradually tapered off into a stream of shuddering whimpers, and I leaned forward, lightly brushing my lips with his. He gave a little gasp of surprise, his body stiffening as if he would resist, before leaning in to meet my touch. Soft, tentative, his lips caressed mine as if for the first time, exploring, tasting. Senses heightened by the fresh blood in my veins, his kiss felt like a lightning storm, each electric strike cascading through my skin.

Tenderness quickly turned to passion as I shifted my weight to straddle his knees, and our kiss deepened. I pressed so tight against him, we could fuse. Tongues slipped between sharp teeth, and he groaned, his skin heating as he tasted blood there. He sucked hard at my lips and tongue as if to clean every last molecule from my skin before moving along my jaw and down my neck. One hand tangled in my hair, the other teasing up the hem of my kimono, he tugged my head back and hummed into the hollow behind my ear, sending a delicious chill all the way down to my toes.

And then, I felt it. That familiar sting and dreadful pull. Panic surged coldly through me before being replaced by rolling pleasure. My veins lit like fuses, snapping and popping their way toward his lips. I threw back my head, releasing a shameless cry as my body arched into his. Just like before. The same tension, the same heat, only no danger. With every swallow, he took my life into him, but instead of dying, it was as if we'd become entangled, my life wrapping around his, mixing with his, a flowing golden mist enveloping us both.

He released his bite to kiss me again, and this time there was blood in it. His blood mixed with mine, thick and smoky and colored with his experiences. I drank deeply, desperately, and with it came a rush of images so fast and so compact, I couldn't comprehend them. In those moments, it was as if I knew him. Knew him in a more profound way than he could ever express. I tasted his bitterness, his regret, his deep loneliness. I saw the man behind the hard mask, the one he'd worn for so long it had grown into his skin.

He broke our bloody kiss and in a quick, disorienting motion, threw me onto my back on the floor. We savagely clawed at the bindings of each other's clothes until we met skin, flushed and damp with sweat. He was hard, and he pressed it long and hot against me, pulling my legs up around his waist. He rocked his hips just once into mine, and we both shuddered as a hot wave rolled through our pelvises. Slowly, he lowered his head so close to mine I could feel his ragged breath against my lips.

"You want it?" he asked, gliding his hand up my thigh. His pupils were blown wide and ringed with white. Whimpering, gasping, I nodded vigorously, lifting my hips. "Say my name."

I released a long, low whine, my fingers clawing into his lower back. I couldn't breathe, couldn't think, the blood I'd so recently taken running wild through me. The muscles of my abdomen trembled and twitched, pushing my hips up tighter against his. Vision hazy with lust, I opened my mouth but couldn't form the words. Teeth bared, that dangerous glint in his eye, he pulled back, and with one long, slow stroke of his hardness against mine, I came undone.

"Hideyoshi!"

With a satisfied grin, he hooked his elbow under my knee, lifted my hips and entered me hard and fast. The first sensation was pain, a hot, delicious sort of pain that made my blood pump faster. In another time, another life, it might have scared me, but now it didn't matter. Any damage he'd done would quickly heal, the warm rush of magical blood and the tingle of regenerating flesh only adding to my pleasure.

He paused after that first stroke, breathing harshly and gritting his teeth. Brow knotted, his long hair shrouding us in a blanket of black, he started a steady rhythm, slow, but each thrust as hard as the first. I moaned as the heat inside me grew, pulsing, undulating with every roll of his hips, the tatami biting into my back. Sweat beaded on the lines of his collarbone, and I caught it with my tongue.

He groaned as I whispered his name into his skin. The heat inside me grew spiky and volatile as his pace quickened. "Hideyoshi," I whined again as my body tightened around him. I thrust my hand between us, stroking myself to his rhythm. His hand joined mine, and soon I was lost in the sounds and smells of sex, muscles burning, hips straining upward, Hideyoshi growling as we frantically reached for release.

In one great, simultaneous burst, we came with toe-curling intensity. Hideyoshi shuddered as he pulsed inside me, my contracting muscles lengthening his pleasure. My body unfurled with a sound like weeping, releasing all its tension and going weak. Hideyoshi sank shivering onto his side, and I remained curled around him, tangled up in him, unable or unwilling to separate myself.

Fingers wrapped in his hair, I gazed into his sleepy eyes as our breathing slowed. Our hearts beat together in a fast but steady rhythm against our chests, the blood we'd shared looped around them like an unbreakable chain. I traced the lines of his face with my fingertips, savoring this rare moment where his mask softened, but I could already feel it coming down around my fingers.

"Still feel like rampaging through town?" he asked with a sarcastic quirk of his lips.

"No," I answered on the tail end of a sigh. "I never want to move from this spot for as long as I live."

He gave a little snorting laugh, his hand resting lightly on my hip. "That could be a while."

My expression darkened as I flicked my eyes down toward the body at our feet. "What do we do...with her?"

"I'll take care of it," he said drowsily.

"Not now," I said, clutching his arm as he made a move to sit up. "Can we just...stay like this just a little while longer?"

His face went hard, that mask slamming down to hide some unknown emotion that flickered behind his eyes. He froze in place for a moment, as if considering, before giving a sharp nod and settling back down next to me. I tucked my head up under his chin where I couldn't see his face and listened to his heart. Strong and steady and slightly fast. Somehow I knew even when his face kept secrets, his heart would always tell me the truth.

I quickly dropped into sleep, not waking until the sun came up the next morning. I found myself tucked into that saggy futon with my kimono draped over me. I reached into the space beside me and found it empty. Hideyoshi wasn't there, likely already up and readying the horse for the next leg of our journey.

I sat up and stretched with a contented sigh. Hideyoshi. After the intimacy we shared the night before, the polite use of his surname seemed inappropriate. I shifted in the bed, expecting to feel the physical effects of the night before and a little disappointed when I didn't. But his powerful blood still vibrated under my skin and his voice whispered in my veins. A smile tugged on my lips as I thought of him, an excited leap of my heart urging me out of bed and toward him.

I stood and shook out my kimono, filling the room with road dust, and groaned. I'd given little care to my appearance since leaving the okiya, but suddenly I felt the need to look at least presentable. I'd left my home with nothing. I only had the one garment, and between the trudge from Kyoto and falling off the horse, it had become terribly soiled. Throwing it loosely over my shoulders, I poked my head out the sliding door and into the deserted hallway; no workers, no attendants, not even other guests as far as I could tell. I padded lightly down the hall, poking my head into rooms until I found one that looked lived in, the dwelling of our pretty hostess.

Swallowing a hard lump of guilt, I slipped inside. I ran my fingers over a single wall hanging, a splash of black ink in the shape of a waterfall, and bent my head to sniff at a vase filled with small, scraggly wild flowers. I wondered who she was, who loved her, who would miss her.

Shaking off the sudden threat of tears, I made a beeline for a small armoire tucked in the back corner. Pulling it open, I found what I expected. Simple clothes for a simple townswoman, but all a vast improvement to what I was wearing. I found a kimono in muted pink with a white obi and, tossing mine onto the floor, pulled it on.

I'd never been so grateful to be a small man. A bit tight at the shoulders and just too short at the hem, but otherwise the fit was negligible. The addition of a pair of bright-white socks to hide the extra leg, and I was almost attractive.

My mood lifted, I ran back to my room and had just enough time to rake a comb through my wild hair and tame it into a loose ponytail at my crown before Hideyoshi returned. He stopped short when he saw me, a sharp intake of breath sending a splash of heat across my face. He touched the curled end of my ponytail with his fingertips, a faraway look in his eyes, before clearing his throat and returning to his usual stoicism.

"Time to go," he said brusquely before turning on his heel and marching out the door with me following a half step behind.

Once back on the road, we fell into an easy silence, as if something had shifted between us, or within me, alleviating our previous tension. Perhaps in allowing myself to mourn what I had lost, I also allowed myself to let it go. Letting go of my resentment made room for something else. I didn't know what it was, didn't even try to give it a name. All I knew was, whether it was love or some strange biological imperative, I wanted, *needed*, to be by his side. Resistance would only lead to misery.

He was a part of me and there was no going back.

SIXTEEN

Edo

———

WE WALKED WITHOUT REST FOR A DAY AND A HALF, STOPPING TO change horses. I leaned heavily on Hideyoshi's arm, only noticing where we were when the quality of the roads changed. Loose gravel turned to hard-packed earth, and I looked up to find myself in the densely populated post town of Naito-Shinjuku. The air was thick with the smell of horses. Shops packed tightly up against one another, serving girls waving flirtatiously at passersby, and everything buzzing like an angry beehive. The rattle of horse carts and calls of *Irrashai!* from shopkeepers flooded my ears, making me rattle with nervous excitement.

The great stone gate of Yotsuya Oukido loomed in the distance like a crouching dragon standing guard over a wide bridge leading to Edo castle, its white towers gleaming in the sun. Men pulling carts and carrying baskets precariously balanced on rods over their shoulders raced to and fro like worker ants, sweat pouring off their brows. This was nothing like the cultivated fantasy world of Shimabara. This was dirty and real, and it spoke to a longing deep in my soul. I didn't even realize I was squeezing Hideyoshi's arm until he reached down to pry my fingers out of his sleeves.

Hideyoshi stopped off at a butcher, who greeted him in sharp, quick keigo before handing him a small, brown-paper package. I took the opportunity to dispatch a hikyaku with a short letter to Hanagawa letting her know we'd arrived safely and I would write again soon. He then steered us east out of the commercial center. Soon we were surrounded by more open spaces dotted with grand homes hidden behind stone walls, only their sweeping roofs and the tips of manicured trees peeking over the tops. The few people we passed bowed low, making me feel strange and self-conscious. I glanced out of the corner of my eye at Hideyoshi, who seemed unfazed by their deferential behavior.

"Are you...important?" I whispered, leaning over his shoulder. He simply snorted in response.

He brought us to a stop in front of a heavy wooden gate. "This is us," he said, tapping on a wooden nameplate reading *Sakurai*. He laughed, catching my shoulders as I craned my head backward, nearly falling over in an effort to see the top.

"This? But—how—" I stammered.

"My daimyo is very generous."

I could only gape in stunned silence. Samurai were not known to be particularly wealthy, especially in this relatively peaceful time. I expected the modest, utilitarian home of a soldier, not...this. Hideyoshi laughed again and nudged my shoulder with his.

"You can see better if you go in." He shoved an iron key in the lock, and the gate swung open with a deep groan. "Go on. I'll unload the horse."

As if on cue, a little man of very advanced age appeared, spewing a stream of proprieties. Hideyoshi handed him the reins, giving me a little push before working on the saddlebags. I stumbled through the entryway and into a wide, green garden. A house not unlike the one where we'd stayed in Kyoto loomed large before me, flanked by a pair of sculpted plum trees, their branches leaning toward each other in a great natural arch. White flowers covered them and filled the air like snowflakes.

I followed the white stone path to the genkan situated on the left end of the U-shaped building. The wooden amado had been closed over the shoji, giving the house a hard, almost desolate feel. I approached the porch cautiously, tiptoeing out of my sandals and laying a tentative hand on the outer door. It slid open with a whooshing sound, revealing a wide, open room with a tatami floor. I let out a low whistle, remembering the four-mat room I shared with my brothers back at the okiya. I couldn't even count the mats in here. To the left was a seating area, laid out with a small, low table with a cushion on each side and an iron brazier. Everything was so neat and clean, it seemed unreal, like maybe he didn't live here at all.

A hallway led off the back, leading past the kitchen and taking a hard right turn toward what I presumed to be bedrooms. The wood paneling creaked lightly under my feet as I traced the silhouette of a great black crane flying across the shoji, illuminated by the shards of light that made it through the amado. I made my way to where it dead-ended into a narrow doorway and poked my head inside. It was beautiful. Eastern light filtered in through intricately carved ranma above the shoji, and a sliding door opened to the outside at the back. Tall vases filled with fresh flowers, likely procured by the old man upon word of Hideyoshi's return, stood in every corner, and a long, deep closet took up the entire inside wall.

"It's yours if you like it." I jumped at the sound of Hideyoshi's voice close behind me. He flashed me a wicked smile before ducking into another room down the hall, one I could only assume was his.

"I won't be sleeping with you?" I teased.

He poked his head out again, eyebrow arched. "For the days you hate me."

I laughed, and his eyes lost a little of their shadow.

With the package from the butcher in hand, he slipped out the back door. I followed using the door in my room, and we entered the back garden on opposite ends of the engawa. Hideyoshi grabbed a leather glove off a hook set in the wall and pulled it on before opening the package and revealing what appeared to be butcher's scraps. Thin, gristly strips of meat glistened from within the packaging, and he plucked one out with his gloved hand.

I curled my nose. "What are you doing?"

He gave me a quick glance, one corner of his mouth twitching upward, before unleashing a long, high-pitched whistle. He waited, eyes on the sky, until an answering cry pierced the air, a fast, rhythmic call that pinged off the stone walls. He whistled again, an upward-cascading string of notes, and lifted his gloved hand. I gasped as a goshawk burst into view over the walls, its white wings catching the sun. It swooped in low, drifting in and out of sight beyond the tree line before banking sharply upward. I squinted up at it, its speckled white belly lost in the glare of the sun. It released another cry before descending fast, taloned feet thrust forward, and landed on Hideyoshi's outstretched hand.

Hideyoshi clicked his tongue and mumbled soft words of praise as the bird tore into the hunk of meat, swallowing it in one great gulp. His eyes warmed with affection as he stroked the bird's feathers.

Awestruck, I crept down the engawa closer to them. Such a change came over Hideyoshi in that moment, I hardly recognized him. The constant tension he carried melted away, and a softer, gentler man shone through. My chest warmed as Hideyoshi plucked out broken feathers and the hawk nibbled at his fingers, bird and man interacting with absolute trust.

The bird spread its wings and barked a shrill note as I approached, its amber eyes fixed on me. They cut through me, not unlike Hideyoshi's on the day we met, the eyes of a warrior. Hideyoshi whispered a few soft words, and it quickly calmed. I jumped off the engawa as a second cry sounded from over my head. Another goshawk, this one slightly smaller, perched on the eaves.

"Careful. That one's wild," Hideyoshi said before tossing a strip of meat in the second bird's direction. She plucked it from the air and tipped it down her throat in one easy swallow. "His mate, I presume."

"And where did he come from?" I asked, keeping a careful distance between myself and the birds.

"I won him."

"How?"

"With a sword." He sighed at my perplexed expression. "Another samurai, a supposed takagari master, kept him as a trophy. Something he could show off to his high-ranking friends. He kept the bird tied to a post eating scraps while he feasted on the geese it brought down for him."

Hideyoshi's mouth twisted, and anger flashed in his eyes. I imagined the duel that followed, Hideyoshi's blade powered by the injustice he perceived.

"You don't cage him. Aren't you afraid he'll run away?"

"He's spent enough time bound by the whims of men," he answered, stroking the bird's chest with the back of his finger. "He has food and shelter here if he wants it. One day I may whistle for him and he won't come. But at least I'll know he's free." The corners of his mouth lifted in the most genuine smile I'd seen from him. "And we'll never have mice."

A soft feeling curled through me as I watched Hideyoshi interact with the hawks. It wasn't love, exactly, at least not the syrupy love one gives to a pet, but respect. He respected the hawks as equals, as soldiers in a war long past but still fighting.

"I sent ahead for a few kimono for you," he said, sending the hawk on its way with a flick of his wrist. His mate joined him, and the two made a slow circle over the house before disappearing beyond the tree line. Hideyoshi's disposition hardened again as soon as they were out of sight. "They should be in the closet. Pick one and get dressed. We have an errand to run."

"What!" I whined after him as he ducked back into the house. I stomped down the hall behind him and into his room. "We just walked for two days straight—"

"A day and a half, actually," he corrected. "I'm sorry. But it can't wait."

"What can't wait a few hours—"

"Do as I say, Hiro!" he snapped, turning on me with so much venom I raised my hands as if he might hit me. The change from just seconds ago was dizzying, and I found myself staring wide eyed, heart pounding in my ears. He flinched at my reaction, softening almost immediately, though his shoulders remained tense. "Just…get dressed."

I sulked out of the room, blinking and completely cowed. An explosion of irrational anger destroyed the relaxed camaraderie of our journey in less than a second. As I changed out of my dusty kimono, giving my hair a quick rinse in the basin, I tried to figure out what I had done to trigger such a reaction. Was it because I'd questioned him?

Threatened disobedience? Or was it my weakness that had annoyed him?

I opened the closet and found it filled with kimono boxes. Every color, every pattern I could think of, and all supremely beautiful. The geisha Hiro would have been giddy at the sight of it, but my mood was tempered by self-doubt. I picked one in navy-blue painted with swaying bamboo in white silhouette and a pale-blue obi. It was a fine thing that rivaled anything I ever wore in the okiya, but without the attendants to help me, I struggled to control the layers of thick fabric. Hideyoshi appeared in the doorway as I pulled it on, and I frowned in concentration as I fought with the bindings.

With a huff, he stomped into the room. I shriveled as he slapped my hands away and tugged the silk into place. What a disappointment I was. A geisha who couldn't even manage his own kimono. I squeezed my eyes shut, hiding my trembling hands inside my sleeves as he reached once again into the folds of the fabric to retie the bindings.

He paused as his fingers brushed my skin through the light fabric of my nagajuban, and almost instantly his touch softened. He let his knuckles glide briefly over the curve of my hip as he knotted off each little set of ties anchoring the garment in place. He ran his hand slowly along the seam, straightening it anywhere it bunched. He flattened his palm against my chest, over my shoulders and down my back to smooth the fabric before looping his arms around my waist to wrap the pale-blue obi around me.

"Aho."

"I know," he whispered thickly into my hair, resting his head against mine as he skillfully tied the knot at my back. His work done, he let his hands rest on my waist, and I laid mine over them.

I leaned into him. "So what am I getting all dressed up for?"

He sighed, tension creeping back into his voice. "We need to get you a name."

SEVENTEEN

Asagi

DARKNESS SETTLED OVER HIDEYOSHI AGAIN AS WE LEFT THE house, he walking ahead, me just a step or two behind. I didn't know what he meant by getting me a name, but his manner left me with a sense of foreboding. Something was different. His shoulders were set in a hard line, head high and defiant. His wood-soled sandals made a hollow sound and left deep dents in the dirt road as he walked. He projected confidence, but the tension in his jaw and his white-knuckle grip on his sword said otherwise.

I trailed behind him in silence as we headed back toward Naito-Shinjuku, my kimono swishing around me. I pressed my palms against my obi to keep them from sweating as he stomped toward our destination. Like a man walking to the gallows, full of fear and regret, but showing only spite.

"Just let me do all the talking," he said so sharply it made me flinch. "The youkai we're meeting can be a real snake."

"Youkai?" I asked, my brows bouncing upward in surprise. A chill ran through me as I pictured a literal snake, giant and eyes alight with a preternatural glow.

"Did you think we were the only ones?"

"I guess I hadn't really thought about it," I said with a shy laugh. "How many—"

"More than you think," he answered. "You may have even met one and not known it."

I released a long breath, my heart fluttering with nervous excitement. What would they be like? Like Hideyoshi, cold and mysterious? Would they be beautiful, wise and old beyond comprehension? I didn't even know how old Hideyoshi was.

"What's going to happen?" I asked.

"Nothing to worry about," he said with a quick glance over his shoulder. "Just a business transaction."

"What are you buying?"

"I told you," he said, "A name."

"I have a name."

"A surname. You'll never be more than a servant without a family behind you." I wrinkled up my nose, and he rolled his eyes impatiently. "It's just documents. If you ever want to do any sort of business here, have any sort of independence—"

"Independence?" I asked, as if the word were foreign. "I'm yours, aren't I?"

He stopped so suddenly I nearly ran into his back. He turned to look at me with a strange, almost pained expression. "You're not a slave to me, Hiro."

I gasped, blinking in confusion. In the okiya, business matters were never of consequence to me. They were someone else's job, someone else's problem. I never gave any thought to what it took to run the house. I wouldn't even know how to buy groceries. Now, Hideyoshi was telling me he didn't want me to be dependent on him, that he wanted me to be my own man. I wasn't even sure I knew what that was.

Did I even want a name?

Minutes later, we were weaving our way through the tables toward the back of a mostly empty teahouse. The front of the building was completely open to the air, its back wall lined with ceramic pots filled with spirits. The few drab patrons huddled close to the outer edge to catch the breeze lowered their eyes and purposefully turned their backs as we passed, as if making a point to ignore what went on behind.

Even the attendant bowed her head as she slipped among them, refilling raised glasses before disappearing somewhere inside. My heart twitched under a stab of nervous insecurity, and I clutched onto Hideyoshi's sleeve, but he shook me off, his gaze focused on the back table.

A man in a modest but well-made dark-blue kimono sat hunched over a stack of rice paper sheets, an ink stick and suzuri laid out neatly beside them, trying hard to ignore the attentions of the woman leaning on his arm. Shining silver kanzashi tinkled merrily as she brushed red-painted lips over his ear, the sweeping sleeves of her brightly painted kimono nearly brushing the floor as she tickled his chest. She leaned on her hip, legs stretching out from under her, geta hanging loosely off her toes.

She pulled away just long enough to take a deep drag off a pipe, pushing blue, sweet-smelling smoke into the air. The man at her side coughed and blinked, his thin lips curling in annoyance as she returned to his ear, smoke still leaking from the corners of her small mouth.

"Asagi."

The man's eyes flicked up, and he stiffened slightly at the sound of Hideyoshi's voice. The woman's smile dropped, and she peeled herself off her consort, turning narrow, unnaturally colored eyes on us.

"Yoshi-chan. Hisashiburi."

I gasped as a hard, deep voice came not from the man, but the woman at his side. A woman, but not a woman. Eyes the color of rubies jerked toward me, those painted lips curling to reveal small, pointed fangs. Asagi's gaze raked over me as they lifted their pipe again, pinching the end between their teeth.

"What are you doing here?" Asagi asked Hideyoshi without looking at him.

"I'm here on business," he answered, stepping in front of me.

"Mnn-hnn," Asagi said, leaning on their arm in an effort to see around him. "Fresh from your return from Kyoto. And what's this? A souvenir?"

"He needs a name." His voice was calm, but the muscles of his back knotted under his kimono.

"It's not like you to pick up strays." Asagi looked me over from my head to my toes before shifting their gaze back to Hideyoshi. "But then, you've always had a taste for pretty things."

"He's not a stray," Hideyoshi said from between his teeth. He hesitated a moment, jaw working as if tasting the words. "He's mine."

The air went cold. Asagi's teasing, playful manner dropped, their face hardening. "Is he?" Asagi's voice dipped a register lower. Knocking the coal out of their pipe with a sharp strike against the table, Asagi stood, tall, broad shouldered, barrel-chested. All the marks of masculinity once so masterfully downplayed were now on vivid display. Asagi pinned Hideyoshi with a glare that would shrink giants. "You saw fit to share your blood, did you?"

"I don't need your permission—"

Asagi cut him off with the loud snap of a fan opening between them. Asagi held it over their face, red irises even more striking from behind it.

Hideyoshi didn't move, didn't blink, eyes fixed to a point on the wall over Asagi's shoulder. Asagi's attention turned back to me, and I flinched. No flirtation, no sarcastic innuendo, just cold calculation. Asagi stepped around Hideyoshi, towering over me as they walked a small circle around me, examining me, sizing me up. Those red eyes burned holes in my skin. I hugged my arms around myself as if they could somehow protect me from Asagi's unnatural gaze.

Asagi snapped their fan closed and leaned close to me. Their voice lost a bit of its hardness. "What's your name, boy?"

My gaze jerked toward Hideyoshi's back. "H-Hiro."

"And your surname?"

"I...um..." I clutched nervously at my sleeves. "I don't..."

"Are you a slave?"

"No," I said quickly, straightening my back almost proudly. "I'm geisha."

A long silence stretched as Asagi's eyes narrowed. The corners of their lips curled, and their face flushed before they threw their head back and laughed. "A *geisha!*" Asagi said, turning and spitting the word in Hideyoshi's direction. "Are you so lonely, you've gone and made yourself a whore?"

Before I could so much as open my mouth to defend myself,

Hideyoshi appeared between us, puffing out his chest and glaring down his nose. I shrank into his shadow as Asagi's laugh trickled away. A strange energy passed between them as Asagi held Hideyoshi's eyes. The haughty affectation slipped, and their eyes went glassy. They took a shaky breath, lips parting as if on a question. But an iron wall came down before they could ask. Asagi closed their eyes for half a breath, and when they opened, the hard smile was back again.

Asagi threw themself back down beside their poor consort and draped themself over his arm. "The samurai and his geisha. How romantic." Asagi's lips curled around the words, but their eyes wavered. "You want a name? Fine." The old man picked up his brush as Asagi tapped the stack of papers in front of him with their index finger. Producing a small bag of tobacco from their sleeve, Asagi picked up their pipe again and packed the bowl, red eyes squinting at me. "Hiro is a fine enough given name. It actually suits you. But what of a surname? We can't exactly use the one of your *house* anymore, can we, now that Yoshi-chan's stolen you away."

The scribe, brush whisking over the paper, paused midline, watery eyes studying Asagi as he patiently waited for them to finish. Asagi hummed in thought, striking a piece of flint over their pipe and filling the air with the pungent aroma of cloves once again. "Ah! Of course!" Asagi exclaimed in a puff of smoke. "Taken from one house and brought into another. What better way to flatter a *whore* than with a samurai name."

"Sakurai Hiro."

I rolled the name reverently on my tongue. Something fluttered inside me, and I felt breathless. The scribe's brush jumped to life once again, and I watched the characters pour from its tip. Sakurai Hiro. Before we'd come here, I was afraid of the name I'd be given, didn't even think I wanted one. Now, I couldn't think of anything I'd rather have than *his* name.

The scribe's work finished, Asagi picked up a wooden hanko dipped in red ink and pressed it to the bottom of the page. Asagi lifted the paper up with two fingers and held it out gleefully toward Hideyoshi. "Ah!" Asagi snapped it away as Hideyoshi reached for it.

Growling, he thrust his hand into his sleeve and dropped a purse full of coins onto the table.

"Is he anything like you, Yoshi-chan?" Asagi asked, their mirth colored by something else, something deeper. That strange energy returned and made the air heavy.

"He's...better."

A slow smile crept across Asagi's face as they lowered the document into Hideyoshi's hands.

"Then what a pretty pair of demons you will be."

EIGHTEEN

His Name

THE WALK HOME WAS FULL OF CONFUSED ENERGIES. ONCE ASAGI handed Hideyoshi the papers he had purchased, he stuffed them in his obi and stomped out without a word. I was so dazed by the whole undertaking, it took me a moment to realize it was over, and I had to run to catch up. I found Hideyoshi bristling with anger, his jaw clenched and shoulders tight. I wanted to say something to take his mind off the strange person that obviously troubled him so, but all I had was *Sakurai Hiro* spinning in my head.

"Tch!" he spat suddenly, clenching his hand around his sword. "That snide bitch. He's making fun of me. Red-eyed harlot."

"I don't understand you," I said with a dry laugh.

"What business is it of his who I share my blood with?" he ranted, his face red. He didn't look at me. I had the feeling he would continue ranting even if I wasn't there. "Who is he to judge my choice? He rides the coattails of his maker, gaining social standing on the Arakawa name. Keeping humans as slaves and exploiting everyone around him, even his own kindred."

"Human slaves?" I asked, shocked. "Why would they—?"

"For blood," he answered, snarling. "Rather than killing his victims, he enthralls them, keeps them bound to him so he can take from them whenever he wishes. It's the same with his scribe. You can see it in his eyes."

"You can do that?" I asked, wonder slipping into my voice. "Take without killing?"

"Don't," he said sharply, turning on me with rage in his eyes. "When we take, their lives become part of ours. They live within us forever. We elevate them. What he does is disgusting. An insult."

"Why do you do business with Asagi if you hate them so?"

"I have no choice."

"You always have a choice," I said, giving him a poke in the ribs. He slapped my hand away with a growl and continued walking. "Seriously, though. Were you friends? Did Asagi betray you in some horrible way?"

"He's a bitch. Isn't that reason enough?"

"For you? The samurai with a heart of stone? No, this is a special kind of hatred." I chuckled, looping my arm through his and leaning my head on his shoulder just long enough for him to shrug me off. My good mood undeterred by his foulness, I grinned mischievously, my eyes flashing. "Were you lovers, *Yoshi-chan?*"

"Absolutely not!" he exclaimed, nearly choking on his tongue in the process, his face so twisted out of shape he didn't even look like himself anymore.

"Come on," I said with another poke. "You can tell me. I won't be jealous."

"I wouldn't touch that son of a bitch if he were the last man, last *person* on the whole island!"

I laughed and shook my head, unconvinced.

"Asagi takes pleasure in belittling me," he grumbled, speeding his stomping pace as if to put as much distance between himself and Asagi as possible.

"I don't know," I said, catching up and wrapping myself around his arm again, plucking at the bit of paper sticking out of his obi. "They did give me such a wonderful name."

"He just wants to slander me. Dirty my name by giving it to a—"

I froze, heart sinking into my toes and bruised as if he'd stomped on it. He stopped two steps later, his shoulders dropping. "To a whore?" I finished for him in a cracked voice.

He sighed, swiping a hand across his face. I could feel that wall going up between us once again, only this time I'd added bricks of my own. He glanced over his shoulder, the contriteness of his face doing nothing to soothe the sting of his words.

"I'm tired," he said, his shoulders straightening and his back going rigid. "Let's go home."

We walked the rest of the way in a hard silence, his eyes pointed stoically forward and mine lowered to the road beneath my feet. When we reached the house, he went straight to his room. I lingered in the front of the house, my pace slowed by the weight of my thoughts. By the time I joined him, he'd already loosed his hair and stripped down to his nagajuban, his kimono carefully folded into a little pile in the corner. He looked up expectantly as I hovered in the doorway, but I didn't go in. Instead, I turned and headed down the hall to the room at the end, and as I slid the door shut behind me, I could swear I felt him shrink.

I SPENT THE NIGHT TOSSING AND TURNING, SWEATING AND SHIVERING, what little sleep I got plagued by ghosts. I reached a hand out into the darkness, but I couldn't reach him. No matter how fast I ran, I couldn't catch up. No matter how many times I called his name, he would never turn, and I woke up gasping, tears in my eyes and legs tangled in the sheets. I saw every tender moment between us strung together like shining beads, only to be crushed under the boot of self-doubt. I curled myself around the warmth of his mysterious presence in my heart, but it only served to highlight the gulf that existed between us.

It hurt. Everything hurt worse than the pain of the need or the despair that followed. It hurt down to my soul until I had no choice but to get up and stumble through the dark to his room. I went down on my knees next to his futon and stared at his back, watching the steady movement of his shoulders and listening to the slow in and out of his breathing until he rolled over onto his back and found me. He sat up with a start, rubbing his eyes and blinking in the dark.

"Hiro?" he asked, voice rough with sleep. "What are you doing?"

I didn't answer, my mind a tangle. I spotted the paper he'd gotten from Asagi, the red Arakawa stamp shining in the low light, sitting atop his tonsu. The feeling of those moments surged through me again in a great swell and crash. I wanted his name and everything it meant, but just like in the dream, it was out of my reach. Hideyoshi called out to me sharply as I snatched it up and ran with it out of the room. I didn't know what I planned to do with it until I had already lit a lamp.

"What has gotten into you, boy?" Hideyoshi grabbed me by the wrist just as I held the paper over the flame. The edge had begun to brown and curl, and he quickly shook it out.

"I'm giving you back your name."

He groaned and swept a hand over his eyes. "It's too late for this, Hiro. Go back to bed."

"You think I'm a whore," I spat.

"You're letting Asagi poison you."

"What else am I supposed to think when you take such offense to your name next to mine?"

"You—" He cut himself off, taking a step back and turning away to hide his anger. When he turned back, his tone was more controlled, but only just. "You've had a hard few days. You're emotional. Get some sleep, and in the morning, we can talk about this like civilized men."

"Why did you even bring me here, Hideyoshi?" I asked with a shrug of resignation. "Do you even want me, or am I just a burden you've been saddled with?"

"You think I want it to be this way?" Frustration flared again, his voice tight as if he wanted to scream but held it back. "You show up at my house in the middle of the night, uninvited, begging me to use my power to solve all your problems. When I refuse, you play on my affections—"

"Your *affections*?"

"Yes!" His cheeks burned red, and he averted his eyes as if he'd given something away. "I made you. I'm responsible for you, and you... you made a promise to me."

"And I have done everything to keep that promise. But you're like that castle out there." I jabbed a finger in the general direction of Edo castle. "Surrounded by walls and moats so no one can touch you."

"You don't want to be here. With me," he said in a gruff voice.

"I do. I want to be with you. And last night, I thought…" My sinuses burned as I remembered the way he had looked at me. In that moment, it felt so real, but I wasn't sure anymore. "I have pandered to the shallow affections of men my whole life. I don't want to do it anymore. I don't want to feel like a whore."

Silence descended between us once again, dark and imposing. The light of the lamp sent orange shadows dancing over his face, making it all the more unreadable. He closed his eyes and took two deep breaths before continuing.

"You got what you wanted." He pressed the paper containing my new name into my hand. "Burn it if you want. You are released from your obligation."

His words cut me down to the marrow. Everything I thought we'd found on our long walk to Edo charred like paper over a flame. As he turned to walk away, the desperation of my dream strangled my lungs and squeezed my heart. What could I say that he would hear?

"Aho!" I wadded the paper into a ball and threw it at his retreating back. "That wasn't obligation."

I wanted to see something in his eyes—anger, resentment, anything—but that hard shell had come down around him once again.

"Say something."

"What do you want me to say?"

"Anything."

His Adam's apple worked in a slow up-and-down motion, and his eyes drifted away from me. "I don't think you're a whore," he said finally. "If you want to leave—"

"I don't."

He let out a breath, and his spine unknotted.

"But I'm scared."

He turned his eyes back to me. "Of me?"

I shook my head. My throat constricted, and tears fell as I thought of the parents I never met, of the Okaasan I lost. "I'm afraid you don't want me. I'm afraid you'll leave me too."

"Stupid boy," he said, the words more breath than voice. He shook his head before turning to fully face me. "I'm a part of you. As long as you're here, I'll be beside you."

Relief crashed over me like a wave, and I crumpled under it. Hideyoshi appeared beside me as I fell to my knees. I clung to him, pressing into his chest and filling my ears with the pounding of his heart. My anxiety poured out of me with every heaving cry, replaced by a sort of blank calm.

"I want you to have it."

I blinked and lifted my head just enough to see his profile in the candlelight. "Have what?"

"My name. If you want it." His Adam's apple rose and fell with a deep swallow. "I'm not...offended."

I sighed and dropped my head back into his chest. Hideyoshi gathered me up, blew out the lamp, and tucked me into his bed as if I'd been there all along.

NINETEEN

Unlucky

THINGS CHANGED AFTER THAT NIGHT. IT WAS AS IF WE'D COME TO some sort of agreement. Hideyoshi made efforts to calm his whip-crack temper, and I resigned myself to his distaste for physical affection, but it didn't stop me from seeking it. We found ourselves in a constant emotional tug-of-war. Every flirtatious ode met with a sarcastic quip. Every touch met with a scowl. I didn't let it bother me, and I soon learned to sustain myself on the small moments, those rare and elusive instances where his hard shell cracked and I caught him gazing at me from across the room, his gentle touch when he helped me dress, and the dreamy look that fell over him when I sang.

Time passed for me in a love-sick haze. I adapted quickly to the pace of life in Edo while continuing to trade letters with Hanagawa. Apparently, our "little Hiro" had disappeared for a couple of days only to return with about half a dozen of his young friends, all orphans of varying ages. She lamented that they were eating her out of house and home. She complained loudly across the paper about the trouble they caused, but every word was laced with affection, and I made sure my next letter was accompanied by a package of sweets and as much money as I could gather.

Meanwhile, I lived every day only to see that small spark of approval in Hideyoshi's eye. To watch his hard mask soften with the marks of pride. Every time was like unearthing a rare jewel from a mountain using only chopsticks, made more valuable and precious by the effort. And he never seemed prouder than when he watched me take. His eyes would harden to sharp points as he picked a faceless victim from the crowd and then threw a look over his shoulder at me. His silent command. *Sing.* I would thread my voice low and dark into the ear of his chosen one and draw them to my arms.

I took them gently. I didn't want them to suffer, so I sang a song that gave them dreams. They would see the face of their lover, feel their kiss as I pressed my teeth to their neck. They would fold their arms around me and meld their body to mine, unaware that their life was being drained out of them until, with a gentle sigh, they collapsed in my arms.

"You hold them like you love them," he commented once, wiping a drop of blood from my lips with his thumb and gracing me with a rare warm look.

"I do."

The corners of his mouth curled ever so slightly, and he brushed his lips against mine, making my heart leap. These were the moments I lived for, the small victories that made my murderous life bearable. I wanted all our moments to be like this.

We created quite a name for ourselves among the demons of Edo. Over time, my guilt over killing faded. There was only the rush, the high, the full body arousal as their light melded with mine in the most intimate of joinings. The more lives I felt teeming inside me, the more I thought as he did. Being taken was a gift, a favorable end in a brutal time. As the samurai and his geisha, we lured whole companies of men to their deaths with a sweet song. A beautiful image, if not somewhat exaggerated. Somewhat.

We had set up one night in the back room of a brothel, our favorite game. Hide brought the staff and the house mother under his influence, enchanted with a brush of his hand. They led a train of patrons one by one into our room where I would sing them a song while Hide watched, sitting on the floor sipping saké. In those moments, I could almost believe I was just a geisha. It surprised me how much I missed it. My heart fluttered as it had the first time I sang for him, every brush of his eyes sending tingles over my skin. That innocent, naïve boy was still inside me aching to be noticed, secretly reveling in the attention of a mysterious and forbidden stranger.

But oh, how my fantasies had changed.

Blood drunk and high on nostalgia, I could hardly stand as I let my latest victim, a rough-looking young swordsman just searching for a good time, slip from my arms. I held out my hand to Hide.

"Dance with me, Hide," I said, smiling playfully and wiggling my fingers.

"Saké!" he yelled into the house, snorting and turning up his nose.

"Oh, come on," I prodded, prancing over the body at my feet and kneeling next to him. I wrapped myself around his arm and pushed my nose into his neck. My body buzzed, and I ached for affection. "I wanna play."

"You have plenty of toys to play with," he said, trying his best to ignore me as I slipped my hand under his collar and nibbled at his ear.

"They're all broken."

I mewled in his ear, fingers tickling at his most sensitive places, and he had just started to warm when the door slid open.

"Oh, look. A new one," he said as a serving girl carrying a fresh saké bottle appeared with a new patron in tow. "Just in time."

I frowned and jumped to my feet, catching this new boy by the wrist and pulling him to me before he could see the mess we'd made of the room. He was tall with a sturdy frame and dark skin. He could have been a samurai by his bearing, but he wore no swords on his hip. It didn't matter, really. I only needed one thing from him.

I draped myself over him, poured love songs in his ear, and soon we were dancing. Not the partner I wanted, but I made the most of it, looping my arms around his slim neck and glaring at Hideyoshi over his shoulder.

"You are unlucky, Okyakusama," I whispered into the boy's ear as I tipped his head back with a finger under his chin. "If only he had agreed to dance with me, you could have gone home."

"I'm afraid, Geisha-kun, you are the one that's unlucky."

I'd never been stabbed before. It felt like being punched in the gut and having the air knocked out of me. Then came a familiar, sticky warmth. The kind I was used to on my face, on my hands, but never mine. Then pain, hot like a branding iron.

I jerked away, and the knife came out with a sick, wet sound. This was not a normal blade. Brighter. I remembered my first ride with Hide, bandits and a shattered sword. In that same instant, the sharp sound of broken glass cut through the air. Hide had the servant girl pinned to the floor by her neck, but his grip was weak. She broke away, using a panicked crawl to put distance between them. Hide slumped over the little table in front of him, wide-eyed and gasping, a dart protruding from his back.

I looked down at myself with disbelief as the front of my kimono turned crimson. I wasn't healing. Why wasn't I healing? I clamped my hands to my belly and sank to my knees as the blood I'd just gorged on poured out of me. How did this happen? How did they escape the magic of my song?

As if in answer to my unspoken question, the boy grinned and pulled balls of wax from his ears. The servant girl stood over Hideyoshi, staring down at him with a coldness that could only be born from hate.

"What...what did you...Hideyoshi..." Pain made mud of my mind and jumbled my words. Adrenaline spiked through me as my body struggled and failed to close the wound, waking something ominous within.

The boy took the girl's hand and pulled her back. He yanked Hide upright by the hair and pressed the blade to his throat.

"Do you live for him?" the boy snarled in his ear. "Or does he live for you? He's so young, has he even found something strong enough to live for?"

Hide tensed, his fists clenching until his knuckles turned white.

"Perhaps you should watch each other die and find out."

Time stopped, and my vision narrowed to a point. The knife glinted silver in the lamplight. The boy tightened his grip on the hilt. A little stream of blood flowed down Hideyoshi's neck where the tip of the blade just pierced the skin.

And I screamed.

TWENTY

Scream

I SCREAMED. I HONED THE POWER IN MY VOICE INTO A SHARP POINT that pierced their ears like daggers. It ripped out of me and raced through the air like something alive, something angry. They both doubled over clutching their heads, faces twisted and pale.

Fueled by fear and an intense rage, I threw myself at the boy with the knife, knocking it easily from his grasp and tackling him to the floor. The girl fell back against the wall, screaming as I tore into his throat. He didn't scream, making only a wet grunt as he opened to me. Blood poured from him, but I drank none of it. I spat it onto the tatami. He would *not* be part of me. He would *not* be elevated.

I wasn't aware of the girl anymore, only that the screaming abruptly stopped. I was blind. Rage swallowed me whole. The black rose up, and I became the monster. I ripped into the body underneath me even after it had gone still, tearing holes into his flesh with claws and teeth. All I could see were his hands on my maker, so I tore them off, cut his guts open as he had done mine.

"Hiro, stop! You're bleeding!" Hide wrapped his arms around me, pinning my arms to my sides. I fought him off easily, growling and snapping like an animal. "Hiro, enough!"

Nothing remained beneath me but a bloody pulp. My vision

blurred, and my insides went cold. Like a fire had gone out inside me, my strength vanished, and I crumpled into Hideyoshi's arms. He cursed and pulled me off the boy and into his lap. In that desperate moment, all of Hide's walls came crashing down. His hands shook and his eyes glistened as he ripped fabric from his sleeve and pressed it to my wound.

"Am I dying?" I asked between fast, shallow breaths.

"It doesn't matter," he answered, his voice tight. "You'll come back."

As the world went fuzzy around me, I was astonished by what I saw in his eyes: need. I knew he wanted me, desired me even, but this was different. His words were confident, but he was afraid. I lifted a weak hand to touch his face. I wanted to study every line of it. Engrave it into my memory and keep it forever.

"Do you love me?"

"Stupid boy," he answered, catching my hand and pressing his lips to my palm.

A feeling like falling swallowed me, and I plunged into a darkness so deep, a silence so total, it was as if I didn't exist anymore. It was like I'd never existed, like the world I knew had all been a dream. My body had no limit. I didn't breathe because there was no need to breathe. I didn't think because there was no need to think. It felt like dropping into a bottomless pool and dissolving. Empty. Quiet. Cold.

Some last, lingering thought teased at the outer reaches of my thinned-out existence, hard eyes and a soft touch. I scraped at the edges of my memory and pieced together the scraps. A promise. *As long as you're here, I'll be beside you.*

I'm here.

I'm right here.

Where are you?

Like imploding and exploding at the same time, my consciousness snapped together with a whiplash yank and pulled me from the lonely dark. My body convulsed, and my lungs expanded with a burning gasp as I struggled to surface. My heart pumped once, twice, and my very blood seemed to fight against me, but I forced it to move. It warmed my skin and quickened my muscles, and once my body held form again, I reached out blindly for the presence that called me back.

He was there already. Hide with his arms wound tight around me. He shoved something between my teeth, and I bit down on it.

"It's all right. You're all right." His tight voice penetrated the silence, breaking that final barrier and bringing the world back sharp and real around me.

The smell of blood teased my nostrils. His heart pounded loud against my ear. A voice cried out in pain, and it took me a moment to realize it was mine.

I lost consciousness again. I woke up at home, groggy and aching all over. My hands and face were cleaned, my bloody kimono gone and replaced with a gray yukata. Bottles of antiseptic lay on their sides on the floor amid piles of gauze. I touched my abdomen and found it packed with bandages.

Hide sat on his knees beside my futon, his head on his chest and snoring softly. His cheeks were pale, and the skin under his eyes looked bruised. He was still recovering, too, from whatever they had done to him. He looked transparent, like they'd sapped the color out of him. I touched his hand, and he jerked awake.

"How do you feel?" he asked, pulling back the comforter to inspect my wounds. The mask was back up, but it bothered me less after having seen what was behind it.

"Fine. Hungry." I flinched as he poked at my belly. I was mostly healed, but still a bit tender under his touch. "What happened?"

"Hunters," he answered after a pause, gritting his teeth.

"Hunters? What kind of hunters?" I asked, eyes wide. He arched an eyebrow at me, and I gasped. "Youkai hunters?"

"You're surprised?"

I released a sigh along with a dry laugh. "I guess not."

"I should have known," he snarled. "After they found us on the walk from Kyoto. I should have known they were watching. I was foolish."

"Hideyoshi…"

"The brothel was a mistake. I shouldn't have——"

I squeezed his hand, and he stopped. He closed his eyes, sucked in a breath, and let it out slowly, tightening his fingers around mine. I shifted into a more upright position, wincing as pain needled through my abdomen. "Why is this taking so long to heal?"

"It's the blades. They're made from silver and some other process we don't understand," he explained. "All we know is that they leave wounds that can bleed for days, some so severe that they never heal properly."

"They did something to you too." I lifted a hand to touch his cheek.

"It was nothing," he said, batting it away. "A poison-coated dart wielded by the servant girl."

My heart jerked. "Poison?"

"Mn. Deadly to humans, but on us, it acts more like a tranquilizer. They use it to slow us down and sap our strength." He shifted in his seat and released a weary sigh. "It's not pleasant, but it will pass."

"So they bleed us, poison us, but to what end? They can't kill us unless we let them."

Hide closed his eyes for a moment and took a deep breath. When he opened them, they were hard and sharp as daggers, his voice flat and matter of fact. "They torture us. Hold us captive. They take until we have nothing left." He paused, and something shifted in his eyes, some dark truth he was holding back. "There are things worse than death."

Goose bumps raised across my flesh as I tried to imagine what could be worse than the nothing I just came from. What fate could scare a man—or a monster—so bad, they would choose eternal darkness?

"They tried to kill me in order to kill you."

Hide frowned and turned his face away, but didn't protest when I laced my fingers through his.

"They won't take me, Hideyoshi," I said, voice thick but firm. "As long as you're here, I'll be beside you."

Hide sighed a little and brought my knuckles up to his lips before pulling himself off the floor. Watching his unsteady walk, I couldn't help but wonder what would have happened if things had gone differently, if that boy had managed to cut his throat and I watched him die. Would I have had the strength to escape the dark, not knowing if he would be there when I returned? Would he?

"What's that?" I asked, noticing for the first time a large wooden trunk in the corner.

"Oh, this?" He knocked nonchalantly on the lid, and the room filled with high-pitched screams coming from inside.

"What have you done, Hideyoshi!" I jumped up from my bed and whipped open the lid. Inside, along with the remains of the mutilated boy Hunter, was the serving girl from the brothel, caked head to toe in dried blood and screaming madly. I shot Hideyoshi a cross look.

"What? They did start it."

"Remind me never to get on your bad side," I said with a dry laugh. I turned back to the girl and offered her my hand. "Come on out of there." She flinched and started screaming anew, eyes so wide I thought they'd fall from their sockets. "Oh, stop. I'm not going to hurt you. Would you rather stay in there with him?" I asked, gesturing to the body underneath her. She swallowed her screams and shook her head. "Then give me your hand."

She took my hand hesitantly, and I lifted her out of the box and set her on her feet. She immediately pulled away from me, pressing her back to the wall and shaking. She was small, her round face still carrying the softness of adolescence, and my heart softened a little toward her. She reminded me of a bird fallen too early from the nest. Her eyes darted from me to the trunk and back again. Screams threatened to boil over once more, and she clamped her hands over her mouth as I reached over and snapped the lid shut.

"I know you must think I'm a monster," I said gently, "but think about this: What would you do to protect something you love?"

She gasped and went very still. We weren't that different, she and I. I saw it in her eyes when she stood over Hide after he'd been poisoned. A vacant look that told me she only saw the past. She had lost something important and would use any manner of cruelty to prevent it from happening again.

A memory twitched in the back of my mind. Yamaguchi with his throat torn open.

"What do you want to do with her?" Hide asked as I fetched a fresh towel from a little pile next to the wall, set out from when he was tending to me. I dabbed at the blood on her face and hands, cooing words of comfort as she twitched at every touch. "If you let her go, she might try again."

I wiped the last of the blood from her face and moved on to her trembling hands. I couldn't blame her. Something had been taken from her. A husband, a brother, a son. Despite the fragile peace I'd made with it, I knew what we did was monstrous. To prevent someone else experiencing her loss, she'd allowed herself to be pulled into madness and become a monster herself.

"Look at her, Hide." I pushed a strand of hair away from her manically shifting eyes. "She can't hurt anyone anymore."

"You have a kind heart, Hiro, but may I suggest a better use for her?" he asked with a cold grin. He slipped his hand over hers, and I stepped back, giving him a curious look. She resisted only a little when he pulled her close to him. Her eyes glazed over, and his magic took hold. He lowered his lips to her ear and whispered, "I want you to go back to your Hunter brothers. I want you to tell them what happened here. Of the demons, Sakurai Hideyoshi and Hiro, and our great *kindness*. Tell them if they *ever* try to take what's mine again"—he paused, the words coming out a snarl—"I will not be so kind."

A shiver went through her as Hide released her. We sent her on her way that morning with a new kimono and a package containing the boy's head. We both knew Hide had taken a huge risk, that she could lead them back here with an army. But Hide was fiercely possessive, not just of me, but of the city he called home, and he would risk everything to protect what was his. He had sent his message. Now, all we could do was wait for an answer.

We didn't have to wait long.

TWENTY-ONE

Crazy and Brave

THE LONGER I SPENT IN THE SHADOW OF EDO CASTLE, THE MORE I fell in love with the city at its feet. The long, meandering streets packed full of people, the myriad shops and merchants ready to help someone find whatever their heart desired, and of course the constant flow of travelers and tradesmen drifting in and out like a slow tide. Stories and curiosities from the farthest reaches of Japan and beyond washed up on our doorstep, and if I ever got bored, all I had to do was go outside.

The longer I lived there, the better I got at spotting others like us. Villagers, shopkeepers, doctors with young faces and old eyes tucked seamlessly into the landscape, providing services and safe havens that only we would need.

Hide and I, along with much of the youkai population it seemed, frequented a little izakaya tucked into a dark corner of a lonely back road in Takatanobaba. It was not unlike any other, with hard-faced cooks sweating behind a bamboo-planked bar and servers shuffling between rows of tightly packed tables, but it had the dangerous atmosphere and subtle tension only found in a room full of demons. Flashes of fang and white eyes often accompanied heated discussions about clan politics and war stories.

Hide and I had taken residence in the backmost corner, which had the double advantage of being secluded and having a direct line of sight to the door. He glowered into his saké glass as I leaned on his arm, mischievous fingers tickling at his thigh under the table in a desperate bid for his attention. The same old game.

A hush went through the room, and I became aware of a distinctly human presence. It happened from time to time. Though humans instinctively avoided the place, the occasional weary traveler still stumbled in searching for a quick meal, only to be driven out by the strange energies of the patrons before even being served. I separated myself from Hide and leaned out into the center aisle. Several others had done the same, and I had to push aside the hem of a server's kimono to get a clear view.

"Kuso," I cursed under my breath as I scrambled to my feet. Hide stopped frowning long enough to arch an eyebrow at me. "It's the girl."

The blood-soaked girl we'd sent from our home with a man's head in a box, no longer befouled but looking like a proper lady. The inexperienced huntress who'd poisoned my maker had stumbled into the hornet's nest. I quickly pushed through the crowd of gawkers and placed myself in front of her before she could venture any deeper, arms crossed tightly over my chest.

"If you plan to try again, you couldn't have picked a worse place," I said with as much venom as I could manage.

"He wants to see you," she said in a monotone. "Both of you."

Hide had slid up beside me, and we traded a puzzled look. Something was off. She didn't look at us, but past us, eyes glassy. She didn't shrink back in fear or fidget with mania, but swayed lightly, drifting on unseen currents like a ghost, like she was there but not there.

"Who?" Hide asked sharply. "Who wants to see us?"

"Now," she said simply, turning on her heel and ducking back out through the door.

We both stared dumbly at the empty space where she had been before Hide made an irritated sound and traipsed out after her.

She was already halfway down the street by the time we made it out the door and fell into step behind her. Hide's hand rested easily over his swords, but his jaw was set, his eyes boring holes into her back.

"Something's not right. Did you see her eyes? It's like…" I couldn't finish. It was too ludicrous to even consider.

Hide took my arm and hooked it through his, pulling us closer together. His hand lingered over mine a moment longer than it needed to before returning to his swords.

"Do you think it's a trap?" I whispered, clinging to his sleeve.

"Of course it's a trap."

Moments later, we exited the dark backstreets of Edo and approached the gate of a brightly lit estate. The girl pushed the gate open and stepped aside with a bow. She gestured for us to enter but averted her eyes as if she herself didn't dare to even look past the stone walls.

Inside was a modest estate with high, green-tiled roofs and a lavish garden. Ornamental trees lined the walls so densely, one could imagine themselves in a forest, the only sound the soft trickle of running water and hollow *thonk* of bamboo against stone. The whole front of the house was open to the night and lit with so many oil lamps the air shimmered. Smoke curled from brass incense burners, tickling my nose with something earthy and not altogether unpleasant that made me feel light, like stepping into a dream.

I clung tighter to Hide's arm as he led us down a white stone path toward the house. His soldier's eyes clocked every pinch point, every escape route. Something about the methodical movement of his eyes made me feel safe, and the wild pounding of my heart settled into something steadier.

As we drew closer, a man appeared in the front room, sitting cross-legged and leaning back on his arm. He was not exactly small, but more compact, with somewhat long hair that fell into his eyes and grazed his shoulders. He moved in a slow, almost lethargic fashion, as if he'd never in his life felt the need to rush. He sipped something hot from a tall ceramic cup, and the steam curled around his short, square nose and made his cheeks flush. His gaze caught ours over the rim of the cup and flashed darkly.

He had a face like a bulldog, crinkling in a hundred places as his lips curled into a smile and he gestured for us to enter. Everything about him was easy and casual, yet the hair on my arms stood on end.

Hideyoshi hesitated, every muscle coiled tight, before stepping up onto the engawa.

He pointed at a spot on the tatami in front of him. "Sit."

"What is this?" Hide asked sharply.

The corners of the strange man's mouth lifted slightly. "Tea."

After a brief hesitation, we took a seat on our knees, Hide first and then me just behind him, and even this amused our host. The subtle hierarchy of our relationship. He set out a pair of cups and retrieved a teakettle from atop a small wooden box beside him—the box we'd sent along with the boy's head.

"I apologize for the abruptness of my invitation. My name is Kyo," he said as he poured the tea, his voice low and slick and tinged with a guttural accent I couldn't place. He gave a short bow, his eyes never lowering. "Yoroshiku."

"You'll forgive us if we don't drink," Hide said.

Kyo's lips curled again, revealing crooked teeth framed with pointed incisors. He filled his own glass from the same pot and took a demonstrative sip.

"Why are we here?"

"It takes a strange mix of crazy and brave to challenge me the way you did," he answered, his face settling into a pensive glare. "I'm just wondering," he said, pointing to each of us in turn, "which is which."

"You influenced that girl," Hide said. Kyo's mouth stretched into that strange smile again. "Why? What is she to you?"

Kyo shrugged. "A tool. Nothing more."

"Like him?" Hide asked, gesturing to the box at his side. Kyo's smile dropped. "Are you planning some kind of revenge?"

"He had a job, and he failed," Kyo said with a coldness that pierced my bones.

"To kill us?"

"Yes."

"You're the leader of the Hunters," I breathed, no longer able to hold my silence.

His gaze snapped to me so fast it made me flinch. "'Leader' might be a bit of an exaggeration," he said after another sip of tea, unhurried, the silence in between drawn tight as a bowstring. "I set things in motion."

"But you're…like us."

Kyo's expression pulled taught, and something in the air snapped. My skin crackled with an unseen electricity, and my blood vibrated. Some deep, animal part of my brain cried out in alarm, urging me to run, but my muscles locked, rooting me to the spot as if the tatami beneath me had grown into my skin. I was suddenly aware of being in the presence of something old and powerful beyond my comprehension, and it shook me to my core. My fingers found the edge of Hide's kimono and curled up in it, as if this small bit of contact with my maker could somehow shield me from the darkness in his eyes.

"I am youkai, but not like you."

"Then why…"

"Because we are a plague on this world," he said, his eyes going hazy and out of focus. "A scourge, a mistake that needs correcting. We take the very essence of humanity into ourselves in an effort to tame the beast, but it's always there, lurking behind our sadistic nature, making us slaves. Humans need to be protected, so I teach them how. I teach them how to turn our dark hearts against us and slay the beast. I teach them how to set us free."

A long silence fell over us. The dark thing coiled inside me, itching and craving even now. I resisted the truth of Kyo's words, but they haunted me. Did I take at the will of the monster, or did it take at mine?

I trembled so fiercely I could barely stay upright. Hide watched me carefully from the corner of his eye, never faltering, but the hair on the back of his neck grew damp.

"That's a rather hypocritical view, isn't it?" Hide asked. "You make the choice for others yet allow yourself to live."

Kyo leveled his gaze on Hide, devoid of anything but pain. "It is my burden to live until I am the last. My…penance."

His words fell heavy on our heads. Penance. I closed my eyes and listened to the voices teeming in my blood and wondered what my penance should be for taking their lives. But then, I thought of all the faces in the izakaya, laughing merrily. I thought of the ones that cowered in dark corners, so afraid of what they were they couldn't move. I thought of the ones turned against their will, who never wanted to hurt anybody.

I thought of Hideyoshi.

"It's not fair," I said finally, voice trembling. Hide shot me a sharp look, but I just couldn't stay silent. "It's not fair," I repeated, but this time, my voice didn't shake. Hide's face went ashen as I pulled myself to my feet. Kyo rose to meet me, an amused smile curling his lips, and even though I towered over him, I felt small. "We're not beasts or monsters—we're people with as much right to live as anyone else. This is something that happened to us, not who we are."

"What about the people you take?" he asked. His words held an edge, but his voice never raised. "What of their right to live? What of the piles of bodies you leave behind after just one night? How they would stack up over a century."

"Do you worry over the cattle felled by wolves?" Hide asked.

"Even wolves are hunted to protect the herd," Kyo replied with an amused smile.

"You must know it is an unwinnable fight," Hide said.

"It would be foolish of you to underestimate my patience."

We dropped into another ominous silence. Kyo's scrutinizing gaze remained leveled on me, his posture relaxed, expression alight with anticipation.

"There has to be another way," I said, unperturbed. "Some sort of balance." I started to pace, jagged spikes of adrenaline making my hands shake. "Everything kills in order to live. In that respect, we are no different from any other animal on this earth."

"Animals with all the base desires of men," Kyo said.

"And all the virtues."

"You think *virtue* can muzzle the beast?" he asked, the corners of his mouth turning up and a spark in his eye. "Even ones like yours who so love gorging themselves in the back room of a brothel?"

"Yes," I answered, swallowing hard. "I'll prove it to you. You teach humans to protect themselves. Let us teach youkai."

Kyo took a step toward me, and Hide was on his feet between us. The light wavered around us, making my head swim.

"Crazy and brave," he said absently, crossing his arms over his chest. "You might just be useful after all."

WE WENT HOME IN A DAZE. HIDE FELL DOWN ONTO A MAT WITH A bottle of wine and immediately set to drinking. I paced the space in front of him, my mind a vicious tangle. The more time we spent in Kyo's house, the more I was sure he wouldn't let us leave, yet he had with little more than a brusque grunt of dismissal. I had to wonder why. Did he have some plan for us? Had we become his tools to be used and ultimately sacrificed like that dead Hunter? I played the conversation over and over again in my head, wondering when exactly the trap had snapped closed.

I set things in motion.

The most frightening part of it all was that it made sense. The urge to protect humanity from glutinous predators wasn't an ignoble one. I'd found a hundred different ways to justify what we did, but the end result was the same: the death of an innocent. Yet I couldn't stand by and watch the mass genocide of my own kind.

My kind. Had I lost so much of my humanity that I didn't even identify with them anymore?

Kyo, the Hunter leader, he was my kind. Or was he? *I am youkai, but not like you.* Just the thought of him made my hair stand on end. The power that radiated off him. In my short experience, I'd never felt such a thing, like he could set the air on fire if he willed it. It triggered a deep, instinctual fear in me, as if all the voices in my blood cried out simultaneously. The threats he uttered in such a calm, almost congenial manner as if it were all a game.

"He's a monster," I said more to myself than anyone else.

"If he's a monster, then so are we."

I wrapped my arms around myself, shivering as if summer had turned to winter in a breath, and Hide beckoned to me. I stopped pacing and slipped my hand into his. He pulled me down to the floor next to him, holding me tightly against him with an arm around my shoulders, and I laid my head on his chest.

"Maybe we are," I said.

"Hiro—"

"I felt like a monster that night," I said, squeezing my eyes shut, "when the Hunters attacked us. Tearing apart that boy. I don't even really remember doing it. Like watching myself from across the room. Sometimes, I lay awake at night and wonder when killing became so easy. When I started caring more about the high than the price. Does that not make me a monster?"

"So control it," he said firmly, lowering his face to look into my eyes. "Take those parts of you that scare you and break them off. Put them in a cage. Release them only when you have no other option. Make the monster a slave to you."

I swallowed hard, pushing my nose farther into Hide's chest. I thought of all the things I'd be giving up: the mind-obliterating high, the drunken power. Most of all, I thought of the look in Hide's eyes when he watched me, smoldering over the edge of a cup of saké. The feeling of a girl's body pressed between us as we shared her and the hot passion that followed. Giving it up meant a door closing between Hide and I, and more than any Hunter threat, that terrified me.

TWENTY-TWO

A Message

WHITE LIGHT DRILLED INTO ME FROM EVERY DIRECTION, BRIGHT AS A *firework that didn't burn out. So bright it shone through my eyelids and my hands that covered them. I cried out against it, screamed until my throat ached, but the sound was swallowed up before it could escape. Silence pierced my ears and slapped at my skin. I flung my hands out into a place with no definition. I could have been floating in space, could have been pressed into the ground or falling from a cliff. Panic seared my skin until my hand finally slapped against something tangible.*

It felt soft and wet and vaguely sticky. Blood. Everywhere. I was soaked in it. It was in my mouth, on my skin. I smelled it in the air. My vision, once white, was now red. My body, once weightless, was now heavy as lead. My veins burned, and my skin itched. Something like a twitch passed through me, followed by a flash of images: twisted faces, dismembered limbs, disemboweled bellies, fangs torn from their sockets, flesh ripped from bones and screaming, screaming, screaming.

I am youkai, but not like you.

"Hiro, wake up!"

I woke up gasping and choking. Something wrapped tight around me, and I fought against it, but it only held me tighter.

"Hiro, look at me."

I squeezed my eyes shut, and gory images played behind my eyelids.

"He's killing them!" I cried, hands knotted in my own hair. I pulled, and the sting was the only thing that felt real.

"It's a dream, Hiro." A familiar voice sounded against my ear. The smell of blood gave way to sandalwood and incense, fresh flowers and wine and...

"Hideyoshi." I cracked my eyes open. Darkness lay all around us, soft compared to the bright light of the dream. I blinked up at him, but the horrible images remained, superimposed onto his face. I collapsed into his chest, and he held me tight as I sobbed and shook, running fingers through my hair and whispering words of comfort into my ear.

"It's all right," he said. "It was just a bad dream."

"He was killing them," I panted. "I could...feel it."

"Who?"

"Kyo," I answered, his name sticking in my throat. "I couldn't see him, but I know it was him. Youkai tortured, their fangs torn out..."

My stomach knotted as I struggled to make sense of what I was feeling. It was a dream, but it felt different, more real somehow than any dream before it. My blood still sizzled with the same contradiction of fear and need. I stared at my hands, expecting them to be red. And the feeling that someone else had been with me the whole time lingered.

"He's watching..."

"You're safe," he assured me as I continued to tremble. "There's no one here but you and me."

"I could taste the blood. Smell it." I swallowed hard and took a deep breath. "I can still smell it."

He held me tighter, rocking me gently until one by one the horrors of the dream let go of me. My thrumming heart slowed. I no longer tasted blood, my vision no longer swam with images of torture, but I still couldn't rid myself of the smell as if it had adhered to my senses. Slowly, I lifted my head, scrubbing at my face with my sleeves. Something still wasn't right. I looked up at Hideyoshi, expecting his usual calm, stoic expression, but he had gone stiff. The sharp call of the goshawk pierced the night.

"Hide, I still..."

"Yeah." Brow furrowed, eyes dark, he reached for a robe and pulled himself out of the futon. "Stay here."

Protests caught in my throat, I clung to his hand as he slipped away from me. He gave it a quick squeeze before shaking me off and disappearing down the hallway. Everything went deathly silent, no birds, no chirping insects. The wind shifted, and I smelled it again. This was not a dream. Thick, sickly sweet and real, the scent was unmistakable. My chest tightened as I crawled on my hands and knees toward the door.

"Hide?" I peeked my head out and found the hallway empty. Using the wall as support, I pulled myself to my feet and slid along it to the front room. The front shoji was open, and I had to cover my mouth and nose against the smell—thick and metallic and slightly rancid like bad meat—that rushed in with every gust of air. I could just make out the outline of Hide's back in the darkness beyond it, crouched down on one knee. The hawk barked from a branch overhead, and he quickly stood when he heard me approach.

"Go back inside, Hiro," he said, pushing me backward just as I reached the engawa.

"What happened?" I craned my neck in an effort to see over his broad shoulder.

"Just turn around," he insisted. "You don't need to see—"

In a burst of anger and desperation, I shoved past him and into the garden. Out here, the smell hit me like a wall, making my eyes tear and nearly knocking me over before I reached the edge of the porch. Staggering, blinking, hand over my mouth to keep from retching, I peered into the darkness at a distinct mound that had formed in our garden. My stomach knotted, and as my eyes adjusted to the dark, the mound gained definition. Hands, feet, faces took shape. Human bodies. Drained of blood. Ten, maybe fifteen of them piled in front of our house like some grotesque offering.

A moan escaped my throat, and I swayed on my feet as my bones turned liquid. Hideyoshi appeared at my side, catching my elbow and lowering me down to the porch. "Stupid boy," he growled. "I told you to stay inside."

"What...what is this?" I asked between gasping breaths.

"A message." His voice was low and gravelly, his usual stoic expression trembling around the edges. "Look."

He handed me a small wooden box that just fit in the palm of my hand. Dark wood had been sanded and varnished until it was smooth as glass. A dragon carving adorned the lid, its eyes inlaid with red stones. It rattled as something shifted inside it. Palms sweating, I cracked open the lid. The hinges creaked a complaint, and something small and pearl white reflected the moonlight. Two...no, four almost cylindrical objects, tapered and wickedly pointed at one end, lay within.

Fangs.

I slammed the lid closed, and Hide had to take it from my hands as it started to slip. Fangs, cleaned and polished like jewels, boxed up like trophies. Along with the pile of human corpses, one of our kind had been taken, taken and tortured, and this was all that remained. Just like in my dream. Hide then handed me a little piece of rice paper, folded into a neat square as if it had been tucked inside. Written on it in perfect calligraphy: *One night.*

Hide sat silently beside me, taking my hand in his. I think he expected despair, but rage boiled up inside me, rage and disgust. That dangerous part of me scratched and stirred, and my heart went eerily cold.

"Who do you think they were?" I asked in a flat voice, my gaze resting on the box in Hide's hand but not really seeing it.

"Doesn't matter."

"It matters to someone." I clenched my fists in my lap, wadding the paper in my hands into a tight ball. "Is this what we can expect from now on? Each night's body count stacked up on our lawn?"

"Not if we stop it."

"I saw it, Hide," I said, the images from my dream striking me again and bringing fresh tears to my eyes. "I saw what he did to these people."

"It was a dream, Hiro," he insisted. "You smelled the blood, and your mind did the rest, that's all."

"It didn't feel like a dream."

Hide's brow creased as he studied me, considering my words. Disbelief hung like a veil over his eyes, but he didn't voice it.

"What do you want to do?" he asked.

"I want to hang him from a tree and watch the crows peck out his eyes," I answered, surprised at my own coldness.

Hide laughed, a loud burst of sound in the tense silence.

"Well, that sounds like a job for tomorrow," he said, pulling us both to our feet. "For now, I want you to go inside, have some wine, and try to get some sleep."

"But—"

"I'll take care of this," he said, gesturing to the mess over his shoulder. "Go."

I did as he said. I went inside and poured a glass of wine, but didn't drink it. Instead, I sat at the low table in the main room, my hands wrapped tightly around the glass, and thought about what Hide had told me. *Break off the parts that scare you.* But the parts that scared me, the parts that raged and thirsted for blood and violence, were the only parts that held any comfort in times like this. The only parts not susceptible to fear, sadness, all the messy emotions that left me weak. It made me think of Okaasan and how I couldn't help her. It made me remember Hide's warning as we stood in front of the okiya for the last time. *Your presence endangers them.* My mind drifted to the box of letters from Hanagawa I kept tucked away in my room. How long before the Hunters traced me back to her?

As the air filled with the smell of smoke and burning flesh, I clung to the rage, pushing my softer self into the cage until I went silent inside.

"Hiro." I blinked, and Hide appeared in front of me, his hands resting on my forearms. He narrowed his eyes as he studied me. "You all right?"

"Yes," I answered, shaking the cobwebs from my mind. My hands trembled again, and I lifted the glass to my lips.

He took the glass from me as it lowered, finishing it off himself before setting it aside.

"I'm scared."

He swallowed hard, his gaze falling to the table between us. For a moment, I saw all the same fears rolling around inside him, saw his jaw clench and his lips shake. Then, the wall came down, solid and final, and something inside me burned. I felt like I'd been dropped in that white space again with nothing to grab on to, and the wine in my belly turned sour.

With a deep breath, he stood and moved toward the bedroom.

Hideyoshi shot a strange look over his shoulder when I didn't follow. Something strong, wild and insistent boiled up in me, making my skin hot and my blood shake. The monster, high on violence and the smell of blood, rolled and complained, unsatiated. Instead of locking it away, I clung to it, the only thing that felt solid, the only thing that had any answers.

I stood up from the table, but instead of following Hide back to bed, I went straight out the front, past the still-smoldering pile of bodies, and out the gate. The sky was ink black, the street all but deserted at this time of night. I was vaguely aware of Hideyoshi's stomping footsteps behind me, but I focused instead on the firefly glow of human hearts.

A man appeared on the road ahead of me, stumbling drunk and filthy as if he'd been sleeping on the streets. He shone like a beacon in the night, and like a ship at sea, I drifted toward it. Hide called my name sharply as I picked up my pace, head lowered, a predator on the prowl.

Like a wild dog, I pounced. I hit his back hard, and he went down face first on the dusty street. He floundered in the dirt, cursing loudly as drunken eyes swiveled in their sockets in search of his attacker.

Hide once praised me for my gentleness, but there was nothing gentle about what I was about to do. He let out a loud *oof* as I dropped my knee into his lower back, pinning him to the ground. The smell of wine and sweat and living blood flooded my senses and made me swoon. The fissure in my mind grew wider as I grabbed his topknot and pulled his head up. His neck stretched long and bare before me. My veins tingled. My mouth watered.

"Hiro, stop!"

Hide's words passed through me as if I were made of glass. The monster inside me roared, and I plunged my fangs into the drunkard's neck. He thrashed uselessly against me, his cries vibrating the night air. I pulled hard, and they became choked as his blood streamed out of him and into me. It hit the back of my throat with a bright euphoria that burned away my earlier despair until nothing was left but blood and ash.

"Hiro!"

Hideyoshi's hands came down hard on my shoulders and yanked me back. I fell on my side next to the drunkard, now pale and lying motionless in the dirt. Blood oozed from a deep tear in his throat. He looked like he'd been mauled by an animal. It wasn't far off.

Hide took a moment to ensure the man was dead before snatching me up by my collar and dragging me into the nearest alleyway.

"Stupid, stupid boy," he spat as he tossed me up against the nearest wall. "Have you learned nothing?"

I laughed a giddy, joyless laugh. The blood made my joints loose, and I slumped against the wall, arms wrapped around myself. I'd learned one thing. It still felt good, the blood and the violence. I'd made the monster a slave to me. I'd thrown it up between me and all the things I didn't want to feel. I'd used it as a shield, and now that it had retreated, it left a cold space behind.

"Do you have any idea how many people could have seen you?" Hideyoshi's face flared red, and his irises turned white. He wanted to pace, but the confines of the alley wouldn't allow it, so he was stuck twisting like a flag in the wind, body cutting jagged lines in the shadows, fists balled at his sides.

"I only wanted you to see me." The giddiness faded, and tears blurred my vision. "I need you, and you're so far away."

He closed the space between us and grabbed me roughly by the shoulders, forcing me to look at him. "I am right here." He pushed the words between his teeth. At this distance, I could see all the cracks in his armor. A tear dropped from my eye, and he brushed it away with his thumb. The white faded from his eyes, the anger leaving with it, and he pressed his forehead against mine.

A sob lurched out of my throat as all the feelings I'd tried to drown in blood resurfaced. I clung to him, bringing him as close to me as our bodies would allow. His arms encircled my waist, and I buried my face in his neck, world blacked out by the veil of his hair.

"What did I do?" I asked as much to myself as him. "That man did nothing wrong. Why did I do that to him?"

"To punish me, I think," he whispered into my hair.

"I'm sorry."

He released a long sigh and pressed a kiss against my temple. "Let's go home."

I thought he would pull away, but instead he hooked an arm behind my knees and swept me up. Nestled against his chest, I focused on the steady rhythm of his heart and let the high of the blood wash over me again, strong and dizzying as hard liquor.

"I'm sorry, too," Hide said after a long silence.

I blinked, momentarily disoriented. "For what?"

"That I can't be…like you."

I tipped my head back far enough to give him a questioning look. He glanced down at me for a moment before clearing his throat and refocusing on the road.

"You're so open." His mouth twisted as if every word took tremendous effort. "Everything you feel flows through you like water. Both good and bad. Before I was…like this, I was still a soldier. Death was commonplace, often by my hand." His throat worked through a hard swallow. "I couldn't allow myself to feel those things, so I put my heart in a box. To protect it. I think I put you there too."

"Hide…"

"You *are* there," he said, face stern. "You are. Even when it's hard for either of us to see."

A burst of warmth flowed through me from the top of my head to the tip of my toes. It wasn't quite an "I love you," but it was maybe close enough. A laugh bubbled up inside my chest and my eyes burned again, but this time the tears were different.

"What's funny?"

"Nothing," I said, pressing my lips right up against his jaw. "That just might be the sweetest thing you've ever said to me."

Hide huffed, his cheeks going very pink, and I laughed again.

"It's all right," I said, relaxing against him again. I laid my hand against his chest, over his heart that now raced a little. "I think I love enough for both of us."

TWENTY-THREE

Training

"GET UP." I JERKED AWAKE AT THE WEIGHT OF A SWORD DROPPED across my bare chest.

"What the—" I blinked and rubbed at the sore spot on my sternum, squinting groggily through the dimness at Hide in full dress towering over me. He wore a patterned gray kamishimo over his black kimono, the pointed shoulders and wide skirt making him appear even more imposing. "What's going on?"

"Sword training," he said, tapping his foot impatiently, one hand on his hip, the other resting on the hilts of his swords. "You have to be able to defend yourself."

"Can't it at least wait until the sun comes up?" I groaned.

He snorted and, hooking his hand under my armpit, dragged me roughly to my feet, and threw a kimono at me.

"Get dressed and meet me in the garden," he said, spinning on his heel and marching out. "You have two minutes."

Two and a half minutes later, I emerged, bedraggled and yawning, hair thrown into a haphazard knot at the base of my neck. The sword hung loosely from my fingers, and I used the hilt to scratch the back of my head as my gaze swept the lawn in search of Hide. The trees that flanked the house swayed lightly in the wind, cicadas chirping merrily.

Bright-purple flowers bobbed their heads, but no sign of Hide. I was about to give up and go back to bed when the snap of a bamboo shinai and a sting across the back of my legs knocked me flat on my face.

"You're late," he said, leaning over me, the shinai resting casually on his shoulder. "And you're dead."

"Hideyoshi!" I gasped as my lungs seized and struggled within me. "A little warning next time."

"You think a Hunter will give you warning before he stabs you in the back?" he growled, grabbing me by the collar and hauling me to my feet.

"Stop messing around," I whined, brushing the dust off my clothes. "It's absurdly early in the morning and this is my first—"

Snap! Snap! Snap!

I reeled as a succession of strikes landed across my shoulders and ribs, leaving me doubled over and gasping.

"Dead again," he said, eyes narrowed and razor sharp. "Are you even trying, Hiro?"

I staggered backward, floundered for my sword, and yanked it out of the saya. My heart raced, and my face felt hot. Gripping it with both hands, I raised it in front of me and glared at Hide down its point. His eyes flashed, and with a click of his tongue and a quick step forward, he struck my wrist, sending the blade clattering to the ground.

"You really are helpless, aren't you?" He took a step toward me, and I flinched, holding my wrist, eyes burning with frustration. The corner of his mouth twitched upward, and he raised his hands in submission before bending to retrieve my dropped sword. He placed the sword in my hand before slipping around behind me, resting his hands on my hips.

"Right foot forward," he said, nudging my heel with his toe. "Hips square, weight centered over your hips and on the balls of your feet. Use the muscles in your calves to propel you. You should glide over the ground. None of this stomping around like a mule."

He pushed my hips forward, and I tried to do as he said, tripping over my own toes. He pulled me back, and I fell backward into his chest. With a huff, he set me back up straight and pushed me again, over and over until I learned to balance my weight, my straw sandals kicking up grass and dust.

"Wrap your right hand high on the hilt, just under the guard," he said, placing his hand over mine, guiding it into the right position. "That's your power. Your left goes here." He took my left hand and placed it in position toward the end of the hilt. "This is your stability and your leverage."

My face heated as he slid his hands up my arms to my elbows.

"Keep your arms and shoulders relaxed, wrists facing inward." He gave my elbows a little nudge, manipulating my arms into the proper position. "Your sword should be centered with your body, the end at the level of your opponent's throat."

His hands came to rest on my hips again. "Arms straight, hips square. Every movement you make starts here. Align your blade with your body. It is both your weapon and your shield. Don't forget that."

I nodded, my mouth too dry to speak. Giving my hip a little pat, he moved back around in front of me and raised the shinai. I studied his stance, shifting my weight lower to match his, spacing my feet one slightly forward as he did, squaring my shoulders as he did. For a long time he just stood, still as a statue, and then in a burst of movement almost too quick to see, he attacked, raising his sword over his head and pushing himself forward off his back foot. He glided across the grass as if his feet didn't even touch the ground. The shinai whipped through the air. More out of reflex than anything else, I quick-stepped backward and brought my hands up, shifting my sword over my head and perpendicular to my body to block his strike. The shinai hit the sharp edge and shattered in a shower of splinters.

He brought his broken sword down, a slow smile spreading across his face as he examined the tattered end. My heart raced with a flush of triumph. "Good," he said softly, more to himself than to me. He threw the shinai away and, squaring himself up again, slipped his hand around the katana at his hip and pulled it from the saya. "Again."

"Whoa, Hide—"

"I said, *again*." The wrappings of the hilt creaked under his grip.

"But...a real sword..." I stammered, breaking out into a nervous sweat. "Aren't you going to show me some moves first or something?"

"I find it best to learn by doing."

"But if you hit me—"

"You'll heal."

"It'll still hurt!" My heart thundered in my ears, my eyes glued to the sharp edge of his blade. He smiled again, that slow, menacing smile.

"Better not let me hit you."

I barely got my sword up in time to block a one-two-three bevy of blows. The hard clang of metal on metal vibrated through the bones of my arms, setting my teeth on edge. First from above, then from the left, then below, the last coming so close it cut the loose fabric of my kimono. Like the first time, he left no time to think. Sweat gathered in my hairline and poured down my back.

"Again," he said sharply, repeating the pattern. "Again." The same pattern, but faster. "Again." Faster still and with an added strike.

Over and over the same thing. Each repetition built in speed and complexity until my muscles trembled and my heart raced. My feet tangled up in each other, sending me down on my back once again, the point of Hide's blade pointed just millimeters from my nose.

"Good," he said, sheathing his blade and smiling casually. "Dead, but good."

"You're crazy," I panted.

"And you're not so helpless after all." He dusted his hands off on his hakama before holding one out to me.

"No, I think I'll stay down here."

"Let me tell you something, Hiro," he said with a laugh. "I started sword training when I was seven years old. I scarcely had the strength to keep the end off the ground. I would watch my father practice and think I would never be as strong as he was." He paused a moment, his eyes going a little far away. "I know it seems hard, now. Like the sword is fighting against you, but you have to trust me, Hiro. Kikentai no ichi. Sword, soul, and body are one. Your body knows what to do. Your mind is just getting in the way."

"What is that supposed to mean?" I asked, sitting up on my elbows.

"You're afraid," he said simply. "Afraid of being hurt or killed, and it's slowing you down. Let that go. Trust your body to protect you. Once you stop *thinking*, the sword will become part of your arm, and nothing can stop you."

His eyes sharpened and his face shone, gleaming and pink with exertion. I became suddenly aware of how alive he looked, the sound of his heart, his quick, heavy breathing. Not just from physical strain, but excitement, enjoyment. This was what he was, not demon or monster or youkai, but *swordsman*. A swordsman who wore his soul on his hip and, despite his supernatural advantage, lived each day as if it were his last. As I reached out my hand and wrapped it around my discarded sword, I felt the weight of my samurai name, felt it hardening like carbon steel on my bones. I took his hand and allowed him to pull me up, straightening the collar of my kimono and thrusting my sword back out in front of me.

"Again?"

WE SPENT THE WHOLE DAY IN PRACTICE. HIDE ATTACKING, SHOUTING a quick stream of instruction at me and then attacking again: weight lower, shoulders straighter, hands higher. My supernatural body took surprisingly well to the new activity, and soon I matched his every swing. I felt myself taking on the attitude of a swordsman. By the time the sun passed its zenith, I walked like him, moved like him, more aware of my surroundings and my position within them than I had ever been. Senses that were once small and contained now swelled to encompass all of me. I saw, heard, felt with my whole body.

I felt him, too, in a way I wasn't prepared for. In all our time together, I'd never seen him so open. He yelled louder, but he also smiled quicker, and even his frustration came from a place of care. The ability to protect myself was the ultimate goal. He followed heated admonishments with gentle touches and patient guidance, and when his teachings clicked into place, he brightened like a lamp had been lit inside him. The fact that I had been the one to light it filled me with so much pride, it was intoxicating. I'd resented his lessons at first, but once started, I didn't want them to end. It was like seeing the real Hideyoshi for the first time.

That night, we went out. The sword still hung heavy and awkward against my hip, but after the day's lesson, I could at least move with confidence that I wouldn't cut off my own thumbs. I found my hand drifting to its hilt, my muscles twitching with the memory of my lesson. Hide watched me from beneath the rim of the round straw hat pulled low over his face, and his mouth twitched with quiet amusement.

"Itching for a fight, are you?" he asked. He tipped his head to the side, exposing sparkling eyes.

"No," I answered, cheeks warming. I yanked my hands off my sword and clutched them in front of me instead. "I don't know... maybe." I pulled my lip between my teeth, a little spark of adrenaline shooting through my heart. "Today was fun, though, wasn't it?"

A quick smile flashed across his lips before he could stop it, and he looked away, clearing his throat. "It's not a game, Hiro," he said, face somber and voice serious. "Your sword is a tool of life and death, and you should never draw it unless you intend to kill whatever is on the other end."

"What if all you want to do is protect what's behind it?" I asked. "Can't it just be a shield?"

A strange, almost soft expression crossed his face before a sound diverted his attention down the adjacent side street. I squinted through the dark along his eye line as the air around him went tense. He stood completely still, poised like a cat, his hand on his sword.

The wind shifted, and I smelled it: blood. Moments later, a girl darted from an alley and into the street, kimono dirtied, her obi coming undone and flying in a long trail behind her. The heels of her hands, and probably her knees, were scraped as if from a fall, leaving gory red splotches along the wall as she stumbled and tripped over her broken geta right into a small knot of passing farmers. Baskets of vegetables fell to the ground, tripping her up further. Her eyes latched onto us, a scream strangled in her throat. I lunged toward her, but Hideyoshi swung his arm into my path, holding me back.

I opened my mouth to protest as her pursuer appeared, stealing my words away: a youkai, long and lean and very, *very* drunk. Whether it was on blood or on booze, it was hard to tell. His appearance was that of a young man, though his energy spoke to something older. The air around him shivered, energized by his power. He smiled, exposing long fangs, and licked his lips as he trailed the girl in a halfhearted game of chase, calling out slurred obscenities. She was obviously not his first, or even third, kill of the night. The smell of blood hung so thick on him, it made my eyes water even from this distance.

The pursuer grabbed the girl by the collar just as she managed to untangle herself from the farmers and pulled her into an adjacent alley. Cursing their lost yield, the farmers followed a few steps, sharp tools raised. They stopped just outside the alley, angry expressions dropping as they realized what was actually happening.

A current of strange energy passed through Hide. His eyes widened momentarily before narrowing to sharp points, his lips curling around his fangs. "Shameless," he muttered under his breath.

"He would kill her in front of all those people?"

"He's too drunk or too arrogant to care."

My stomach turned as the high-pitched notes of her struggle pierced the air around us and the men watching continued to do nothing. Not that it would make a difference.

"We have to do something."

"It's none of our business," he said gruffly.

"If Hunters are watching—"

"All the more reason to not get involved," he said, jaw set, words squeezed between clenched teeth. "Let that one be their target. Not us."

"Hide…" He didn't answer, his entire attention focused on the man in the alley. I wrapped my hand around his restraining arm, and his muscles were hard as stone. "I don't want to see her body on our lawn."

Hide hesitated before slowly lowering his arm. His eyes met mine for a long moment, hard and full of warning, before nodding toward the growing crowd of spectators.

"Maybe do something about that first."

I nodded and advanced toward the knot of townspeople, Hide just a few steps behind, face hidden behind his hat. The farmers had been joined by the patrons of the adjacent shops, their staff leaning out of doors and windows to get a look. I drifted through them with a song on my lips, just a casual traveler humming to himself. Each note was heavy with magic, and before I'd reached the second bar, the crowd had dispersed and staff returned to their work, unsure of what had drawn their attention in the first place.

The youkai noticed the girl's eyes before he noticed us creeping up behind him. He had her cornered in the junction between a shop and a storage shed, his fingers curled in the collar of her kimono. He turned, nearly falling over with the action.

"Care to join me for a drink?" he said with a flamboyant wave of his hand.

"I think you've had enough," I answered.

His playful sneer hardened into a scowl as his glassy eyes raked over me. He had the lean bearing of a soldier and the round, soft face of a noble. His gray kimono had twisted out of place, and the collar bore a number of dark-brown stains. The girl, all but forgotten, whimpered and tried to squeeze past him, tripping over her obi in an attempt to escape.

"What business is it of yours, *boy?*" He snatched her back up by the arm and pulled her in front of him, his features twisted into something grotesque. She screamed as he grabbed her by the hair and forced her head back, stretching out her neck. I felt more than saw Hide's hand tightening on his sword.

"Please, help me!" the girl cried. "He's a monster!"

"You've drunk enough to keep you high for the rest of the night," I said, struggling to keep my voice steady. "Enough to live on for a week. What difference does one girl make?"

"Maybe I just want something sweet to wash it all down," he answered, dipping his nose into her neck and triggering another stream of high-pitched squeals. It was only a matter of time before we drew yet another crowd. The monster shone in his eyes, and it sent a prickle up the back of my neck.

"Let her go," I said firmly. "You don't know the danger you bring on all of us with your shamelessness."

He threw his head back and laughed. Reason mattered little to him. We weren't talking to a man, after all. His smile dropped when he noticed Hideyoshi standing close behind me. He lowered his head to get a better look beneath his hat. "I know you." He pointed a long finger at my maker. "You dare draw your sword on me, Samurai?"

Hide's jaw clenched, and his grip tightened. "Don't make me."

The man's mouth twisted into a snarl. "You want her," he growled, letting her drop to her knees beside him, "come and take her."

In a flash of motion almost too quick to follow, he lunged forward with his fangs bared. Hideyoshi appeared between us with his short sword drawn. The monster crashed headlong into him, sending Hide's straw hat flying. Heedless of the blade's bite, his attacker pushed forward, one hand on the sharp edge, the other over Hide's on the hilt. Blood poured from his palm as the skin was cut, healed, then cut again. I stumbled backward as they wrestled for the upper hand in the confines of the alley. They snapped and snarled at one another until Hide finally managed to push him back, pressing him against the wall.

"Hiro, the girl!"

I broke out of my daze as the girl scrambled to her feet. I caught her quickly from behind, wrapping my arms around her shoulders as she fought against me in wild panic. Lips pressed to her ear, I hummed a tune, and little by little she relaxed, her arms going slack. She leaned back into me.

"Forget," I whispered between the bars of my song. "There are no monsters, only bad dreams."

I loosened my grip on her gradually, allowing her to regain her balance before leaving her on her own. She blinked twice, glassy eyes rolling over her shoulder toward me before starting a hazy path down the road ahead of us.

The fiend in Hide's grip growled anew at the loss of his meal, redoubling his fight against his captor, but Hide had leverage against him. Back foot firmly planted in the dusty road behind him, he leaned forward, forcing his blade tight against his rival's chest. Blood ran in a thin river down his arm as he struggled to hold the sword back.

"How dare you!" he spat in Hide's face.

"Charming," Hideyoshi said, rolling his eyes and blinking away the spray of spittle that landed on his lashes.

"I'll take what I want, when I want," he seethed. "If you think you can stop me—"

The air shifted. I sensed someone else with us in the alley. Before I even made the decision to act, my sword was drawn. I pressed my back against Hideyoshi's as a blade flashed through the air and landed hard against mine, the metal shining too bright in the sparse lamplight. A swordsman, human, eyes hot with hatred, cried out and pulled back for a second blow, and I easily parried, pushing him back into the center of the street.

Hide called my name sharply as a second swordsman appeared. The monster in his grip forgotten, he turned his blade on this new attacker, fending off a bevy of strikes aimed at my back. The air rang with the sound of swords as we moved in tandem, our backs toward each other, blades swinging with perfectly matched precision.

A strangled cry sounded from behind me, followed by the wet, sucking sound of pierced flesh. My foe's eyes widened, his attention drawn momentarily over my shoulder, before crying out in rage and taking a wide swing. I responded with a swing of my own, backing it with so much force it sent his sword flying and the swordsman to the ground. He scrambled backward on his elbows, arms flailing in the dust for his weapon. I stopped him with a point leveled at his nose.

"Do you see this?" Hideyoshi shot at the cowering youkai behind us, his usual stoic tone colored by anger. Hide snatched up the dead man's silver sword, shoving it in his face. He shrank away. "This is what happens when you take what you want, when you want."

"You are a hypocrite, Sakurai Hideyoshi," he hissed.

"Perhaps," he said, his voice cooling.

Hide's rigid posture softened as the adrenaline eased out of his system, his shoulders slumping slightly as he turned back to me. A small crowd had gathered again, and Hide pinned them all with a shriveling glare. His name was whispered somewhere in the crowd. The samurai that had killed a thousand men. Fearsome and beyond question. What they saw was a fight among swordsmen, not monsters. One by one, they averted their gaze and wandered away.

The Hunter still lay on his back, trembling under the point of my sword, and Hide looked down on him in disgust. "Finish him, Hiro."

My breath caught as the Hunter squirmed and whimpered under his glare. "F-Finish..."

He placed a gentle hand over mine as the end of my blade trembled. "He may seem defeated, but he will only return to try again."

Sweat broke out on the back of my neck as I looked down my sword at the quivering boy before me. He was young, so young, his shoulders narrow, his features still soft with boyhood. The beard that had just begun to come in darkened his lip and jaw. He could have been so many things, a soldier, a businessman, a father. He could have had a future full of pain and triumph, happiness and regret. But instead he ended up here under my blade. My heart cried out with the injustice of it.

And then, I remembered my dream.

Blinded by blood and torture, I gripped my sword tight in both hands and brought the point down into his throat until I felt the ground beneath it. He didn't scream, just sort of sputtered, his body spasming for a moment before going still. Tension left me with a great exhale, and I fell to my knees beside him. I went numb, blind to everything except the weight of Hide's hand on my shoulder.

"Good boy."

"I won't stand for this, Hideyoshi," the youkai said in a weak voice, picking himself up and straightening his clothes. Even he seemed a bit deflated now that the threat was gone.

Hide didn't answer, pulling a cloth out of his kimono to clean his sword. As the fiend slunk back into the shadows, I stared at the dead Hunter in front of me, my throat tight and eyes watering as if I might get sick.

"He was…just a boy," I croaked, biting back a sharp rush of emotion.

"He was a Hunter."

"He was human," I countered, "and I killed him."

"You kill people every day," he said.

"This is…different," I said, swallowing hard as I pulled myself to my feet and extracted my sword. It didn't feel good. It felt like murder in a way all my previous kills hadn't. I examined the blade, gleaming red in the moonlight, and as if it would give the boy's death some kind of meaning, I lifted it to my lips. Hide caught me by the wrist, stopping me before I could run my tongue over the edge.

"He doesn't deserve to be a part of you," he said coldly.

He tossed me the cloth and hefted the first Hunter's silver katana in his hand before snapping it off under his foot.

"What are you doing?" I asked, giving him a puzzled look as he swiped up the second and gave it the same treatment.

"They want to take trophies," he said, "so can we."

Steeling into the night, we hunted. We took one, just one, sharing her between us with a new reverence. The thing inside us moaned and complained, but we paid it no heed, giving in instead to a higher calling.

The next morning, Kyo found a pair of broken-off silver swords embedded in the planks of his front gate.

TWENTY-FOUR

Alliance

"HOW MANY TIMES HAVE I TOLD YOU TO KEEP YOUR ELBOWS IN!" Hideyoshi barked at me from above as I sulked on my rump, nursing a rapidly healing gash across my upper arm. Sweat coated my skin, my kimono marred by grass stains and sticking uncomfortably to my back.

"You didn't have to cut me!" I snapped back.

"Perhaps if you feel the pain, you will learn," he snarled. "A cut on the arm is a samurai's shame. But you're not samurai, are you? You're *geisha*." He spat the word as if it tasted bitter, and I flinched, the implied insult stinging worse than the wound he'd dealt me.

"You're a real beast, you know that?" I said, petulant tears welling in my eyes. I sucked in my breath and nearly swallowed my tongue as he raised the point of his sword level with my cheek.

"Get up."

"No."

"Get up and try again," he said, grinding the words between his teeth.

"Not until you calm down."

"Don't test me, Hiro. I said—"

A loud *thwak!* echoed through the courtyard, and his sword dropped. Hide spun around to confront his attacker, fire in his eyes. "Asagi!"

Hideyoshi cursed, one hand grasping the back of his head. We'd been so absorbed in our own fight, we hadn't noticed them stomp through the gate, which still stood open behind them. Red eyes burning, they raised their fan above their head for another strike.

"What are you thinking?" Asagi asked, punctuated by the slap of their fan across Hide's shoulders. "Did you really think you could meddle in other people's affairs without consequences? Do you have any idea who you've just insulted?"

"What are you—" *Thwack! Thwack! Thwack!* "Cut it out!"

"You're interfering with other youkai," Asagi spat. "Stealing what they've taken and letting them go."

"Word travels fast," I said, pulling myself to my feet and scrubbing at the fresh stains on my rump. Asagi eyed the blood on my sleeve with a scowl before turning their attention back to Hide.

"I'd think that would please you," Hide said, a snide twist to his lips. "Sparing a human and making life difficult for we indiscriminate killers."

"With discretion, maybe, but not in the middle of the street for *everyone* to see." They emphasized their point with another slap of their fan. "Do you care at all about your reputation? You hunting your own kind now, is that it?"

"What business is it of yours?" Hide asked.

"You've struck over your own head. He was a daimyo—"

"*Was,*" Hide spat as he snatched up his sword and snapped it back into its saya. "He gave up his title before he turned."

I blinked. *Daimyo?*

I know you.

"Wait. Did you—"

Hide cut me off with a look. This was a conversation for later.

Asagi rolled their eyes. "Is. Was. Doesn't matter. He has influence, Yoshi. Influence he will use as a weapon against you. You've broken the one rule among youkai."

"What rule is that?"

"Mind your own *damn* business," Asagi said with another swing of their fan.

Hide blocked the strike with the back of his hand. "What is this? Concern?"

"For you? Please," Asagi scoffed. "Nothing would give me more pleasure than to see you beaten at your own game."

"Then what?"

"What are you really up to?" Asagi stepped up so close to Hide their noses nearly touched.

I opened my mouth to respond, and Hide raised his hand to silence me. "What is it to you?"

"Are you trying to claim territory? Taking all the blood of Edo for your own?"

"I'm not an animal."

"Then why?"

Hide fell silent, clenching his teeth. Asagi took a step back, a hand on their hip and eyes narrowed.

"If I know you—"

"You don't know me," Hide said sharply.

Asagi's eyes lowered for half a breath before lifting again. Something passed between them that triggered a spark of jealousy. Asagi's expression shuttered, and I shivered at the familiarity.

"It's not entirely self-serving, is it?" Asagi's question was sincere, lacking its usual venom.

"Maybe I've had enough of blood in the streets."

"Yet you've no problem with it in your own garden," Asagi countered with a pointed look in my direction.

"Youkai are killing for sport, for their own pleasure—"

"You among them, if you do recall," Asagi said, jabbing a finger at Hide's nose. "If you plan to upset the balance of power—"

"There *is* no balance," he barked.

"And you aim to what? Crown yourself king among demons?" Asagi asked, arms crossed tight over their chest. "You can't even control your own heart. What makes you think you can control the masses?"

"Because he won't be alone," I said, unable to hold my tongue any longer. Two sets of eyes jerked in my direction, and I flinched, shifting uncomfortably under their weight. Asagi took a small step toward me, bending slightly at the waist to get to my eye level.

"You're new, so I'm going to give you a little lesson. Something I learned the hard way." Asagi's brows lowered, and their eyes darkened. "Your actions have consequences. Sometimes life-altering consequences. Consequences you could have never predicted. And you will have a long, *long* life in which to reflect and regret." They paused, and for a blink, I saw a different Asagi, a gentler Asagi, a glimpse, perhaps, of who they were before time made them hard. "It *will* change you."

My heart shuddered. Consequences. There had already been consequences. I often spent nights staring at the ceiling considering all the choices I'd made since I met Hideyoshi, all the lives they affected. Now, our arrogance had attracted the attention of something monstrous, and the wrong choices could potentially destroy us all.

Asagi straightened with a huff, all their walls coming back down tight around them like a clamshell. "Petty squabbles among demons of the night are none of my concern," Asagi said, "but how long before it spills over into the light? You will start a war."

"The war has already started."

Asagi blinked and took a step back. I pinned Hide with a hard look, and he released a sigh before disappearing into the house. Asagi trailed him with their eyes. They tucked their fan into their obi and pulled out a long pipe, lighting it and smoking in nervous little puffs until Hide returned with a small fabric bundle. Asagi's face blanched, and they recoiled as Hide unwound the cloth, revealing a broken piece of a silver blade.

Disgust, shock, terror flashed across Asagi's face lightning quick at the sight of the blade. They touched trembling fingers to their lips, closed their eyes, and turned their face away. For a long moment, Asagi was silent, and despair trickled over their effeminate features.

"They've come for us. Twice." I laid a hand on Asagi's arm, and they flinched away. "They're here, and they are fearless. Consequences or not, we have two choices: hide or fight."

Asagi opened their eyes slowly, taking a deep breath to steady their voice. "You should pay a visit to that wretched izakaya you're so fond of. That *former* daimyo is taking pleasure in dirtying your name." Asagi swung their attention to Hideyoshi but didn't quite meet his eyes. "I would like...the opportunity to get the humans in my care to safety."

"Better hurry, then," Hide responded. He probably meant it to sound menacing, but it fell flat.

Asagi reached out a hand as if they would touch Hide's arm, but stopped short, wrapping it around the pipe instead. "I hope you know what you're doing, Yoshi."

Asagi snapped their fan open and, tucking their face behind it, made a hasty retreat in a rush of silk. Hide fell into a sullen silence, and I was left fidgeting in the middle of it all. Sword training seemingly forgotten, he dropped into a cross-legged position on the engawa next to a waiting bottle of wine.

I peeked outside the gate in time to catch a flash of red disappearing around the corner. Something itched in the corner of my mind, and Asagi's fading silhouette felt like an opportunity missed. The Arakawa name and the social standing it lent, ill-deserved or not, meant influence, influence that still carried weight among the monsters they despised, influence that could be turned in our favor.

With a decisive stomp of my foot, I took off after Asagi. I caught up with them quickly, falling into step just a few paces behind. Hearing my approach, they shot an annoyed huff over their shoulder and picked up speed, but I didn't give up.

"Asagi, wait!"

"If you haven't noticed, I'm in a hurry," they growled without turning.

"Look, I don't know what happened between you and Hideyoshi to make you two hate each other," I said, ignoring the dry laugh they buried behind their fan, "but I think we can help each other."

"And why would I help? Do you have any idea what they do? What they can take from you?" Asagi's voice cracked. "You'd be lucky if they killed you. You should get as far away from him as you can."

"It was my idea."

Asagi's face fell with genuine disappointment. "Then you're an even bigger fool than he is."

"I get it. You're scared." Asagi scoffed. "Getting involved makes you a target. But ignoring them means living in fear. Both put your humans at risk."

"Get to the point."

"The point is, there's no upside for you," I said with an exasperated sigh. "What if I can change that?"

Asagi stopped so abruptly I nearly fell over to avoid running into their back. They flicked their fan over their nose a few times before snapping it shut and turning, hands on hips and red eyes burning. They arched an eyebrow and tapped their foot, scowling as they waited for me to continue.

"Help us. Just show the other youkai of Edo that you're behind us," I said, pleading. "We need them to understand that we're working in their best interests. You are respected here."

"Respected," Asagi scoffed. "I provide something they need. That's all."

"They will listen to you."

"And if they don't?"

"Then they don't," I answered.

Asagi squinted red eyes at me, leaning slightly into my space. "What are you not telling me?"

I remembered Hideyoshi's warning, his earlier hesitation to share the truth. "Nothing."

Their eyes glistened, and their usual haughty posture melted. "There are lives involved here I won't risk."

"With the Hunters gone, they will no longer be in danger."

"Yoshi doesn't trust me." A strange emotion flickered through Asagi's eyes.

"Is there a reason for that?"

Asagi's crimson lips twisted, but they stayed silent.

"Leave him to me," I said with a grin.

Asagi frowned deeply. They flipped their fan open again, hiding their face behind it as they considered. Ruby eyes shimmered as they flicked back and forth behind it. They squeezed them tightly closed for a moment, taking a long deep breath, before closing their fan and pinning me with a hard look.

"They are all that I have." The sarcastic edge had gone from Asagi's voice. "I know what Yoshi and the others think, and it's true that my lifestyle is not without sacrifices, but they are *not* slaves." Asagi bit down on the word, eyes glassy, as if they desperately needed to believe it was true. "They are...family. They are loved. If you go back on your word..."

"I won't."

Asagi took another deep breath through their nose before spinning around and taking up their fast pace away from me.

"Is that a yes?" I yelled after them.

"No," they called back over their shoulder.

TWENTY-FIVE

Slander

VOICES LEAKED OUT ONTO THE STREET, TENSE AND ANIMATED. A crowd had gathered at our little izakaya, and every lamp in the place burned at double height, giving off a harsh and unnatural glow that jumped and seethed with the energy of the mob. Shadows moved behind slatted windows. I recognized the lanky man we accosted on that first night, raising his voice like a politician to stir up the crowd. Hide stood beside me, his long hair tied in a careful knot and his hands on his swords, scowling as he cased the entrance.

"His name is Matsudaira." Hide ground the name out from between his teeth. "Though, he goes by Hashiguchi now. Hashiguchi Toshiro."

"Matsudaira?" I echoed in surprise. "Matsudaira Suketada? The daimyo of Tango province? That's near Kyoto."

He shook his head. "Matsudaira Sukemasa. Suketada is his son."

I know you.

"You served under him?"

"I protect Suketada's holdings in Edo and sometimes act as escort when he travels between here and Tango."

The muscles in his jaw twitched, and the air around him turned brittle. It was standard practice for daimyo to spend alternating years between their own provinces and Edo. They were required to keep residences here, sometimes even leaving families behind to ensure their loyalty to the shogun. Hideyoshi's job was to watch over them on his behalf, and judging by our home, he'd been generously compensated. Hashiguchi might have changed his name, but he was still Matsudaira by right. Hideyoshi's loyalties ran deep, and the guilt of his disobedience played heavily in the stiffness of his shoulders and the line of his back. In the time we'd been together, this was the first time his human life had brushed up so close against the youkai.

"They aim to starve us!" A deep voice from inside cut through the night. "To drive us from our homes! They think they can bully us into submission and claim Edo for their own."

"Asagi was right," I said under my breath, my hand slipping around Hide's elbow. "He's in there slandering us. What do we do?"

"What do you think?" He tightened his hand around the hilt of his sword and took a step toward the entrance.

I stopped his forward motion with my hands on his forearms. "All you'll do is prove him right. Besides, that sword will do you little good unless it's made of silver."

A growl rumbled through his throat, and his brow knotted. He crossed his arms tightly over his chest and glared down his nose at me, but I didn't budge.

"We saved his life, and all he cares about is the blood he was denied."

"Not every problem can be solved at the end of a sword, Hideyoshi."

His posture relaxed a bit, the murderous fire in his eyes lowering to a dull ember. Voices inside continued to rise, and each strike on his reputation hit him like stones until he couldn't take it anymore and he shoved past me.

I jumped back into his path, hands planted on his chest. "Wait, what are you doing?"

"Telling them the truth."

"What truth?"

"That the only reason he's not being tortured by Hunters right now is—"

"Do you hear yourself?" The knot in my stomach pulled so tight it made my voice shrill. I thought about Asagi and the terror in their eyes when we showed them that silver blade. "You'll start a panic."

"Maybe they should panic." The fire in his eyes flared to life once again. "You said you wanted Kyo and his Hunters gone. What better way to make them leave than with an army at our backs."

"That's not an army. Most of them aren't even soldiers. At best, half of them will flee, and the rest will go killing anyone carrying a sword on the chance it might be silver."

"How can you want to protect them when they shit on your name?"

"We're facing genocide, and all you care about is your reputation? This is bigger than us." Tears sprang to my eyes. His face twisted in my blurred vision into something grotesque and horrifying. "Damn your pride, Hideyoshi."

"Where are you going?" he snapped as I pushed past him and stomped away. "Hiro!"

Dust from the road filled the air as I spun on my toes to face him. "Did it ever occur to you that we are only allowed to exist because people don't really believe in us?"

He balked, brows knotted in confusion.

"I grew up on stories of monsters and demons waiting in the shadows to suck out our souls. Stories meant to teach us to be strong, be honest, be virtuous, or be punished. We all heard those stories, but no matter how much they frightened us, we never really *believed* them."

"What are you getting at?"

I stabbed a finger over his shoulder at the izakaya. "If you go in there and tell them about the Hunters, if you clear your *good* name, there will be blood, innocent and guilty alike. Maybe even enough to make people believe in monsters. What then?"

Hide screwed his face into a bitter knot. Another burst of noise escaped the izakaya and his shoulders tensed, but he didn't turn. His eyes held mine, hard and darker than the night sky above us. He took one step toward me, then another, and the air hardened to stone before he stomped past me up the street toward home.

TWENTY-SIX

Immortality

WE DIDN'T SLEEP AT ALL THAT NIGHT. HIDE LAY IN BED IN AN anxious knot, his eyes squeezed stubbornly closed. The events of the night played in repeat across his brow. He twitched and grunted, his fists knotting in the fabric of my yukata and squeezing me tight against his chest. By the time the orange light of the sun leaked through the shoji, we had given up altogether. Hide pulled himself up and disappeared out of the back of the house without a word. Shortly after, the air filled with the flat *thwack* of a weighted bokken against a canvas heavy bag.

Feeling lost and fairly crushed, I headed to the kitchen to make a pot of tea. I struck a flint over the brazier and coaxed the coals to life. They glowed a bright, friendly orange, releasing puffs of sparks as I moved them around with a poker. I hung the cast-iron pot on a hook over the fire and wafted my hand through the little puffs of steam that leaked from the spout, overwhelmed by a memory of Okaasan kneeling over the brazier with me tucked against her hip as she taught me how to make the perfect cup of tea. The water had to be just the right temperature, hot but not quite boiling. The leaves had to be packed into the filter just right. Too loose and the tea would be weak. Too tight and the leaves would burn.

So much had changed since then. The boy in those memories felt like someone else, Okaasan herself like something imagined. I realized suddenly that I didn't even know where she'd been buried, and the thought left me feeling bereft. In my mind, she still lay alone in the place where I left her. The last evidence of my human self was fading into dust.

But she wasn't alone. Hanagawa was there with her ever-growing family of orphans. It seemed like every letter she sent contained new names, and my heart swelled at the image of her in her oiran finery surrounded not by men who didn't care about her, but children who loved her and needed her. The okiya had become a home when it could have been a tomb, and no amount of money or candy or toys I could send would be enough to express my gratitude.

Things were about to change again. This life to which I'd finally grown accustomed would be turned on its end, and it shook me to my core. The only comfort I had was Hideyoshi. My rock, hard in all the ways I was malleable. No matter what happened, he would be my foundation, the solid ground upon which I stood, and even though I was terrified of what this new future held, I knew he wouldn't let me fall.

I removed the teapot from the fire just as it started to boil and drizzled the water over a well-packed filter of green tea leaves into a pair of painted ceramic cups. Leaving one behind, I picked up the other and made my way out the back door. A single lamp burned beside the heavy bag hung from a thick branch of a tree. Hide had thrown off the shirt of his jinbei, and it lay wadded up in a corner. The wooden sword he wielded whipped through the air, all his frustrations etched into the muscles of his bare back. He hadn't even bothered to tie his hair, and it rippled around his shoulders with every swing.

"I made you some tea," I said, tentatively lifting the cup in his direction. He didn't stop, didn't look up. The air shook with another loud *thwak*. "Hide, come inside." *Thwack*. "Hide, please..." *Thwack*. "Hideyoshi!"

The bokken stopped mid-swing, and his shoulders went rigid, making me take an instinctive step back. A second later, he released a long sigh, his arms dropping limp to his sides. I flinched again at the white in his eyes when he turned, but it quickly faded as he tossed the wooden sword aside and drifted, slightly crumpled toward me. He laid his hands over mine on the cup but didn't take it, and though his face remained stoic, emotions zipped around beneath the surface like an electric current through his fingertips.

"I'm sorry," I said.

"For what?"

"For what I said before. About your pride."

His eyes pinched, and he brushed a hand over my cheek. He parted his lips as if to speak, but no words came. Instead, he took the cup from me and dropped down onto the porch with a heavy sigh. I sank down beside him, hands clutched at my knees.

"You really want to do this on our own?" he asked.

"I don't think we really have a choice."

"Are you scared?"

"Of course I'm scared."

"Good," he spat before taking a long sip of his tea. "At least you've still got some sense left in you."

"You think this is a mistake?"

He sighed. "Yes. But I also think you're right." I shot him a sideways look, and he released a dry laugh. "Those people…they're a bunch of overexcitable idiots fueled by gossip and spite."

A laugh burst out of me before I could stop it.

"They have no discipline. No discretion, obviously."

I nodded in agreement, and a shiver ran up my spine at the thought of them running white-eyed and snarling through the streets. Senseless bloodshed would only feed the Hunter's cause, every witness a new recruit, until there was nothing left but Hunter and youkai and a bloody war with no end.

I studied his profile for a long time before asking, "What do we do?"

Hideyoshi released a sigh, interrupted by the sharp barking call of the goshawk. We both looked up in time to see him do a slow circle over the house and drop onto the branch Hide's heavy bag was mounted on, the limp body of a mouse dangling from its beak. He spread his wings wide, painting an impressive silhouette against the rising sun, before making the short hop to the eaves over our head and dropping its mouse directly into Hideyoshi's lap.

"What is that?" I yelped and pulled away as Hideyoshi plucked the mouse up by the tail, a smile on his lips.

"A gift, I think." He glanced up at the goshawk, who beat his wings as if in affirmation before taking off back into the tree line. "Maybe he's trying to make me feel better."

"Gross. Get rid of it."

Hide laughed and dangled it in my direction as I slid farther down the engawa. "Well, that would be rude."

"Sakurai-san!"

Our heads jerked up at a raised voice from the front of the house. Hide's brows lowered, and he looked up at the sun that had barely crested the trees.

"Expecting someone?" I asked.

He grumbled, tossed the mouse aside and, snatching up his shirt, stomped into the house. His back cut a jagged line as he whipped open the front shoji. I nearly ran into him when he stopped short, immediately dropping into a low bow.

"Matsudaira-dono."

Three men stood in our front garden, all wearing formal kimono and swords on their hips. Two wiry swordsmen in dark-blue kamishimo took a flanking position, faces tense and alert like coiled vipers. The man in the center was set apart by the tall, black eboshi standing like a pillar on top of his head and the white fan tucked in his obi. His plump face was serene, marked only by a slight pinch between his brows.

The daimyo, Matsudaira Suketada.

"My apologies." Hide's words took on the clipped cadence of keigo. "I am not properly dressed to receive you."

"No apologies necessary," Matsudaira-dono replied with a wave of his hand, his soft cheeks lifting in a smile. "I've come early in the morning and unannounced. But I'm afraid I have business with you that cannot wait."

My geisha instincts immediately kicked in, and I stepped up beside Hideyoshi, offering a bow of my own. "You are welcome, Matsudaira-dono. Would you like some tea while Sakurai-han dresses?"

"That would be nice. Thank you."

Hide cast me a grateful look before disappearing into his room. The daimyo stepped lightly onto the engawa, and I stepped aside, head low, as he slipped out of his shoes and into the main room of the house. I arranged a zaisu and chabudai in front of the tokonoma, and he lowered himself onto the mat as I slid open the remaining shoji, letting in the sweet morning air.

"'Han'…" Matsudaira's voice was deep and smooth as heavy cream. "Are you from Kyoto?"

"Yes."

"Have I seen you before?" He touched the tip of his finger to his lips and raised his eyes to the ceiling. The question wasn't really for me. "Do you work near the capital?"

Work. I remembered the story Hideyoshi had told me on the walk from Kyoto, about how he'd learned of me from his daimyo, and a shard of panic prodded my heart. I ducked my head, running through every face in my memory. Had I served him before?

"No, Matsudaira-dono." My ears heated with the lie. He made a low sound in his throat, and his gaze slid over me in a way that made my skin itch. I pushed the last shoji aside and bowed. "I'll be back soon with your tea."

I exited perhaps a bit faster than was appropriate and headed to the kitchen. It took me less than a minute to stoke the fire I had started this morning and heat water in a cast-iron pot. Tension hung in the air with the steam as I collected all the tools I would need onto a lacquer tray: a squat, black container of tea leaves, a filter, and a tall ceramic cup painted with bamboo leaves.

When I returned, I found the daimyo waiting patiently, back straight, hands resting on his thighs. An odd, distant expression clouded his features. His gaze rested somewhere in the distance, and his chin drooped almost to his chest as if his neck couldn't carry the weight. I shuffled my feet as I entered, and his head jerked up at the sound, his serenity restored.

He didn't speak to me as I knelt beside his table and brewed his tea. Water at just the right temperature poured over a perfectly packed filter. He watched me, every move monitored down to the position of the kettle against the glass, calculated attention that made my palms sweat. I placed the cup in front of him, and he lifted it to his nose, his gaze seeking out mine as he breathed in the earthy aroma. His eyes were a deep brown, soft and sparkling.

"I'm sorry to make you wait, Matsudaira-dono." Hideyoshi's voice knocked against the silence as he reappeared.

He'd tied his long hair into a topknot and changed into his usual black kimono and hakama, only this one slightly more ornamented. He wore a haori emblazoned with the imperial seal on the shoulders, and little bits of gold from his under collar and woven into the haori-himo caught the morning sun.

Matsudaira-dono put down his cup and acknowledged Hide's bow with a slight nod. I retreated to the edge of the room as Hide eased to his knees directly across from him, back rod straight and eyes respectfully lowered.

Matsudaira-dono took a long drink of his tea and placed the cup gently back on the table. That heavy look flashed across his face again before he spoke.

"I'm here about my father."

Hide's eyes snapped up.

"He's missing."

"I was under the impression your father was dead."

Matsudaira-dono released a melodramatic sigh. "Yes, well…"

Hide and I traded a look as Matsudaira-dono took another long sip of his tea. Nervous spiders crawled up my spine. What was going on here?

"It's true my father was in ill health when he passed his title on to me." Matsudaira-dono's eyes remained on his teacup as he spoke, his tone flat. "It was reported soon after that he died, and it was what he wanted everyone to believe. The truth is he went into seclusion, getting away from public life as a form of treatment for his disease."

Treatment. Hide and I glanced at each other again. Hashiguchi Toshiro. He went into seclusion because he had turned.

Hide's face hardened, and he curled his hands into fists at his thighs. Exactly how much did he know? Matsudaira-dono betrayed nothing but concern and perhaps contriteness for his deception, yet danger crackled in the air around him.

"We've kept in contact through letters, written under a fake name, of course, and delivered by a trusted attendant. Yesterday, my attendant went to deliver a letter and found his home empty. He waited most of the night, but my father never returned."

"Pardon my rudeness, Matsudaira-dono," Hideyoshi started, "but it's only been one night. He likely spent the evening elsewhere and will return soon. Do you have reason to believe—"

"Just call it a feeling," Matsudaira answered brusquely.

A muscle in Hide's jaw twitched. Questions piled up behind his eyes, but he didn't dare voice them. "You want me to find him."

"Yes."

The corners of Hide's mouth pulled down sharply. "Why me? Clearly you have...others that already know of your situation."

The air solidified as we all made conscious efforts to ignore the pair of samurai pacing up and down the engawa pretending not to listen in.

"I trust you," Matsudaira-dono said with a small smile. "And your reputation is...intimidating."

Hide released a long breath through his nose, his gaze shifting back to me. Matsudaira-dono, ever observant, followed his eyeline.

"If you're worried about your companion," he started, eyebrows bouncing, "you don't have to be. I'll leave one of my men here to watch over him."

"No need," Hide answered quickly.

"I insist."

Those spiders in my spine began to bite. Matsudaira-dono had finished his tea, and it took me a moment to realize he'd been holding the cup toward me. I swallowed hard, the inside of my mouth sticky as flypaper. I returned to Matsudaira's side and cast a sidelong glance at Hideyoshi as I brewed Matsudaira-dono's second cup. We both knew why he was leaving a guard behind, and it had nothing to do with my protection.

I was to be a hostage.

It wasn't an uncommon practice. Just as the shogun held leverage over him, he would hold leverage over us. Still, it rankled. Hide's eyes burned with resentment as he nodded his assent.

"Good." He took a long drink of his freshly brewed tea. "You'll want to get underway immediately. A man's life is at stake, after all."

Hide touched his forehead to the tatami before rising and heading toward the back of the house. I did the same and hurried after, catching him just as he reached his room.

"This doesn't make sense," I said, voice low. "We saw Hashiguchi at the izakaya. How does a man vanish in the space of a few hours?"

"He doesn't." He threw off his haori with a muffled curse. "We'll likely find him passed out behind a whore house."

"I don't like this, Hideyoshi."

He didn't answer, shoving clothes and provisions into a canvas bag as if they'd done him some slight.

"Do you think he knows?"

He stopped packing, his back to me, and his shoulders dropped. "I don't know."

"You shouldn't go."

"I don't have a choice."

"Of course you have a choice."

He spun on me, his eyes white. "I can't refuse my daimyo."

I flinched, and he backed down, exhaling his frustration. He turned back to his bag but didn't continue to pack, his hands clenched in the fabric. I laid a hand between his shoulder blades, and when he didn't pull away, pressed my nose into the back of his neck.

"Keep an eye on him," he started, his voice low and hoarse. "The man he leaves behind."

"Don't worry about me." I kissed the spot behind his ear. "Just make sure you come home."

He leaned into me for a breath before straightening his back and marching past me and back into the main house. Matsudaira-dono had abandoned his tea and now stood outside with his men, their heads together and speaking in hushed voices. They pulled apart as soon as Hideyoshi's feet hit the tatami.

Matsudaira-dono smiled and gestured to the path before him. With one last glance at me, Hide slid into his shoes and walked out. I tried to keep my expression neutral, but those spiders were all over me now, itching and biting, and all I wanted to do was lock the gate and prevent him from leaving.

But he left. The dark shape of his back disappeared through the gate, followed closely by Matsudaira-dono and one of his samurai guards. The other stayed stationed on the engawa, arms tightly crossed over his chest. I took a deep breath and did my best to push my dark intuition aside and focused on my own little problem.

"Would you like some tea?"

The samurai flinched as if I'd flicked him on the end of his crooked nose, his wiry frame wound tight as a spring.

"Let me guess. You're not supposed to talk to me."

He narrowed his eyes into dark slits.

"Look. You don't want to be here. I don't want you here. But here we are. We might as well make the best of it, ne?" I shrugged and started back toward the kitchen. He knew I knew the real reason he was here. Now he would know I wasn't afraid of him. "Would you prefer wine?"

I didn't look back but kept my ears tuned to the front room. A grumbled curse came, followed by shuffling steps on the tatami. A triumphant smile tugged on my lips as I fetched a jar of nihonshu and two glasses. When I returned, I found the samurai had claimed the seat his master had vacated, a clear expression of our perceived ranks.

With none of the formality of my earlier interaction, I kicked a mat toward the table opposite him and plopped down. I filled two small glasses—mine first, then his—my gaze pinned to the katana he had propped against the table. A white hilt with a black wrap. The wakizashi still sat at his hip, and his collar bulged in the particular shape of a dagger.

The samurai lifted the glass to his nose, gave it a sniff, then tipped it back. The monster in me followed the line of his throat, the veins like ropes glowing from within. My mouth watered and fangs tingled. I could take him easily, dump his body in the river, and no one would know.

Except Matsudaira-dono.

"I have an idea," I said, shaking off my murderous fantasy. "Let's play a game."

He arched an eyebrow at me, and I flashed an innocent smile.

"We used to play this all the time in the okiya where I grew up." I grabbed the little pot containing the tea leaves, dumped it out, and turned it upside down on the table between us. "Konpira Funefune. Do you know it?"

Konpira Funefune was a game based on rhythm. The participants sat across from each other, an upturned bowl between them, and alternated touching the bowl with their palm to the beat of a song. If one person picked up the bowl, the other knocked the table with their knuckles on the beat instead. The music got progressively faster as the game continued, ending when someone either knocked the bowl or slapped the table.

The samurai crinkled his nose but nodded. I laid the flat of my hand on the bowl. He straightened his back, brow lowered, all attention focused on the bowl. I started to sing.

"Konpira Funefune, Oite ni hokakete, Shura Shushushu."

I added no magic at first. Just the song and the game. We tapped the bowl back and forth, keeping a steady beat. He kept up well. Back and forth, back and forth until he picked up the bowl.

I slapped the table.

"Oh! I lost!" I feigned a mix of disappointment and delight, giggling and covering my mouth with the back of my hand. I swept up my wineglass. "Time to take my punishment."

His eyes widened as I downed the entire contents in one swallow. "Careful. You'll get drunk."

"He speaks," I said with a laugh. "I guess I'll just have to beat you next time."

One corner of his mouth quirked, and he set the bowl back down between us. He laid his hand over it and waited.

"Konpira Funefune, Oite ni hokakete, Shura Shushushu."

The samurai pulled the bowl away, and I knocked the table. The song quickened.

"Mawareba Shikoku ha, Sanshou Nakanogori, Zouzusan Konpira Daigonken, Ichido mawareba."

He pulled the bowl. I knocked the table. The tune sped up again. I pulled the bowl. He knocked the table. Back and forth and back and forth until—

"Kuso!" The samurai cursed as the flat of his hand hit the table. I hooted in triumph before topping off his glass. He glared at me over the rim, deep creases forming around his eyes, but dutifully drank it down.

I placed the bowl back between us. "Again?"

A sizzle of adrenaline flashed across my skin as he nodded and leaned forward, his entire being focused on the bottom of that little bowl. His guard down.

"*Konpira Funefune.*"

Slow and easy, the only sounds the wind rustling the trees outside, the tapping of our fingers, and my voice.

"*Oite ni hokakete.*"

His rhythm faltered, and I pretended not to notice. The wind stilled.

"*Shura Shushushu.*"

My heart raced, but the song remained steady. The samurai's eyes glazed over, his tapping more and more off beat until he stopped altogether, hand hanging in the air as if he'd gotten stuck. I waved my hand in front of his face with no response.

I had him.

It was easier than I thought it would be. Maybe it was the wine. Maybe he didn't know about us at all, and I was being paranoid. Surely a Hunter would have known, would have prepared, would have avoided the game that allowed me to use my magic. My voice cracked around the song as my attention shifted to the sword at his side, and my throat went dry. There was one very easy way to find out.

My heart pounding a hard counter beat, I wrapped my hand around the hilt of his katana. I slipped my fingers easily over a wrap worn almost smooth from handling. Was he like Hideyoshi? Had his sword killed a thousand men, or only threatened monsters? I pulled, and it slid from the saya, a finger width, two fingers, the breadth of a hand.

Silver.

I jumped back but didn't let go, and the sword came with me. The morning sun flashed in shards of white off the silver blade, its curve wicked and smelling of blood. It rattled in my shaking hands. My stomach twisted. My blood burned.

The samurai—the Hunter—blinked back into awareness as my spell faded. His hand still hung over the bowl, and he touched it as if the game were still in progress, his brows knit in confusion. He saw me but didn't quite comprehend.

I'd been sitting across from him. Laughing, drinking. Now I stood over him, fangs bared and holding his sword.

He jerked up onto one knee, his hand flying to the wakizashi at his hip. I lunged forward and pressed the edge of the katana to his throat.

"I know it's made for monsters," I growled, "but I'm sure it will kill a man just fine."

He froze, his Adam's apple bouncing up and down his throat. His expression remained neutral, but his voice shook. "I was told only to keep you here. That's all."

"By Matsudaira?"

He nodded, a quick twitch of his head.

"Do he and his other man have silver swords too?"

Another nod. My eyes burned, and I swallowed a knot of panic.

"And Hideyoshi? What are they—" My voice cracked, and I took a breath to steady it. "What do they want from him?"

He didn't answer, his gaze sliding away from mine. I pressed the blade harder against his neck, and he hissed.

"I don't know. We get orders, and we follow them. It's not for us to know anything else."

I thought of that boy Hunter whose head ended up in a box. "Orders from where?"

"I don't know." He gestured to the door. "I don't even know the man I came with. He came to my home, showed me his silver sword, and told me we were to see Matsudaira, that we should act under his direction until the job was done."

"What job?"

He shook his head, expression blank. The hilt wrap creaked under my grip. He didn't know. He didn't know anything. He didn't even know who his masters were. Did any of them know? It made both perfect sense and no sense at all. Of course they didn't know. How could they trust a leader that was the very thing they hunted?

My head spun and my vision blurred. Puzzle pieces slotted into place, but the image remained hidden. There was a bigger picture unfolding, but I could only focus on one thing.

"They're going to take him from me."

The end of the sword trembled, taking little bites out of the samurai's skin. If they killed him, would he come back for me? My chest tightened. My lungs seized.

Sometimes it's easy. Sometimes it's hard.

In a flash of motion, the samurai drew his wakizashi and sprang to his feet. Cups flew and broke. Tea spilled. Swords clashed. He was good, fast. But I was faster. *Don't think.* My body acted on its own, parrying one, two, three blows before countering with a hard downward sweep. My toes dug into the tatami. The blade cut through the air in a long, white arc.

A spray of blood hit me full in the face, hot and sticky. The dark thing inside me writhed as my tongue slipped out unbidden to catch the drops that landed on my lips. The samurai stumbled backward, his sword falling to the ground as he grasped his throat. Red seeped through his fingers, down his chest, dripping in thick drops to the floor.

I lurched forward and grabbed him by the arms as his knees buckled. I sank with him to the floor, my hand pressed over his and panic searing my veins.

"Tell me where they went."

He made a wet, choking sound, and his face grew paler by the second. His eyes rolled, and I gave him a rough shake to bring his focus back to me.

"Tell me!"

The tatami around him turned red, then brown, and then almost black. He gripped my sleeve and his mouth gaped. I leaned closer. A shiver ran through him, and he expelled a great cough, spraying my cheek with blood and foam before going still.

"No." I shook his shoulders, slapped his face. The gash on his neck opened like a mouth to sneer at me. *Your actions have consequences.* "No, no, no. Don't die. Tell me. Tell me where they went. Tell me!"

My voice raised in pitch with every word. The samurai's head bounced off the tatami as I shook him, but he didn't wake. He wouldn't ever wake.

What have I done?

I scrambled backward away from him as if distance could erase my mistake. The air turned coppery and thick. I squeezed my eyes closed and clapped a hand over my mouth and nose. A sob climbed up my throat. They were going to take him from me. Hideyoshi was in danger, and I'd just killed my one chance at finding him.

Break off the parts that scare you.

Numbness crawled through my chest like an ice flow as the monster inside me begged for release. I bit down on my tongue, crushed my knuckles into the tatami, anything to keep myself grounded. The blind rage and bloodlust tempted me, but I couldn't succumb, not now. Not when Hideyoshi needed me.

A familiar cry broke me out of my reverie. Hideyoshi's loyal bird. Had he seen where his master went? Would he show me? One of the Hunter's swords lay just an arm's length away, and I reached for it with a trembling hand. Dried blood cracked around my knuckles as I wrapped my fingers around the hilt. The blade glared at me, reflecting back my own white eyes.

I can't let them take him.

I pulled myself up onto wobbly legs, retrieved the sword's sheath, and thrust it into my obi at my hip. I took a deep, ragged breath, panic turning the air into razor blades. Turning my back on the dead man, I closed up the shoji one by one, sealing him inside. Outside on the engawa, the air didn't smell like blood. I could pretend he wasn't there. I would have to deal with him eventually, but for now, I focused on the sky. I had higher priorities.

"There's a house just outside the city."

I jumped and spun around, sword drawn, at the sound of a familiar, oil-slick voice. Kyo stood just inside the gate, hands clasped behind his back and his expression impassive. The trees seemed to bow toward him, drenching him in dappled shadows.

"Follow the main road west out of Naito-Shinjuku until you crest a hill overlooking a rice field. You'll find him there."

"What are you doing here?" I asked in a shaky voice. "Why are you telling me this?"

He shrugged and took a languid step toward me. He slithered through the shadows like an eel. "An act of goodwill, maybe. I want you on my side."

"I will never be on your side," I hissed from between my teeth.

His eyebrows bounced, and he bobbed his head in a placating nod.

"You gave them their orders."

"Did I?"

"How do I know you're not sending me into a trap?"

"You don't."

My heart pounded, and tears burned behind my eyes. He took another step toward me, and I moved down from the engawa to meet it, sword thrust out. Even I knew my stance was sloppy. A smile tugged at his lips.

"You can't kill me, Hiro. Not even with that."

He walked past me and to the house, his relaxed posture never changing. The shadows followed him, curling around him like a dark mist. He pulled back one of the shoji enough to poke his nose inside, grimacing before turning back to me.

"You live for him, don't you?" he said after a dense silence.

The tears I'd only just been holding back poured hot down my face. The end of my sword trembled, suddenly heavy as stone.

"If he dies with nothing to come back for, it would weaken you, wouldn't it? For me, that's isseki nichou. One stone, two birds. On the other hand, two youkai who live only for each other would be formidable, indeed," he said with a faraway look. "Maybe the closest thing that exists to true immortality."

I couldn't hold the sword up anymore. The tip dropped and made a sharp noise against the stone. Could he love anything that much with his heart stuffed in a box? His bird called out from somewhere high above.

Kyo stabbed his thumb over his shoulder. "Don't worry. I'll take care of this. Go." One corner of his mouth lifted into a crooked smile. "Find out if you're immortal."

TWENTY-SEVEN

Trap

I DIDN'T KNOW I COULD RUN SO FAST.

Chest heaving, muscles burning, I sprinted out the gate and through the streets of Naito-Shinjuku, dodging horse carts and pushing through the morning crowds. I ignored the squeals of surprise as I burst through the pack, bloodied and moving at an unnatural speed with one eye on the sky. I didn't care who saw me or what they thought. I had only one thing on my mind.

Hideyoshi.

Following Kyo's directions and the shadow of Hideyoshi's goshawk, I put the sun at my back and headed west. It crawled upward, painting the sky orange as it went, and I struggled to focus in the strange light. The road shimmered and bent in odd ways, tripping me as I dodged blurry silhouettes. Mirages reached out for me like vengeful ghosts. I kept running until the buildings thinned and gave way to rolling fields of rice and vegetables cut by a dirt road. I slowed as I hit a sharp incline, keeping my body low and hugging the edge of the field until I crested the hill.

A farmhouse appeared just over the hill. It was a small, modest building, its paper walls stained gray by the weather. A light flickered from within, producing a sickly yellow glow. A man I recognized as one of Matsudaira's guards leaned against the doorframe, picking at his nails with a silver knife.

My throat tightened around my already wheezing breaths. Open field stretched to either side of the road as far as I could see. No cover. The sun was rising at my back. The guard would see me the moment I crested the hill. I could only assume Matsudaira was inside, maybe even with more guards. Where was Hideyoshi?

I whipped my head around in search of something, anything that could get me closer. A soft chirp brought my attention to a post by the road. The goshawk sat perched on top of it, plucking at the straps of a wide-brimmed straw hat left hanging on a nail. Hands shaking, I snatched it up, tied the straps under my chin and pulled it low over my eyes. I couldn't hide. So I wouldn't.

Swallowing the lump in my throat, I turned toward my objective. I straightened my hat and my clothes as if one stray wrinkle would give the whole ruse away. With the sun burning an eye-watering yellow behind me, I pulled myself up tall and took my first shaky step over the hill.

Sing.

I picked a song, a traveling song with an easy, carefree melody, and let it drift over my lips as I crested the hill. I dropped my head and took a wavering path as if I were drunk or weary. The guard at the door squinted at me, hand over his eyes to block the sun, but all he saw was a shadow, the details blurred by the brightness. He tucked his knife into his obi and straightened, aware of but not yet alarmed by my presence.

My skin vibrated as the magic in my blood awakened and focused on the guard. I lifted my voice, filling it with positive intention, and fired it like an arrow to his ears. *All is well. You have nothing to fear.* His face went slack, and his alert posture relaxed. I moved a few steps closer and raised a beckoning hand still crusted with blood. *Come to me.*

Clothes stained and face covered with gore, I must have looked monstrous, but the magic in my song painted the image of a spirit born of sunlight. His arms dropped slack to his side, and he swayed a bit before taking an unsteady step forward, then another. Weathered face alight with awe and adoration, he reached out.

My monster stirred in its cage as the guard slid his hand into mine.

My heart raced and my mouth watered. I traced the blue veins in his wrist with my fingertips. The light inside him called to me. *He doesn't deserve to be a part of you.* I knew it to be true even as I drew him closer to me. But he was here in my grip, so warm, so soft, and I was so hungry.

Break off the parts that scare you.

My consciousness sank into a dark place as our bodies pressed together. I tipped his head back and found that river of light that ran within him. My song turned into little more than breath, and the guard shivered as I brushed my lips down the line of his neck. He gave himself up willingly, head falling back and body arching into mine.

The sharp smell of blood jerked me back to reality, not human blood, blood colored with darkness. The same blood that mixed with mine. My gaze snapped up to the farmhouse in time to see the paper walls colored by a spray of red before the lamp went out.

"Hideyoshi!"

I gasped as fiery pain bloomed in my side. *It's a trap!* The guard, freed from my spell during my distraction, plunged his silver knife between my ribs. My vision went dark, and the only thing I was aware of was the crunch of the man's neck in my grip.

The guard's body dropped heavily to my feet, mouth agape, fingers and legs twitching but beyond his control. I fell to my knees beside him. His blade was still embedded in my side, and a fresh burst of pain blackened my vision as I pulled it out. A dark stain spread across my torso and down to my hip. I coughed a great spray of blood. He'd nicked my lung.

The doors of the farmhouse slid fully open, and five men—five!—fanned out across the road. I tried to see past them into the house, but my vision blurred. I was bleeding. I had to stop bleeding.

Breathing ragged and shallow, I tore at the dead guard's clothes until I freed his obi. I ripped it in half, wadded up one section against my open wound and used the other to tie it around my torso. I pulled the knot as tight as I could, sending another bright flash of pain through me that made my stomach turn.

I had to get to Hideyoshi.

The Hunters drifted toward me, swords drawn, but kept a wary distance as they formed a circle around me. Their faces twisted at the sight of their dead companion, his neck bent at an awkward angle.

Head spinning, veins burning, I coughed another spray of blood and struggled to my feet. The Hunters tensed but didn't advance when I pulled my sword. My entire right side screamed with the effort. I blinked through the fog. *Hide. Where's Hide?*

The circle tightened. My heart pounded as their silver swords crept ever closer.

Don't think.

One of the Hunters released a raging battle cry and advanced. I took him down with a downward strike, immediately spinning on my back foot to parry an attack from behind. The air exploded with a clash of swords, flashing red in the morning sun.

A third Hunter rushed at me from the side, and I used every ounce of my remaining strength to stop his blow. He was big, bigger even than Hideyoshi, with arms thick as tree trunks. He brought his knee up hard into my side, and stars filled my vision, but I stood strong, forcing him away with swipe at his midsection he barely dodged.

A pair of Hunters descended on me in a flurry of silver. I reacted on instinct, deflecting a series of blows and taking one opponent out of the fight with a strike to his sword arm. I remembered what Hide taught me: trust your body. I tucked my fear and despair into a box and gave up control.

But it wasn't enough. With every second that passed, more of my strength leaked from the hole in my side. The Hunter's sword came down in an overhead strike, and though I managed to block it, the force took me to my knees. My muscles turned to jelly. He didn't let up until he had me bent over backward, the sharp of his blade resting against my neck.

My vision tunneled. Something went numb inside me as my lungs filled with blood and the Hunter's blade bit into my skin. No. I couldn't let it end this way. I wouldn't let them take him.

"I will tear you apart," I said, and then it all went black.

TWENTY-EIGHT

Isseki Nichou

I WOKE WITH A COUGH, EVERY CELL BURNING WITH NEED AS MY BODY struggled to repair itself. Blood from my punctured lung crawled up my throat and spilled from my lips. I couldn't move, bound in an upright position with my hands over my head, a wall at my back, tatami under my knees. Something cold and hard chaffed around my wrists—chains.

"Hide—" More blood forced from my lungs as I fought to breathe. I was sticky all over with it. A sharp pain pinched in my neck when I tried to lift my head.

"Hide…yoshi." I blinked my eyes open, and everything rocked like a ship at sea. Swirls of light and shadow danced before me, along with movement somewhere. It felt close, but sounded far away.

I flinched as a strange hand gripped my chin and forced my head up. A face swam into view. Dark skin. Patchy beard. Bandage on his forearm. A Hunter. At least I had made him bleed.

"Still alive, youkai?"

I groaned and tried to pull my face away. I wrapped my fingers around the chains suspending me, and they scraped over my head. I followed the line of them to a ceiling beam.

"Hide…"

I coughed, and the Hunter pulled away to avoid the spray of blood.

A dark smile stretched across his face. He took a couple of steps backward, laying his hand on a closet door.

"Is this what you're living for?"

He whipped the door open, unleashing a pain worse than any wound he could have dealt me. Hide sat within, slumped in an unnatural position, covered in blood, unbound, unmoving. His hair had mostly fallen loose from its knot, but I didn't need to see his face to know he was dead.

A scream built in my chest. The Hunter darted forward and wrapped his hand around my throat, cutting it off with a squeeze.

"Use that voice, and I'll cut it out."

He released me slowly and stepped back, eyes narrowed as he watched for signs of defiance. Tears cut sticky paths through the gore on my face, and my chest burned with every short, gasping breath. *Hide...* The Hunter smirked and returned to the closet, pulled Hide out by the collar, and dropped him onto the tatami in front of me. He landed on his side, one arm twisted beneath him, his pale hand curled toward the sky.

"Did you think he was living for you?" the Hunter asked, gesturing to his prone form. "Because that doesn't appear to be the case."

Find out if you're immortal.

The world lost all focus. The Hunter continued to pour his poison in my ear, but I couldn't hear him. All I could see was that hand, the one that had just hours ago touched my face so tenderly. The palm I had kissed a hundred times. I closed my eyes and searched for his light in my heart, praying that somehow he could hear me.

Please, Hideyoshi. I'm alone in the woods. I need you. Don't leave me.

The flame he put inside me flickered, weak but still there. I clung to it and repeated my plea like a prayer. Time stretched and bent around me, infinite and empty. The world around me became meaningless. He was there in that cold nothing, and I could so easily slip into it with him. *Isseki nichou.*

The flame jumped. I opened my eyes. He moved.

A finger twitched, followed by a full body shudder. The world snapped back open as he gasped, groaned, tried to move.

"Hide!" His name exploded past a wall of blood.

He jerked and moaned at the sound of my voice. He reached blindly in my direction, nearly touching my knee before the Hunter intervened with a growl of disgust.

"How many times do I have to kill you?" He kicked Hide's shoulder with his heel, forcing him onto his back.

He fell limply, face tight with pain, blood oozing from a dozen different places.

My heart stopped as the Hunter drew his sword. Hide's head lolled, and a sound that could have been my name struggled past his lips. The Hunter gripped his sword in both hands and aimed its point downward at Hide's chest. His dark eyes flicked toward me, one corner of his mouth twitching upward.

It was then that I realized what our immortality meant. More than years, more than power. It meant they couldn't kill us, but they could make us watch each other die over and over and over again.

In the end, death always wins.

The sword came down. Hide spasmed and made a choked sound, his hand wrapping weakly around the blade before falling limp again. Blood ran from his mouth, making a widening circle on the tatami.

I felt them clawing at me, the wicked hands of death, and I wanted to give in to them, to follow my maker into the dark. I turned my face away, buried my nose into the crook of my arm, unable to bear the sight of his lifeless form. His sightless eyes cracked open. My hands gripped the chains, and the beam overhead creaked.

Break off the pieces that scare you...

Reality splintered, became further away as the demon inside me rose up in all its fiery rage. Some hidden reserve of strength burned through my muscles and coaxed my tired body into motion. From the cold comfort of my prison, I watched it rise to its feet, watched the Hunter shrink back as the beam popped, cracked, gave way with a vicious yank on the chain. My wound tore and my lungs filled with blood, but I felt it as if through layers of cotton cloth—muted, present, but unimportant.

The Hunter's smug expression dropped, and he scrabbled for his sword. He tried to draw it back, but Hide sprang to life again and grabbed the blade. Blood poured from his hands, but he didn't let go. I looped the now-slack chain in my hands, and the Hunter screamed as I threw it around his neck like a noose, tighter, tighter.

I pulled him back into me, stretching his neck at an awkward angle. He clawed at my arms, kicked at the empty air. His pulse thudded against my lips, and he gave a great wheezing cry as I tore into him. His flesh opened to me like a fountain, and I drank him down like wine. I swooned. My starving cells danced in ecstasy.

A sick pop and he went limp in my arms, his neck broken. His heart stopped, his blood ceased flowing, but I didn't stop. I twisted his head and wrenched it from his shoulders, drinking the blood that spilled from it. I did the same with his arms, his legs, tearing him to pieces as if he were made of rice paper. I ripped into his gut and drained his organs.

Giddy with a sick euphoria, I let the gore slide from my hands. It felt good, this violence, like it had with Yamaguchi, like it had with that boy Hunter and the innocent man on the street. My veins rang with it. My heart got lost in it.

"Hiro!"

Hide lay on his side, pushed up on one elbow, his other hand clutching the hole in his chest. His eyes were wide, wide as the ones in that Hunter's head as it gaped at me from across the room. I expected pride. I saw horror.

The dam broke, and reality flooded back in. I stared at trembling hands bathed in blood. It wasn't me that tore into that man—it was some other thing. Yet his voice cried out in my veins. His life powered my vengeance.

The doors flew open, and two more Hunters appeared, swords drawn. They stopped short at the sight of me, and their blades wavered. I could only imagine how I must have looked to them, white-eyed and surrounded by the pieces of their dismembered cohort. But the monster had gone, slipped back into its cage fat and satisfied, leaving a trembling boy behind.

It didn't feel good anymore. It felt wrong, like murder, and I felt broken. My human heart had become a slave to the monster.

My muscles seized. I staggered backward and landed on my knees beside Hideyoshi, shaking so hard my teeth chattered. "No...no more..." I clapped my hands to the sides of my head, and my heart hammered an unsteady beat in my ears. The smell of blood clogged my nose. I couldn't breathe.

The tatami creaked as Hideyoshi struggled to his feet, pain twisting his features, and planted himself between me and the Hunters. He clutched his chest, and blood dripped from his clothes. The tip of a silver sword dragged the ground as if he scarcely had the strength to lift it.

"Now," Hide said between gasping breaths, "would be a good time to scream."

I pulled myself up straight and took as deep a breath as I could manage. I took all my fear, all my pain, and condensed it into a hot ball in my chest. Eyes watering, lungs burning, I released it all in a great exhale of sound that tore through me like something alive.

The Hunters jerked backward as if I'd struck them. One even dropped his sword, and his hands clapped to his ears as my pain bored into them. The other let loose a cry of his own, lurching forward with his sword raised in a clumsy, desperate attack. Hide dispatched him with a clean cut across the abdomen that sent him writhing to the floor, his guts spilling out the gash.

My scream cut off in a fit of coughs, and I slumped forward, dizzy from the effort. The unarmed man tried to flee, but Hide caught him by the neck and forced him to his knees. The Hunter's face went slack as Hide's magic seeped into his skin, his fight weakening until he was practically limp in his grip.

"Where is he?" Hide growled.

The Hunter blinked glassy eyes. "Who?"

"Hashiguchi Toshiro."

The Hunter's face twisted as if resisting Hide's influence. "I don't...know..."

Hide's grip tightened. "Tell me."

Fat tears leaked from the Hunter's eyes. "Are you going to kill me?"

"Yes," Hide answered, bringing his nose even with the boy's. "But how you die is up to you."

The Hunter's gaze darted to the pieces of his dead companion, and a choked sob escaped his throat before he went limp again. When he spoke, it was in a monotone. "A blacksmith. In Sakamachi. Second floor."

"Good boy," he said, loosening his grip on the Hunter and giving him a pat on the cheek. For a moment, I thought he might even let him go. He dropped down to his knees, his grip transferring from the Hunter's neck to his hair. The Hunter released another sob and a garbled string of pleas as Hide pulled his head back to expose his throat. It struck me then that as much as the boy hated us, he feared us, and now he would die in his nightmare.

Hide groaned loud and low as his fangs pierced the Hunter's neck. Normally, he would have spit out the blood he took, an insult, an assertion that the Hunter was unworthy of being a part of him, but the severity of his wounds meant he couldn't afford to be prideful. He took him fast. A spike of hunger had me doubled over when he dropped the Hunter's bloodless body to the floor. For a long time, he didn't move, eyes closed, lost to his own monster.

"Hide?"

He opened his eyes slowly. One hand still clutched his chest, but some of his color had returned. He straightened his back with a wince, and his gaze drifted over to me. His eyes were clear and sharp as a katana's blade, and it sent a wash of relief over me. As if my fear was the last thread holding me together, I unraveled in a fit of choking sobs.

Hide rolled his eyes. "Calm down, Hiro."

"I thought…you were…"

"Stupid boy." He clicked his tongue and slid on his knees across the tatami to kneel in front of me. I scrubbed at my cheeks and ducked my head, but he forced my face back up with a hand on my chin. "What did I tell you?"

"I—I don't—"

"I told you as long as you were here, I'd be beside you."

I swallowed my tears and shook my head. His grip softened, and he brushed a sticky strand of hair out of my eyes.

"You're a mess." He examined the cut on my neck and the growing patch of blood on my side. His brows lowered over his eyes. "You shouldn't have come."

"They were going to kill you."

He nodded. "Mn."

A shiver ran through me. The image of him crumpled in that closet flashed before my eyes, and I knew with absolute certainty if he hadn't come back, those Hunters would have killed me too.

Isseki nichou.

"Can you stand?"

I nodded. "I think so."

"Good." He pulled himself to his feet easier than I would have thought possible and offered his hand to me. "We have work to do."

TWENTY-NINE

Betrayal

WITH THE HELP OF THE BLOOD WE'D TAKEN FROM THE HUNTERS, Hide and I regained some measure of strength, and our wounds, though still open and angry, mostly stopped bleeding. The cut to my neck was actually quite shallow, and I poked at it gingerly as I studied my reflection in the surface of a water bucket. The wound on my side was much worse and oozed with every breath. I spat great clots of blood and had to restrain the constant urge to cough.

Hide, of course, refused to acknowledge his injuries, though his pain was evident in sweat pouring from his temples and the stiff line of his back. He sent me outside to clean up while he searched the house. I was secretly grateful. Now that the rage and bloodlust had passed, the sight of the carnage made me sick.

I told myself it was hunger that drove me to tear that man apart, a way to get at his blood without the help of his heart, but it wasn't true. I remembered the feel of his flesh ripping in my hands, his joints popping like chicken bones. I shivered, not with revulsion, with satisfaction, with pleasure.

I splashed water on my face, and it fell back into the bucket tinged red. I repeated the action over and over, scrubbing at my skin until it burned. There was no end to it. It dripped from the ends of my hair and off my nose, as if I'd be covered in blood forever.

Gravel crunched behind me, and Hide appeared at my side. "Found my swords." The two blades rattled as he leaned them against the edge of the well next to a pile of kimono. "And some clothes."

I nodded, my eyes still on my distorted reflection. "What happened? After you left the house."

Hide released a long breath. "Matsudaira led me here. Said it was his father's house. He waited on the road and sent me and his guard inside. They were already here. Waiting."

"Matsudaira-dono betrayed you."

He nodded, expression blank, but his fingers curled against the wood frame of the well. The relationship between a samurai and his daimyo was one based on honor as much as money. Hideyoshi had promised him his life in service, a promise he should have treasured and protected. Instead, he used it as a weapon against him, and it cut deeper than a hundred silver swords.

"Do you think Hashiguchi was part of it?"

"No. They have him. I saw it when I touched that Hunter." His scowl deepened. "Son of a bitch probably gave me up, along with our mutual connection to Matsudaira."

"So what do we do?"

He closed his eyes and pinched the bridge of his nose.

"Kyo came to the house."

He jerked his head up, a wild look in his eyes.

"He told me where you were."

"Why?"

"I don't know." I shook my head. "'Goodwill,' he said."

Hideyoshi scoffed.

"What if this is all some kind of game?" I ignored a splash of pain in my chest jerking my heart into an irregular rhythm. "What if he's been playing us from the beginning? What if it's a test?"

"Of what?"

"Of our resolve to stand together. To...live, maybe. He asked me if I lived for you, then sent me here to watch you die. There's something bigger going on here, I just can't..."

I set things in motion.

I braced against a wave of dizziness. Hide steadied me with his hands on my shoulders and guided me into a seated position on the ground. I leaned back against the well, the heel of my hand pressed against my forehead. Water splashed out onto the grass, and the well pulley squealed as Hide pulled up a fresh bucket and set it at my feet. He settled down beside me, hissing a little as his wounds tugged, and took one of my hands in his.

It was covered in blood, caked around my knuckles and under my fingernails. The hand didn't even feel like mine, and the realization made me tremble.

Crazy and brave.

"I think something's wrong with me."

"What are you talking about?" Hide plunged a cloth into the bucket and dabbed at the blood on my hands. It came away in watery shades of red.

"What I did. To that Hunter." Bile crawled up my throat, and I swallowed around it.

"It doesn't mean anything."

"But—"

"There's nothing wrong with you," he said sharply, tightening his hand around mine. "You back a wolf into a corner, you get bitten. That's all."

His eyes were hard and stubborn, and they held mine with a comforting steadiness that smoothed the rough edges of my despair. He was right. He had to be. I couldn't imagine a world in which he could be wrong.

I released a breath and melted into his side. Hide wiped at my hands and forearms, his touch gentle and meticulous. Little by little, the blood disappeared, the water ran clear, and I felt like myself again. The coldness that had opened up inside me faded, and I sang, no words, just a melody, low and melancholy. It flowed from my heart and over my lips. It was the only way I knew how to tell him how much I loved him, the only way I knew he would hear. And I did love him. I pressed into his warmth and shivered at the thought of it not being there.

"What are we going to do?" I asked in a hoarse voice. "About Hashiguchi."

Hide snorted. "I'm beginning to think we've saved him one time too many already."

I sat up. "We can't just abandon him."

"Why not? He clearly doesn't care about us. Have you forgotten that girl in the alley?" His whole body went sharp as a brandished sword. "I think maybe he's brought this on himself."

"Then we all have," I snapped. Guilt slid coldly through my veins. "Can you honestly say you've never taken undue pleasure in killing? That you haven't taken more than you needed? I can't."

His expression went hard and unreadable. He stood, his back to me like an impenetrable wall of darkness.

"To say he deserves to die this way is to say we all do."

"And what about the next time?" He spun around, his eyes flashing white. "You can't save them all. If you go up against the Hunters, there will be consequences. People will die." He snatched up his sword and held it out in front of him. "This is not a shield, Hiro, no matter how much you want it to be."

My shoulders dropped, and my eyes burned. My throat clenched as images from that horrible dream filled my mind.

"I can't just leave a man to be tortured. I can't."

He released a hard breath and dropped his arm back to his side. He squeezed his eyes closed for a moment, and when he opened them, they held traces of the same fear and need I'd seen in him after we'd been attacked in the brothel.

"Your soft heart will bring you nothing but trouble."

"I can bear anything as long as you're with me." My voice cracked, and a tear ran hot down my cheek. "Will you stay with me?"

He clicked his tongue and turned his face away. I half expected him to curse, haul me onto my feet by my collar, and drag me home. Instead, he yanked a kimono off the top of the pile he'd pilfered from the house and threw it into my lap.

"Get cleaned up," he growled. "We should go while we still have surprise on our side."

THIRTY

Father

WE TOOK AGAIN ON THE WAY BACK, AN UNLUCKY TRAVELER WE CAME upon on the road back to Edo. We shared him between us right there in the middle of the road with the sun beating down on our heads. It was almost a dare. *Here we are. We're not afraid of you. Come for us.*

While the fresh blood restored some of our strength, it did little for our wounds. Hide bore the pain proudly, back straight, the only evidence of his suffering a slight shortening of his stride. I was not so proud. I hunched and clutched at his sleeve, panting with every step. I pressed my other hand to the wad of fabric packed between the layers of my kimono, the only thing keeping blood from seeping through.

Sweat beaded on my forehead as the low buildings and busy streets of Naito-Shinjuku came into view. It looked different somehow, darker, meaner, every sword-bearing man a potential threat not just to me, but everyone like me. The more I ran the details of it through my head, the more insidious, the more ingenious it became. Matsudaira and those two swordsmen didn't even know each other, yet they banded together under a common purpose. That anonymity was quite possibly their greatest defense. A centralized group could be traced, rooted out, and felled in one great sweep like a field in harvest. Individuals would have to be dug out like ticks, one by one. Fear and bitterness battled it out inside me, making me feel ill. I wanted to hide, but I also wanted to rip each sword from its sheath until I'd found every silver blade and crushed them under my feet.

I ducked my head against Hide's shoulder. Like that first terrifying walk after the change, I followed him blindly. For some reason, I couldn't stop thinking about the first life I took, the duality of emotions it created in me. Was that when it started? That hairline fissure inside me. I needed to be strong, but my mind felt made of porcelain spiderwebbed with fine cracks that could shatter at the slightest knock.

You back a wolf into a corner, you get bitten.

The wind shifted, bringing with it the smell of plum blossoms, and I knew we were home. I didn't look up until the gate slammed closed behind us.

"Where's the guard?"

My throat closed. My muscles trembled with the memory of our brief fight, my ears rang with the sound of his last breaths. Hide's eyes narrowed as he watched the color drain from my face.

"Hiro, did something happen?"

My eyes burned, and I turned my face away. I swayed as he slipped out of my grasp and stepped onto the engawa. He hesitated with his hand on the shoji, the muscles of his jaw tight, and I closed my eyes. I didn't want to see his reaction, didn't want to see the mess I'd made, yet there it was painted on the backs of my eyelids.

The shoji scraped open. Silence stretched tight and infinite.

"There's nothing here."

My eyes snapped open. I leaped to his side, mouth hanging in disbelief. I'd slit the man's throat, watched the tatami changed color as he bled out. How could there be nothing?

Yet there was nothing. The sitting room was laid out as it had been before Hide's departure. The mats had been replaced. Even the dishes had been washed and arranged on the chabudai as if awaiting our guest. Like it had never happened.

"I don't under—"

A flash of memory. A crooked smile. *I'll take care of this.*

"Kyo."

Hideyoshi's stony expression went molten, and a little color drained from his face. He opened his mouth to speak but was cut off by footsteps from outside the gate. My stomach flipped.

"Matsudaira." Hideyoshi's mouth twisted into a snarl, and his hand went to his sword.

I grabbed his wrist and pushed him backward deeper into the house. "You can't kill him, Hideyoshi. He's your daimyo."

"He tried to kill me." The color that had left his face now blazed hot on his cheeks. "Now he's here for you."

"Maybe." I kept my voice low, gesturing for him to do the same. I'd managed to steer him all the way down the hall to his room and push him inside. "Let me talk to him. Maybe I can figure out what's really going on."

"There's nothing to talk about."

"Don't you want to know why he betrayed you? After all this time?" I remembered my conversation with the guard and Matsudaira's slumped posture when he thought no one was looking. The guard said he'd been given a job. Maybe Matsudaira had been given one, too, one he was hesitant to complete. Maybe I could find out the real reason he was here.

Hide's resistance softened, his face going almost unreadable except for the slight twitch in the corner of his right eye.

"I'll be fine. I used to talk to men for a living, remember? I know when to push and when to get out. Besides, I think he likes me." I smiled with more confidence than I felt, and he responded with a short, snorting laugh. I squeezed his hands as a bird call rang from above and the boards of the engawa creaked under heavy footsteps. "Trust me."

He released a breath and nodded. I left Hideyoshi hidden in his room and slipped down the hall and back to the front of the house just as Matsudaira pushed his way through the gap in the shoji. His expression was tense, and his gaze jerked to every corner of the room before settling on me.

I bowed, careful not to wince at the pain in my side. "Matsudaira-dono. Welcome back."

He jumped a bit, like a kid caught with his hand in the sweets. "Where is Ito-san?" he asked, words tight and clipped.

"Who? Oh, the man you left behind?" I kept my features neutral, almost serene, and clasped my hands behind my back to hide the dark stains under my nails. "He left."

"Where did he go?"

I shrugged. "Didn't say. Perhaps he figured I could take care of myself." His tension eased a bit. Could that be relief? One would expect a daimyo to be annoyed at the disobedience of his subordinate. I drifted over to the chabudai and plucked up the teapot. "Would you like some tea? I was just about to brew a fresh pot."

Matsudaira's brows lowered as he studied me, fingers twisted in the loose fabric of his hakama.

"Did you find your father?"

He tightened his fingers. "No."

"Oh." I kept my voice light but sympathetic. "You must be very worried. But Hideyoshi is quite loyal. He won't quit until the job is done. I'm sure he will find him for you."

His throat worked around a thick swallow, the poise of the daimyo fighting against the fears of the man.

I lifted the teapot and arched an eyebrow. "Perhaps you would prefer wine."

He made a sound almost—yet nothing—like a laugh. "Yes. Yes, wine would be good."

I nodded and drifted back to the kitchen to fetch a bottle, casting a glance down the hall as I passed. Though Hideyoshi remained dutifully hidden, I could picture him pacing the little room like a caged animal, his hand clenched around his sword. My own blood burned with the heat of Matsudaira's betrayal, and it took everything I had to maintain my hospitable demeanor. I paused a moment in the kitchen, gripping the wine bottle so tight I feared the glass would break, and took two deep, steadying breaths.

Matsudaira had settled himself back at the chabudai when I returned, his katana leaned against the table and his wakizashi still on his hip. Apprehension tingled across my skin as I wondered what they were made of.

Plastering on a smile, I lowered to my knees beside the table. I poured his glass first, the milky liquid giving off a sharp, sweet smell as it went into the glass. His gaze tracked my movements, though I got the impression he didn't really see them. Shadows hung under his eyes, and there was an almost gray cast to his lips. How long had it been since he'd slept?

When it came to entertaining, I'd learned many things in my time as a geisha, how to carry a conversation smoothly and naturally, filling every pause and brushing away awkwardness. Possibly the most important, though, was when to remain silent. I poured my own glass and leaned back on my heels. Matsudaira emptied his first glass quickly and was most of the way through his second before he spoke.

"He's not really my father."

I put down my own nearly untouched glass and leaned forward.

"He's only a few years older than me, in fact." He released a soundless laugh and drained the remains of his glass. A little pink spotted his cheeks and the end of his nose. He held the glass out toward me, and I filled it again.

"He must really trust you."

His eyes darkened, and his glass stopped half-raised. "He was sick. Likely to die without producing an heir. That's all."

"Even so." I took a small sip of my wine, watching him carefully over the rim of my glass. "He gave you his name, entrusted you with his family legacy. That must mean something."

He took a deep drink of his wine. Despite the bile rising in my stomach, I heard Okaasan's words in my head. *Comfort him.*

I laid a hand on his arm and gave it a gentle squeeze. "And you must care for him as well, to search for him as you are. I can't imagine what I would do if I were in your place. If someone tried to take Hideyoshi away from me."

His back stiffened, and the glass in his hand trembled a bit before he set it down. He knew. And he knew that I knew. Sweat appeared on his upper lip. "The guard…" He swallowed thickly before raising his eyes to meet mine. "He didn't just leave, did he?"

I shook my head. A shadow fell over us, and all the color drained from his face as Hideyoshi appeared in the hallway. The arm under my hand—his sword arm—twitched, and I tightened my grip.

"I'm sorry." His voice came out breathless and husky. "I just wanted Sukemasa back."

"How long have you known?" Hide asked from between his teeth.

"About you? Not until they told me."

"And your father?"

He shook his head, and his face crumpled. All his fighting spirit leaked away, leaving him hunched and hollow-looking like an old tree, rotted from the inside out. "I don't know. Maybe I always knew. He'd been sick for so long, and then one day he just wasn't. I grew up on stories about men who made deals with youkai for longer lives."

He made a sound like a sob, though no tears fell, and he clenched his fists on the table. I let out a long breath, released my grip on his arm, and reached for the hilt of his wakizashi. He didn't resist, didn't move at all, as I pulled just enough to expose the blade.

Steel.

"I'm not one of them," he said, tone defeated.

"Then why?" I asked.

"They told me they would release him in return for Sakurai Hideyoshi."

A ball of molten lead formed behind my breastbone, heavy and scalding. Hide was the target from the start. But why? I pivoted on my hip and found Hide seething with barely contained rage, fist wrapped tight around his sword.

"Who?" he barked. "Who told you this?"

"Those men, the guards I came here with, showed up at my door with an unsigned letter."

"That's how you knew he'd been taken?" I asked.

"Yes."

Hide crossed in front of the table and slammed his fist down on its surface. A shiver of pain went through him, and a spot of blood appeared on the front of his kimono. Anger colored his cheeks, but his lips were pale. "A letter from where?"

"I told you I don't know." Matsudaira's eyes narrowed, a bit of fight returning to them. He pulled a crumpled sheet of paper from inside his collar, flashing just enough of the contents for me to recognize the precise calligraphy running down its length. "Look for yourself. No seal and no signature. And you killed the only people who might have an answer. Or know where Sukemasa is."

Desperation tinged his words, and the hard edges of my anger softened a little. The love he had for his father, his friend, was real, the fight against monsters inconsequential compared to his safe return. He'd been clinging to a small thread of hope, one that required throwing his loyal samurai to the wolves, and now it was gone.

"We know where he is."

Hide made a sharp sound of protest, and I laid a restraining hand on his arm. Matsudaira's eyes widened, and that hope sparked back to life.

THIRTY-ONE

This Means War

"WHAT ARE YOU THINKING, HIRO?" HIDE PACED UP AND DOWN THE engawa, his stomping footsteps echoing through the boards.

I stood with my back pressed against the shoji separating us from our guest, my heart beating like a taiko drum against my ribs.

"He set us up and now you want to help him?"

"You heard what he said. He just wants his father back. He's a victim in all this too."

Hide spat over the edge of the engawa before pivoting and making another circuit.

"Regardless of how you feel about them, we can't leave a man to be tortured."

"Why not? He doesn't deserve our help. Neither of them do."

"Because that would make us monsters."

The statement came out strained and broken, making Hideyoshi's steps falter. The drum in my chest beat so loud it drowned out the cicadas buzzing in the trees over our heads. Bumps raised over my skin as flashes of the earlier carnage flooded my memory. I was close, so close. We both were. We toed the line every day. Hideyoshi might chastise me for my empathy, but it was all that was left of my humanity, and I refused to let it go.

My resolve solidified, and I stepped away from the wall and into his path on the engawa. "If we don't stand up to them, it'll never stop." My words stayed steady despite the dryness of my tongue. "They'll keep taking us, torturing us, killing us over and over again for an eternity unless we do something. Maybe this is our chance to drive them out. To protect everyone by—"

"I don't care about protecting everyone. I only care about protecting you."

The admission came out like a whip crack, surprising us both. Hideyoshi's eyes went wide and his cheeks red before he put his back to me. A shocked laugh bubbled up through my throat, followed by a warmth that started at the flame he put inside me and permeated my skin. I stepped forward, laid my cheek against his shoulder blades, and slipped my arms around his waist.

"I know you're scared." He clicked his tongue and tried to pull away, but I held him tighter. "I'm scared too. But we can do this together."

He sighed deeply and put his hand over mine on his chest. "We can't do it alone," he said after a long silence. "Not in the shape we're in."

"I know."

"So?" He spun around in my arms but stayed close. "What's your plan?"

WE LEFT MATSUDAIRA BEHIND WITH A FRESH BOTTLE OF WINE AND, after quickly tending to our makeshift bandages, headed back out onto the dusty street for Takatanobaba. Word of Hashiguchi's disappearance had gotten around, and the izakaya buzzed with gossip. Many of the same voices that had cursed our name the night before now murmured with speculation on his whereabouts, none of them flattering and none of them even close to true. We slipped in unnoticed, skirting around a tight knot of around a dozen men, expressions ranging from creased worry to flush-faced rage.

"No one's seen him since last night." A small man with a pale complexion paced a two-step pattern around the edge of the group. He looked like a mantis with his hunched back and wringing hands clutched close to his chest. "Something's wrong, I know it."

"Keh! Bastard probably finally got himself caught chasing the wrong girl and had to lie low. Find an angry man's wife, and you'll find him with a finger in her," replied a burly man with a pipe pinched between his teeth and his arms tightly crossed. "It's barely been a day. He'll show up eventually, tail between his legs."

"I don't know." A woman this time, clutching her chest in a way that made me wonder if she was his. A lock of hair had pulled loose from her topknot and curled around her face as if she'd been worrying at it. "Something doesn't feel right."

"You!" All eyes jerked in our direction as another man pointed a sharp finger at us. "You're the ones who attacked him last night!"

I flinched back and clutched Hideyoshi's sleeve. "We didn't—"

"Where is he? What did you do with him?"

Backs straightened and men popped up from their seats. Hideyoshi shoved me behind him as our accuser advanced on us so fast, they nearly bumped noses. Adrenaline spiked through me when they both reached for their swords.

"Stop! Both of you!" I slipped under Hide's arm and pushed between them. I pressed the palms of my hands against the butt of their swords, earning snarls from both sides. "We didn't come for a fight."

"You think you can take from your own kind and get away with it?" another voice shouted from somewhere in the crowd.

"We took nothing," I said. "You don't know the full truth."

"And what truth is that?" hissed the man in front of us, irises white with anger.

"That he was being stalked by Hunters."

A collective gasp went through the room, and all eyes swiveled back to him. His expression wavered before hardening into a defiant mask.

"A convenient lie."

I took a deep breath and tugged a tightly wrapped bundle from the folds of my kimono. I dropped it onto a table beside us, and the wrapping fell away, revealing the broken end of a silver blade.

Voices lifted at the sight of the blade, loud with fear and anger. A palpable division cut through the crowd. The angry man's supporters pulled into a tight knot around him, red-faced with conviction. Others shrank back, wide-eyed and pale-faced.

"This proves nothing."

I turned to Hide and held out my hand for the little box I knew he carried, the one emblazoned with a red-eyed dragon. He extracted if from his sleeve and placed it carefully into my palm. Every eye fixed itself on it, heads craned forward in nervous interest as I cradled it reverently in my hands.

Without word or explanation, I laid the little box down on the bar top and flipped open the lid. A few of the nearby patrons leaned tentatively toward it, eyes straining in the dimness before jerking back with a disgusted gasp.

"Fangs! They're fangs!" The message traveled like wildfire through the crowd. Some shouted obscenities, some stared in silence, tears in their eyes and hands over their mouths.

"They came for us too. The night before we *attacked* Hashiguchi," I started, carefully watching their pained expressions. "They killed me and threatened my maker." A gasp went through the crowd and I continued. "It wasn't even the first time."

"A-Are those..." The woman who had been clutching her chest crept forward, her eyes flooded with tears.

"No," I assured her. "They were left at our house after we were attacked. We don't know who they belong to."

"I..." A soft, tremulous voice rose from the back of the crowd. A young man, his eyes glistening and shoulders hunched, took a shaky step forward. "I think...I might..."

Silence fell over the crowd, dense with grief. I recognized him. I'd seen him more than once working alongside the butcher who provided Hideyoshi his scraps. Someone laid a hand on the young man's arm, and he dropped his face into his hands. My heart ached, and tears stung my eyes.

"This was a message," I said gently.

"A threat," the angry man snapped.

"A warning."

A murmur vibrated through the crowd. Fear clouded their wide eyes and thickened the air. They pulled back, creating a pocket of space around me and Hide.

"We have become too many and too violent," I started, projecting my voice like a stage performer. "And as our numbers grow, so do theirs, the fire of their convictions stoked by our actions."

"Are you suggesting we should sympathize with Hunters?" an angry voice called out from behind a sea of faces.

"No," I said sternly. "I'm suggesting we take responsibility for their existence. Hashiguchi drew their attention when he chased that girl in the street just as we drew their attention by feasting in brothels."

"You think we deserve this?" shouted an angry voice from the crowd. "That we should just give up? Roll over and show our bellies while they take from us?"

Hideyoshi maneuvered me behind him again as the owner of that voice pushed forward through the crowd. The man was built like a bear with a face to match, his heavy steps vibrating through the floor.

"I will not surrender to them," he bellowed. "Nor will I surrender to you."

My heart lurched into my throat, and Hide took a fighter's stance as the beast bared his fangs and went for his sword. Just as he reached it, a pair of arms hooked around him from behind, one around his sword arm and the other holding a knife to his neck.

"Draw your sword and lose your head."

Asagi, tall and imposing despite their feminine dress, snarled into his ear through painted lips. He tried to resist, but Asagi's grip was like iron, subduing him easily despite the difference in size. His back went stiff, eyes wide as his fingers peeled away from the hilt of his sword. A strained laugh burst out of me, and I let my forehead fall between Hide's shoulder blades as I went almost limp with relief.

"Asagi!" the madman exclaimed. "Why—"

"Because he's right. I am not a *murderer* like the rest of you," Asagi said, pointing the end of their knife accusingly around the room, "but every time I hear of your exploits or see evidence of it lying bleeding in the streets, I know it's only a matter of time before they come for me and mine."

"Your slaves, you mean," snapped a disembodied voice from the crowd.

Asagi whipped around toward it, fangs bared, bending the bear's body with him.

"Your recklessness has spurred legends." Asagi's deep voice cut through the chorus of naysayers. "Every living witness is now a potential recruit. Our survival depends on our secrecy, yet you feast like animals, leaving the carcasses to be picked at by crows."

"We're not giving up." I stepped forward again and gestured for Asagi to stand down. They scowled and shoved their captive away, wiping off the front of their kimono as if the man had fleas. "We know where they are and where they're holding Hashiguchi. One way or another, we'll get him back. We'll show them we aren't animals to be slaughtered. And then—"

"And then, we wipe them all out!" Someone threw his fist in the air, and his declaration was followed by cries of agreement.

Panic zapped over my skin as the frenzy escalated, a sea of white eyes reflecting the lamplight. This was wrong. This wasn't what I wanted. Was Kyo right? Was it hopeless? Was the collective selfishness of a horde of bloodthirsty beasts too much to contain? I thought of his heavy face crinkling in glee, his crooked teeth flashing as his lips twisted into a triumphant smile at our failure.

"Do something," Asagi hissed through their teeth as the crowd surged forward.

Hideyoshi pulled the wakizashi on his hip free from his obi and raised it over his head. Adrenaline shot through me, and I caught his wrist before he could bring it down.

"What do you plan to do, exactly?" I called out over the din of the retreating crowd. "Kill everyone holding a sword? Bloody vengeance may feel good in the moment, but it changes nothing. It helps no one."

My voice cracked around a surge of raw emotion. The room went silent as the mob hesitated, bunched up around the door. Hide stepped closer to me and laid a steadying hand on my shoulder. His sharp eyes pinned every one of them in turn, and they shrank. His reputation carried weight even among demons, and it pressed them into submission.

"Asagi is right." Hideyoshi's mouth twisted around the words as if they were covered in barbs. "As long as youkai have existed, so have those who would want to destroy us. An unending war with no winners, only victims."

"But Hashiguchi—"

"We will take him back, make no mistake." Hide stood rod-straight, shoulders back, and chest out. "But we strike with precision. We go in quickly, quietly, and we leave nothing behind. We are ghosts. Things people fear but ultimately don't believe in." He cast a quick glance in my direction, and warmth flashed in my cheeks. "*That* is how we win."

Hope flared in my chest at Hide's words. This was a long game we were playing, but he was right. Time was our biggest advantage. We would keep our presence secret, our activities in the shadows, and eventually, belief in us would fade. We would once again become the things of folktales and children's games. It was the one way in which their disparate structure made them weak. With no concrete threat, the Hunters would die out on their own. They were human, after all.

Well, all but one.

The firecracker tension in the room died down to an ember as they mulled over his words. Asagi released a huff of a laugh, a strange smile flickering over their face before settling into annoyed indifference. Hide simply waited, arms crossed over his chest, the general standing in front of his army waiting for them to fall in line, accepting nothing less.

But they didn't fall in line. Hideyoshi's shoulders tensed, and my stomach dropped as one by one, the crowd turned and trickled out of the room. Asagi scoffed and rolled their eyes before hiding their face behind a fan. Only four men with swords on their hips and the worried-looking girl lingered behind, trading nervous looks.

"Are you...going after Toshi?" the girl asked in a small, tremulous voice.

Hide sighed and glanced at me.

"Yes," I answered, struggling to keep my voice steady.

The girl took a deep breath, nodded, and lifted her chin. "We want to help," she said. "Tell us what to do."

"You." My heart leaped as Hide sprang into action, jabbing a finger at a small, trembly man at the fringes of the group. "Do you know the blacksmith shop in Sakamachi?"

He gave a jerky nod.

"Good. Go there. Get as close as you dare and tell me how many swords you see. All the entrances and exits. If you smell blood. Everything."

The man nodded, gave a stiff bow, and darted out the door. "The rest of you, with me."

The group huddled around Hideyoshi as they discussed their plans in a quick, clipped cadence, the swordsmen nodding along and the girl worrying at that strand of hair in her face and biting her lip. The adrenaline leaked out of me, and I sank onto a mat at the nearest table. My side ached, and I pressed my hand against it. I coughed once, deep and ragged, wincing at the taste of blood. I didn't notice Asagi join me until a full saké glass appeared in my field of vision.

"Are you all right?"

"Fine," I answered, pulling myself up a little straighter.

"You're injured."

I didn't answer, instead taking a deep drink of the wine and swishing it around in my mouth before swallowing. Asagi watched the whole display quietly, brows lowered and lips pinched. If I didn't know any better, I'd say they were worried.

"I'm impressed." Asagi's gaze dropped to their glass as they turned it in their fingers.

"Why?"

"You spoke your heart, and they listened."

"They left."

"They listened," Asagi repeated. "Which means maybe they won't kill anybody."

"Thank you," I said after a short silence.

They huffed. "Don't thank me. My expectations were not high."

"I mean, for helping us."

"Well, don't expect it to become a habit."

Asagi's gaze flicked over to the table where Hide sat hunched with his band of swordsmen, that same tight expression on their face. Their lips twitched as if with words unsaid, their body leaning minutely toward Hide's group.

I laughed, a short, clipped laugh born from exhaustion, and Asagi squinted down their nose at me. "You don't hate him as much as you pretend to, do you?" I asked.

Asagi gasped. They opened their fan in front of their face with a snap, not quite quick enough to hide the twist in their lips. "Don't you have bigger things to worry about?" they barked before jerking to their feet and stomping past Hide's table without so much as a glance and out the door.

THIRTY-TWO

The Raid and the Rescue

"HIRO."

I flinched awake at the sound of Hideyoshi's voice, his hand heavy and warm on my shoulder. Exhaustion and the wine I'd used to calm my nerves had done their work on me, and I'd fallen asleep, slouched against the wall in my corner table. I pushed upright and hissed as the wound in my side pulled.

Hide's eyes darkened. "Are you all right?"

"Fine."

Hide nodded and retrieved his hand from my shoulder to reach for the wine bottle. I resisted the urge to grasp at it and put it back. The knot in my stomach returned. I felt like I was about to be bucked off a horse, and I needed something to hold on to. The three swordsmen he'd been conferring with were still hunched over the same table, pretending not to watch us, along with the man he'd sent ahead as a scout.

"You have a plan?"

"Mn," he answered around the lip of his glass.

I took a deep breath and sat up straighter. "So what do we do?"

"You will go home."

My stomach dropped. "What?"

"I need you to keep an eye on Matsudaira-dono."

I shook my head. "No."

He ignored my protest, eyes on the table in front of him. "Keep him calm. Make sure he stays there—"

"No. I'm coming with you."

"Hiro—"

"Hideyoshi!"

I pounded my fist on the table hard enough to knock over our glasses. The murmur of voices stilled as all eyes turned to us, the only sound the dripping of spilled wine. Hide released a long breath and closed his eyes. I waited, watching the muscles in his jaw work until the voices around us picked up again.

"How many times did you die today?" I asked, voice low.

"Hiro—"

"How many?"

His eyelids lifted, but he didn't look at me. "Three."

My heart shuddered. "Was it hard?"

"What do you mean?"

"To come back." His eyes cut to me, and I took a shaky breath, wiping my nose with my sleeve before continuing. "That time in the woods…you said sometimes it's hard. Was it?"

His eyes trembled before dropping back to the table. He hesitated, rolling his glass between his fingers, before giving an almost imperceptible nod.

"Then why did you?"

"I heard your voice."

My eyes burned, and my throat tightened. I slid my hand over his and released a sigh of relief when he allowed me to intertwine our fingers.

"That's why I'm going with you."

His shoulders dropped, and I knew I'd won. I laid my head on his shoulder, a tingling giddiness bubbling over me.

"Go ahead. Say it. I know you want to," I teased.

"Say what?"

"'Stupid boy.'"

He released a huff of a laugh, squeezing my hand and lowering his nose into my hair. "I may have the perfect job for you actually."

"Really?"

"Mn." I looked up to find an uncharacteristic mischievousness in his eyes. "Can you play shamisen?"

THE SUN HUNG LOW ON THE HORIZON, TURNING THE BUILDINGS along the street into jagged silhouettes. Roofs shimmered with the remaining heat from the day, and the smell of horses and cooked meats mixed into a confusing, stomach-turning concoction in my nose. The two adjoining buildings of the blacksmith's shop sat apart from the others. The shop itself was covered but open to the air on all sides, its great brick kiln glowing red and filling the air with soot as a black-faced smith worked the bellows with his foot. He turned a red-hot blade with a pair of tongs, and I wondered if it was silver or steel.

A narrow, two-story building that doubled as a store and a residence leaned up against the shop like an afterthought. Dark wood walls stained by smoke disappeared into a flat thatch roof. The front shoji were open, and rows of kitchen knives and bladed farming tools glinted in the meager light.

"That's it?" I adjusted the borrowed shamisen strapped to my back and swallowed a sudden attack of nerves. "It doesn't look that menacing."

"They're keeping him upstairs." He pointed up at the slatted windows, the shadows behind them just visible from our vantage point across the street. "Two guards up there with him, plus one in front of the store."

His finger shifted to a restless man smoking a hand-rolled cigarette and kicking at the dust. A single sword rested against his hip, and his gaze bounced over every face that passed.

"You can set up here." He balled his hand into a fist as he dropped it to his side. "Use your voice to keep people away and the street clear. No matter what happens…just keep singing."

"Hide…"

"Just keep singing," he repeated, the words clipped. He turned to face me, his expression stoic, but in his eyes was the same fear, the same need I saw in him in the brothel. "If they come out here looking for you, run. Understand?"

I nodded, a knot the size of a plum in my throat. For a long time, neither of us moved, the swordsman waiting in the street forgotten. Hide lifted a hand to cup my cheek, running his thumb over my cheekbone and across my lips. He followed it with a kiss, a brush of lips so soft and sweet it stole my breath. He started to pull away, and I clutched his collar, bringing him in closer. I pressed my love into his lips, fighting back images of him slumped in that Hunter's closet. I told myself this wouldn't be our last kiss, couldn't be.

But just in case.

"Come back," I said, giving just enough distance to fit the words between us.

He nodded sharply. "Mn."

Then he was gone, the shadow of his back growing smaller as he set a fast pace up the street. Two of his swordsmen coughed and averted their eyes before scurrying after him. The third, blushing all the way to the tips of his ears, gave me a quick bow before joining them. Blinking back tears, I settled onto an overturned produce crate and pulled the shamisen into my lap.

I brought the wide wooden plectrum down across the strings as Hideyoshi and his group disappeared down an alleyway two buildings down. Heads lifted and eyes turned at the music's command. I took a deep breath and closed my eyes as the chord rang through the shimmering evening air. My fingers tumbled over the strings, stiff at first, then finding their rhythm as if they were born to it. I opened my eyes and painted a river with my voice, deep and wide and rushing, the shamisen the rocks beneath it.

They swirled together in a magical concoction that poured into the ears of passersby. One by one, they remembered things undone, felt the heat of the passing day, and sought refuge in shops and teahouses. A few dropped coins at my feet as they passed, and I smiled my thanks, eyes never leaving the blacksmith's door. The street emptied, but the guard remained.

Listen to me.

The guard's eyes shifted in my direction as I focused my song on him. *There is nothing else. Only this.* He blinked a few times and shook his head as if trying to clear a fog. He was a Hunter, likely trained to recognize the effects of my influence, but it was too late. He swayed a bit, his gaze hazy and out of focus. A shadow moved behind him. I kept singing. The shadow grew darker. The guard didn't turn. A pair of hands appeared and jerked him backward into the store, and the shoji slammed closed. A muffled cry sounded from within. The smell of blood followed.

Don't stop singing.

My heart crashed against the beat of the shamisen. Within the bubble of my voice, time stood still, but inside the shop, a war raged, and all I could do was trust Hideyoshi and sing. Sing and wait until he appeared before me again.

A flicker of motion from down the street caught my attention. A man, backlit by the setting sun, drifted down the empty street. I lifted my voice louder, striking the shamisen hard on the downbeat. The shadow paused.

That's it. You have something else to do. There's nothing for you here.

My heart seized when his motion resumed, not away from me, but toward me. The light shifted, revealing enough of his profile to show where his nose was pointed. The blacksmith's shop. Panic zinged through me as I sped my tempo, but his path didn't change. Why wasn't it working? Another shift of light cut familiar features out of the shadow, the wide profile of a kamishimo and the tall pillar of an eboshi.

Matsudaira.

"Kuso," I cursed. Despite Hideyoshi's orders, I dropped the shamisen and rushed forward into Matsudaira's path. His eyes were glassy and trained on the blacksmith's door. I stepped in front of him, and he balked, blinking slowly.

"Matsudaira-dono. What are you doing here? I thought you were waiting for us at the house."

"I…I just needed…" He blinked again, a furrow forming between his brows. He didn't know what he needed but was driven here all the same, aware but not aware. He was under someone's influence, but not mine. Stronger than mine.

"Matsudaira-dono, we have it under control. You should—" I

grabbed him by the shoulders, and he shook me off. We were only steps from the front of the blacksmith's store, and he flung himself toward it, crashing through the shoji before I could stop him.

He froze.

The stink of blood slapped me across the face like a wet rag, making my veins vibrate like the shamisen's strings. The guard who had stood outside when we first arrived now lay slumped against the wall just inside the door like a discarded doll, two jagged gashes across his neck. Fang marks.

The fog cleared from Matsudaira's eyes, and the color drained from his face. His jaw dropped, and a long, thin sound escaped him as he stumbled backward, fell into a display counter and sent blades crashing to the ground with an ear-piercing clatter. In response to the noise, one of Hideyoshi's swordsmen appeared from a back room, sword drawn.

"Stop! He's with us!" I threw myself between them, hands raised. The swordsman stopped when he saw me, white eyes narrowing, and slowly lowered his bloodstained sword.

"What's going on down there?" Hideyoshi's voice called down from above a set of stairs that ran up along the backside of the store.

Sandaled feet appeared on the top step, white socks spotted with red. Then a dark kimono, hanging heavy and stained even darker. The *snak* of a sword sheathing sounded, and then his head and shoulders appeared, face smeared and spitting blood I knew by its smell wasn't his.

"Hiro, I thought I told you—" He stopped short on the last step, gaze landing heavily on the man cowering behind me.

"I couldn't stop him," I said, answering his question before he could ask. "I don't know why."

Hide's jaw clenched. Matsudaira cleared his throat and tapped me on the shoulder. Some of his color had returned, and he smoothed his hands over his kimono in an effort to regain some dignity. He was a soldier, after all. The sight of death and blood were nothing new.

It was everything else.

Hide fully descended the stairs and bent into a low bow. "Matsudaira-dono."

"Sakurai-san." His voice held a slight tremor despite his more composed appearance.

"Pardon me, Matsudaira-dono, but what are you doing here?"

"I…" Matsudaira's eyes went cloudy again, a wrinkle forming between them. He pressed his fingertips against his brow for a moment before giving up. "Did you find my father?"

Hide's expression remained unreadable. "Yes."

Matsudaira's eyes brightened. "Where is he?"

"Upstairs."

Matsudaira took a step toward the stairs, and Hideyoshi raised a hand to stop him. "I'm sorry, but…"

"But what?" Irritation crept into Matsudaira's voice.

"I recommend you wait down here."

"Nonsense. I want to see him." He pushed forward again, but Hide didn't budge. "Why are you stopping me? Is he…" He swallowed thickly, going a little pale again. "Is he dead?"

"That's a complicated question."

"How is it complicated?" he snapped, his eyes watery. "Is he dead, or isn't he?"

Hide released a long breath before turning back up the stairs with an implied invitation to follow. Matsudaira took it, falling into step behind him. I brought up the rear, my chest tight and skin cold. The scent of blood grew stronger as we went. Hide reached the landing and stepped aside to allow the rest of us through.

Two more bodies lie in a pile just off the staircase, full of holes made by both fangs and swords. Matsudaira stepped over them, his sleeve pressed against his nose. A screen blocked off the back corner of the narrow room. Shadows moved behind it, and a dark-brown stain crept across the tatami beneath it.

A thin, pained sound escaped Matsudaira, and he lurched toward the screen. Hideyoshi grabbed him by the arm, stopping him before he reached it.

"All due respect, Matsudaira-dono," he said in response to his cutting glare, "you don't want to see him like this."

Tension vibrated along the daimyo's spine. He shook loose of Hide's grip and laid his hand on the screen, hesitating only a moment before shoving it aside.

Behind it lay the barely recognizable form of Hashiguchi Toshiro.

Like a bug crushed under the hoof of a horse, Hashiguchi's limbs lay splayed and twisted. His kimono had been cut to ribbons, its color completely masked by the blood now staining it. Hardly a patch of skin remained that wasn't colored by cuts or bruises, each one telling a story of torture, starting at his broken fingers and ending with a brutal gash across his throat. How long was he beaten, how many times were his bones broken before he stopped healing?

"Su-Sukemasa…" Matsudaira's fingers twitched toward the body of his friend, but he couldn't bring himself to move closer. His gaze jumped from one injury to the next, finally settling on his face. He blinked rapidly as he squinted, looking through the blood and the swelling, searching for something he recognized.

A girl knelt beside Hashiguchi's body, the same girl I'd seen clutching her chest at the izakaya. She was pale, her cheeks wet, one hand brushing through Hashiguchi's matted hair while the other remained balled at her breast. I swallowed a knot made of needles and moved closer to Hideyoshi.

"Where did she come from?" I whispered out of the corner of my mouth.

"She came ahead of us posed as a kitchen maid. We needed her to…"

My stomach clenched. "To what?"

"To tell us if he was still here."

"What do you mean, *if?*" Matsudaira snarled. His grief had congealed into anger, and he hurled it at Hideyoshi. "How could he possibly survive this?"

"I told you. It's complicated." When Matsudaira only glared at him, he released a long, tired sigh. "There's a place in between life and death. The place where we have to make our choice."

"What choice?"

"To live or die."

"So we're waiting for him to make a choice?" Matsudaira's voice shook, and his fists balled at his sides.

"If he's still there, he's already made it."

At this, Hideyoshi's gaze shifted to the girl. She lifted watery eyes and nodded.

"He wants to live," Hide proclaimed.

Hope alighted in Matsudaira's eyes again despite the disbelief in his voice, and his attention swung to the girl. "And you know this how?"

"She's his bloodline," Hide answered for her. "She can feel him. He wants to come back, but his body is too drained and too damaged. He's stuck."

A shiver ran through me. Memories of my almost-death prickled around my temples, the black and the cold. I imagined him there alone with nothing but the pain of starvation and the memory of torture. How long could someone remain there before they went insane? Before they made a different choice?

Matsudaira's shoulders dropped. "What do we do?"

"He needs blood."

The daimyo's eyes snapped open wide. "Take it," he said, yanking up his sleeve and bearing his wrist. Any bitterness I still had for him evaporated in the light of his self-sacrifice. "Take as much as you need."

"It's too late for that."

"But you just said—"

"Your blood isn't enough." Hideyoshi kept his expression carefully neutral. "He needs stronger magic. It will take the blood of one of us— of a youkai—to give him the strength he needs."

Matsudaira blinked and took a step back, the sudden reminder of our difference sending a flash of panic through his eyes. His gaze jerked to each of us in turn, his throat working as if the question lodged itself deep inside it.

"Please."

Hideyoshi put his hand on Matsudaira's elbow, tugging him away from the brutal scene with surprising gentleness. "You should go downstairs."

"No."

"This will be…violent. You could be in danger."

"I don't care."

Hide sighed but nodded his consent, casting a meaningful look in my direction. I stepped up beside Matsudaira, taking Hide's place at his elbow, and urged him toward the back wall as far away from Hashiguchi as we could get. He leaned into me, and I did my best to prop him up with a gentle hand on his back. Emotions fought across his face: desperation and disbelief and fear. A line of sweat fell from his temple, and he didn't even notice me blot it away with my sleeve.

On Hide's wordless signal, the girl rolled up the sleeve of her kimono, pulled out the knife tucked in her obi, and cut a long, deep gash in her wrist. Matsudaira flinched at the sight but didn't move. The girl cradled Hashiguchi's head in her lap, his blood painting splotches across the pale fabric of her kimono, and pried open his swollen lips. A drop of her blood fell on them, and the cracked skin stitched itself together instantly.

The girl lowered her wrist until it was flush with Hashiguchi's lips. Her blood ran into his mouth, a bit of it leaking from the corners. We all held our breaths. The girl whispered something we couldn't hear, something meant for him alone. Tears fell from her eyes as she stroked his hair with her free hand.

His muscles twitched, a shiver of his lips followed by a reflexive swallow. Matsudaira gasped, digging his fingers into my arm. He took another swallow. A violent spasm and a deep, shuddering moan followed. Bruises faded, superficial wounds healed. The crack of bones snapped back into place as his fingers twitched and curled.

All at once, Hashiguchi lurched into violent motion, back arching off the floor and limbs flailing. He clawed at the offered arm, gnawing on the girl's wrist like a wild dog with a discarded bone. She flinched and squeezed her eyes shut, a swallowed cry lodged in her throat, but she didn't pull away. She bore the pain while her maker took from her with animal ferocity.

White eyes rolled in Hashiguchi's sockets, locking onto Matsudaira. No surprise, no recognition, lay there. He shot upright. His legs curled under him, and the girl locked her arms around his torso before he could launch himself forward.

"Sukemasa!" Matsudaira released my arm and pushed forward. I put myself in his path, restraining him with both hands on his chest. "Let me go."

"Hold on to him, Hiro," Hideyoshi cried. He was now on his knees with the girl, struggling to restrain Hashiguchi.

Matsudaira struggled against my hold, face flushed and tears streaming down his cheeks. He no longer had any care about the dignity of the daimyo, blind to everything but the pain of his father. "Why won't you let me go to him?"

"He'll kill you if he gets hold of you," Hide answered. "All he sees is blood. He doesn't even know who you are."

Matsudaira's motion halted as the snarling, hissing reality sank in. This was what we all were at our core, what we fought to control every day. A mindless, bloodthirsty monster.

The girl thrust her arm back in front of Hashiguchi's face. "Take it, Toshi," she said, her voice a thin wail.

Hashiguchi's eyes rolled again, and he curled his fingers around her slim arm. He bit down, hard and savage, the tearing of flesh accompanied by moans. Little by little, his body calmed. His fighting legs stilled. His face relaxed. His mouth on the girl's arm turned almost tender, like a suckling pup. Awareness leaked into his eyes, and they lost their white color.

"Yui-chan?" He stopped drinking, but his lips were still close enough to brush her skin. His gaze lifted to her pale face, and she smiled weakly. Her skin had taken on a wan tone and dark shadows hung under her eyes. The wound on her arm knitted itself together slowly as Hashiguchi pulled away.

"Toshi…" She swayed a bit, and Hashiguchi grabbed her shoulders before she could fall.

"What did you do? You gave too much." His hands trembled with pain as he brushed her cheek, leaving a smear of blood behind.

"Su-chan." Matsudaira strained forward again, eyes shining with tears.

I glanced over at Hideyoshi, who gave me a nod, and I released him. Matsudaira immediately fell to his knees at Hashiguchi's feet.

Hashiguchi blinked and squinted hard. Pain still pulled down his features and stiffened his muscles, but he leaned forward anyway, releasing a little gasp of disbelief. "Suketada-kun? What are you doing here? You shouldn't be here." His gaze shifted to me and then Hideyoshi, suspicion clouding his eyes. "You!"

Hideyoshi's lips curled as he pulled himself to his feet and stood beside me.

"Did you bring him here?"

"He brought us, really," Hide answered flatly.

"He shouldn't be here. This isn't for him to see." He swallowed hard. "I could've…"

"We tried to stop him," I interjected, earning a searing glare.

"You should have tried harder."

Hideyoshi rolled his eyes and took my arm, tugging me back toward the stairs. "This is the last time I'm saving your life."

"Wait." Matsudaira leaped off the floor to stand before us. His face still bore the marks of his fear, but it was now colored with awe. He might have even hugged Hideyoshi if it had been proper. "He may be… bad at showing his gratitude, but know you have mine. Anything you want and it's yours."

Anything.

My mind raced. I thought about Hide's words back at the izakaya and the long road we were about to embark on. We needed help from someone more integrated with human society than we could ever be, someone with influence. The journey would be cut in half if we could meet in the middle.

"I want to make a deal."

Hideyoshi's eyes snapped to me, brows low and knotted together. He hissed my name between his teeth and gave me another, more forceful pull.

"Help us stay hidden," I said, quick and breathless.

Matsudaira's brows shot up his forehead. "Excuse me?"

"As the daimyo, you have influence, the ear of powerful people." Hideyoshi had stopped pulling, and I shook him off. "We will do our best to clean up our own messes, but for those we can't…"

Matsudaira's brows lowered, his expression grave. I was asking him to cover up murders, and the distaste played over his lips.

"If you hear whispers of monsters, stomp them out. You've seen now what they do to us. There's no need for Hunters if people don't believe we exist."

He let out a long breath. He glanced back at Hashiguchi, still recovering with his girl in his arms. He lifted his head, resolution solidifying in his eyes.

"You could have killed me today," he started, his eyes on Hideyoshi. "I would have deserved it for my betrayal. But instead, you helped me." He pulled in a deep breath before squaring up to the both of us and bowing low. "You have my word. On the name of my father and my unborn sons. You will have the protection of the Matsudaira clan for as long as you need it."

"Thank you." I returned his bow and, when I lifted my head, found the others doing the same. Relief coursed through me so strong my eyes watered and my knees nearly buckled. Hideyoshi caught me by the arm again, gentler this time, his eyes full of something I couldn't quite name.

"Let's go home."

Hide turned on his heel and headed down the stairs. I followed, casting a quick glance back. Hashiguchi held the girl in his arms. Matsudaira stood over them, looking rumpled but relieved. *Anything you want and it's yours.* The gratitude of a daimyo. As my head dipped below the landing, I couldn't help but wonder how much it would be worth.

THIRTY-THREE

The Beginning

ON THE WAY OUT, HIDEYOSHI SENT ME INTO A NEIGHBORING IZAKAYA for a bottle of wine, which he uncorked and drank on the spot. His shoulders hunched, and he touched his chest from time to time as he walked, a sign his injuries were wearing on him. They wore on me too. Now that the adrenaline had worn off, my side throbbed and my punctured lung burned with every breath.

I was tired. I was hungry. I needed something else, too, something less tangible but more profound, and every time I looked at Hide's back, it ached like a bruise. I couldn't stop thinking about Hashiguchi lying there broken and bloody. How it had nearly been Hide, nearly been both of us. If one thing had gone differently, we might never have walked beside each other again.

With my heart in my throat, I slipped my hand into his, bracing for the moment when he pulled it away. He didn't, and though his fingers remained loose and his attention never wavered from his bottle, it eased a little of the pain. I rested my forehead against his shoulder and remembered what he told me about putting his heart in a box. Our relationship might never be like those fantasies I had in the okiya, and he might never be comfortable with the affection I gave so freely, or tell me he loved me, but it didn't matter. Every time he indulged my whims or got angry at my recklessness, he showed me. With every muffled curse of "stupid boy" he told me. And every time I sang and the lid of that box lifted a little, I knew.

"I love you," I said softly against his shoulder.

"Mn?" He'd made it about halfway down the bottle, and his steps wavered a little.

I laughed and lifted my head. "Thank you. For helping Hashiguchi even though I know you didn't want to."

He scowled and took another long pull off the bottle. "He lives to be awful another day."

"Matsudaira-dono was grateful, at least."

He huffed, and we walked a few more steps in silence. My mind wandered back to the blacksmith's shop, to Matsudaira's shadow walking toward me despite my song.

"Stop," Hide barked, shoving the bottle in my face.

I swatted it away. "Stop what?"

"Thinking."

"Don't you want to know what he was doing there?"

"No."

"But isn't it weird—"

"I don't care," he said. He came to a stomping halt and spun on me. "All I want to do is go home, take a bath, and go to bed, preferably with you next to me. If I hear the name Matsudaira, Hashiguchi, or Kyo one more time, I will burn this city to the ground. I've had enough of Hunter conspiracies for one day."

"I think you've had enough of that," I said, snatching the wine bottle from his hand.

He frowned but didn't argue. Our hands had come untwined in the course of his rant, and he held his out without looking at me, wiggling his fingers in space. I bit back a smile and took it, insides glowing as it tightened around mine.

Just like that, the bruise was healed.

The sun had fully set, yet the moment we stepped through our gate, it was as if the world brightened. On some unspoken agreement, Hideyoshi went straight to his room to wash and change, and I headed out the back door to start a fire under the ofuro. The small room jutted off the back of the house, connected only by a narrow engawa. I pushed the screens open to let in the air before tossing logs from a nearby pile into the recess beneath. A few minutes later, the fire popped and snapped, heating the bamboo tub above, and I'd just finished filling it with water from the well when Hide appeared on the engawa.

His fresh, white yukata was such a contrast to his usual black I almost thought him a stranger. It clung to his damp skin, hugging the plains and valleys of his chest. The knot of the obi hung loose against his hip, allowing the front to gape and show an immodest strip of skin from his clavicle to his belly button, and my fingers itched to chase the thin patch of hair below it.

Hide cleared his throat, the corner of his mouth twitching upward, and my face burned as if I'd dunked it in the tub.

"The water's still warming," I said, voice huskier than intended.

His lips twitched again as he approached, carrying a tray holding bottles of fragrant oils and, of course, more wine. His cheeks were dusky with it already, but I didn't comment, taking the tray from him and setting it down next to the tub.

I chose one of the bottles and sprinkled its contents over the surface of the water. The woodsy, lemony smell of hinoki drifted up with the steam. I closed my eyes, pulled in deep breaths, and it dulled the sharp edges of my anxiety.

When I opened my eyes again, Hide had already disrobed, his yukata tossed into the corner of the little building. On my knees next to the tub, I got an eyeful of his thick, strong legs as they lifted over its tall walls and slipped into the water. Skin the color of papyrus rippled over tight muscles as he settled himself in the tub, hissing a little as his wounds hit the surface of the water.

His wounds, deep and angry and open. A slash across his side, a stab into his shoulder, and the worst of them, a horrible hole almost dead center of his chest. My heart shuddered, and my skin went cold when I saw it mirrored on his back. I had a momentary worry about the water and infection before realizing it was ridiculous. He was fine. We were fine.

He leaned back against the side of the tub, and I positioned myself behind him. His hair was still tied, and I let it loose. Thick, black strands wrapped around my hands, and Hideyoshi sighed as I dragged my fingers across his scalp, releasing knots as I went. He tipped his head back, eyes closed, and one by one, the lines around his eyes relaxed.

I traced the line of his neck down to his shoulders, working the muscles loose. As I slipped my fingers below the water, my gaze found that wound again. I thought of Hashiguchi lying there broken, caught between life and death.

"You didn't tell me."

"Tell you what?" Hide asked, eyes still closed and words slurred.

"That you could…get stuck."

Hide's eyes slid open, his gaze on the ceiling. "It's not something I like to think about."

My fingers drifted closer to the wound on his chest. "It could have been you. I wouldn't even know how to find you."

Hide's face went hard a moment before he released a huff of a laugh. "Lucky for me that Hunter had no aim." He caught my wrist under the water and moved it just a bit to the left. "My heart is here."

My eyes burned, and my throat went tight. It occurred to me then that he hadn't told me for a reason, that it would never be him, that if he were caught in that space between life and death, he wouldn't wait to be saved.

I cupped his jaw, tipped his face in my direction. "My heart is here." I brushed my thumb over his cheek, leaving a thin stream of water in its wake. "Don't you dare forget your promise to me, Sakurai Hideyoshi."

His eyes, usually sharp enough to cut, went soft. I saw his heart there, open and vulnerable, before the box slammed shut again. He inhaled as if to speak, but instead curled his fingers in my hair and pulled our heads together. He brushed a kiss against the pulse point just under my jaw, then my temple, and then the space between my eyes. By the time he reached my lips, I was breathless.

I didn't notice he'd raised up onto his knees until he whipped his arm around my waist and lifted me up. "Hide, what are you doing? I haven't washed!" He ignored me, hauling me up over the edge of the tub and into the water with him, dirty kimono and all. "Hideyoshi!"

"Shut up, boy," he said with a laugh in his voice. He pulled me into his lap as the water sloshed around us and cradled me against his chest.

Kimono sopping, hair frizzy from the steam, I must have looked like something found under the wheel of a carriage, but he still looked at me like a treasure he discovered deep in a cave somewhere. Awe tinged with disbelief. He let a wet curl of mine wrap itself around his finger, and I remembered what he said to me back in the okiya, back when we were strangers.

It helps to be in the presence of something beautiful.

"Do you want me to sing for you, Sakurai-han?" I teased.

The corners of his mouth lifted briefly, and his eyes brightened. "Mn."

I rested my head on his shoulder and closed my eyes. All those old fantasies flooded me, but they looked different now. The grand romances of stories and song gave way to quieter things: drinking wine while watching the moon, the sweep of a long ponytail, the press of a warm body against me at night. Those small moments added up to something profound, the spirit of the mountain brought down to earth.

My voice lifted out of me, sweet and soft. I sang the song from our first meeting. That day felt both close and infinitely far away, the people in it the same yet different. Would I have made the same choices had I known how it would all turn out? Would I continue to favor Hideyoshi if I'd known the violence it would incite? Would I still beg him for a power I didn't understand if I'd known the cost for both of us? With his heart beating in my ear, I could only come to one conclusion: I was exactly where I was meant to be.

WE SPENT THE REST OF THE NIGHT IN THE TUB, DRIVEN OUT ONLY after the fire went out and the water went cold. I stripped out of my wet clothes right there in the ofuro, and we fell into our futon without even bothering to dress, all damp hair and tangled limbs. We spent most of the next day in bed hardly moving. My body ached as if I'd fallen from a horse, but my cough tasted less like blood than the day before and the wound in my side had almost closed. Hideyoshi's wounds had likewise improved, though he sternly refused to budge from his prone position, an arm thrown over his eyes to block out the sun.

Hunger eventually tugged us out of bed and back into the world. The sun was high and beat down on us with all its ferocity. I expected the city to be different somehow, but it wasn't. The same street vendors we passed every day still called to us. The buildings still cut the same squat shadows across the road. Horses and people still plodded along beside us as if the earth hadn't shifted beneath our feet. Neither of us commented on the absence of the butcher.

Despite our best efforts to avoid it, we eventually ended up in Takatanobaba. The day had waned into evening, and the lamps were just being lit, giving the place a golden glow. Hide and I hesitated outside, gauging the energy exuding from within. Tension shimmered in the air along with the light of the lamps, and I pressed my hands against my thighs to prevent them from sweating.

Hide glanced over at me before huffing and stomping through the door. I followed, of course. A group had gathered around one of the tables, fast, clipped voices emanating from it. It loosened a bit as the patrons noticed our entrance, revealing the man at its center.

Hashiguchi Toshiro.

He looked far better than I would have expected, though he was obviously still healing. The misplaced bones in his face had returned to their proper positions. The swelling and bruising were gone. Only wounds dealt by silver weapons remained. Bandages peeked from the collar and sleeves of his kimono, and his back bent under lingering pain.

"You."

Hideyoshi ground his teeth as Hashiguchi struggled to his feet. Yui, the girl who shared his bloodline, supported his arm and chastised him softly as he took two unsteady steps toward us.

"The samurai and his geisha." He looked Hideyoshi square in the eye, the disdain evident in his stare. "Suketada-kun tells me you're quite honorable. That when he came to you for help, you aided him without question."

Hide's fist tightened around his sword, and I held my breath as insults pressed against the silence, releasing it only when he answered with a simple, "Mn."

A little of the distaste leaked out of Hashiguchi's eyes, and he lowered his voice. "I hear you plan to eradicate the Hunters by fooling them into thinking we don't exist."

"Something like that," Hide answered, casting a glance at me.

Hashiguchi cocked an eyebrow. "You really think that will work?"

"Mn."

Hashiguchi nodded, the corners of his mouth pulling downward. I saw the daimyo in him then—a quick mind and careful consideration paired with ruthlessness. "You've taken on quite a responsibility. Leadership is a delicate yet heavy thing. These people will look to you as an example, but also as a judge. You will be forced to make impossible choices with life and death consequences. Are you prepared for that?"

Hideyoshi's brows lowered, his gaze flicking over the crowd who watched us with wide, expectant eyes. My heart sped, and my chest tightened. He was right, of course. We had made lofty promises, but if we couldn't live up to them ourselves, then they meant nothing. We had to live the ideal, lead by example, and be unbending against those who would refuse to follow.

A smile lifted the corners of Hashiguchi's mouth. He took a step back, then with Yui's help, lowered himself to his knees.

"Domo arigatou gozaimashita." He pronounced the words sharp and loud before touching his forehead to the floor, an act of gratitude and submission that made everyone gasp.

Yui dropped down beside him and repeated the gesture. An even deeper silence fell over the room as conversation died away, and one by one, each patron stood and bowed. Some low from the waist, others all the way down on their knees.

My heart in my throat, I returned the bow, the weight of every lowered head heavy on my back. I was both terrified and relieved. We had earned some measure of respect. Now, it was on us to keep it.

I flinched at the sharp strike of a fan across my shoulders. Asagi stood over me, red eyes glaring down their nose.

"What are you doing, Hiro?" Asagi said from between their teeth.

"You wanted to be kings among demons, and now you are. What kind of king bows to their subjects?"

"A humble one."

Asagi's eyes cut to Hideyoshi at his words, their lips twisting strangely before being hidden behind their fan. Hide faced Asagi, head up and shoulders back, as if daring them to challenge him. The air around the two crackled as they stared each other down.

Asagi released a huff of a laugh and snapped their fan closed before turning their back on Hide and addressing Hashiguchi. "You say he's honorable, and I suppose that's true. Perhaps to a fault." Asagi cast a dismissive glance back over their shoulder. "If it weren't for that boy beside him, I'd even worry he'd be an unyielding tyrant. But he's smart. When he speaks, you'd do well to listen. And what he *lacks* in *heart*"— they bit the words between their teeth—"Hiro more than makes up for."

Throughout Asagi's backhanded commentary, Hideyoshi never moved. His expression remained as stony as ever, though his eyes now pointed at the floor and his shoulders had dropped a notch. The crowd, however, raised their heads, and their eyes gleamed with hope. My own heart thrummed with it. We'd done it. They were on our side.

We could do this.

Asagi turned back toward us, fan open over their face again. Their gaze skipped over us both. "Don't screw this up," they said under their breath as they stomped past us and out the door.

At Asagi's exit, the mood lightened into one of almost celebration. Hashiguchi returned to his table with Yui at his side. The swordsmen that had joined us on our raid gathered around tables, reciting exaggerated accounts of Hashiguchi's rescue, each painting themselves as the hero. The fear that had once permeated the place vanished, and even with the sun setting outside, the air glowed.

I let out a long breath, maybe the first since this whole thing started, and turned toward Hideyoshi. He stood in the same posture as before, glaring at the floor. I laid a hand on his arm, and he flinched as if I'd woken him.

"You all right?" I asked.

"Mn."

"It's okay to relax a little."

"Mn."

I laughed and planted myself in front of him, hands on his arms. "Stop."

His eyebrows bunched. "Stop what?"

"Thinking."

The corner of his mouth quirked, and he relaxed a little. "This isn't the end, you know. It's probably just the beginning."

"I know." A dark feeling curled behind my breastbone, but I ignored it. "But today is a victory. You're allowed to enjoy it."

One eyebrow lifted. "Am I?"

"Yes." I smiled wide, and his face lightened a bit in response. "So what do you usually do after winning a great battle?"

"Find the best bottle of wine I can afford and drink until I black out," he answered, a spark in his eye.

"All right, then." I shoved Hide toward a table and then swept my gaze over the room in search of a serving girl. I was about to wave one down when a shadow caught my eye. Not exactly a shadow, but something within it, swimming through it like water, something denser than the dark. It possessed a small but sturdy frame, with skin that shone gold in the lamplight, a hard, bulldog face. The face was one I saw in my dreams, in my nightmares.

I set things in motion.

My lungs seized, and my skin went cold when Kyo emerged from the shadows as if born from them, unnoticed by the crowd, just another monster in a den of monsters. A slow smile stretched his face, his eyes holding mine with feral intensity. The smile of one victorious. My heart hammered against my sternum, and blood rushed in my ears. He bowed low, an imitation, his eyes never lowering, before slipping out onto the street and dissolving into the dark.

Hideyoshi was right. This was only the beginning.

つづく

Thank you for reading! Did you enjoy?

Please add your review! Then, sign up for the City Owl Press newsletter to receive notice of all book releases!

And don't miss more dark paranormal fantasy like SOUL OF THE UNBORN by City Owl Author, Natalia Brothers. Turn the page for a sneak peek!

Sneak Peek of Soul of the Unborn

BY NATALIA BROTHERS

The pleasure of Chris Waller's first morning in Moscow turned into annoyance when his younger cousin, Debra Alley, emerged from her hotel room carrying an overnight bag despite her promises not to stay in the village.

"Just in case all evening trains are canceled." Debra patted her bag.

"That would be convenient for you, wouldn't it?" Chris asked.

"Go pack your trunks. A couple days on a beach—doesn't it sound *mahvelous, dahling*?"

"We'll take that tour, have lunch, and I don't care what your friends decide to do next. You're returning with me to Moscow." Chris slapped at the elevator call button.

"If Moscow is all you want, then what's the point in you wasting any time on Vishenky?" Debra sounded sweeter than a wooing salesman.

"I'm glad you grasped the part about wasting my time."

"You're thirty-three, not ninety. Be adventurous."

"I was—when I signed up to chaperone you across the Atlantic. You mom said, quote-unquote, 'Promise me you'll watch her every step, breath, bite, and blink.'"

Chris understood Debra and her friends' desire to be on their own. Four college seniors, assisted by the English-speaking escort, Valya

Svetlova, wouldn't get lost on their way to the village thirty miles from Moscow. The guide had rave recommendations from her visitors last year. *Vishenky's Legends and Supernatural Phenomena*, some countryside tour offered by the hotel—good luck with that. The whole thing irked Chris only because the airheads had the *Legends* on their list all along, but Debra didn't bother to tell him until last night. Maybe his overprotective Aunt Rita had a point when she had initially refused to pay for her daughter's trip to Russia.

"Playing babysitter in front of your students...." Debra clicked her tongue. "Must be embarrassing."

"Let me tell you about embarrassing. Your mother also asked me to make sure you don't lose your purse and check your room for a deadbolt lock. No food from street vendors, and, please, don't stay out after nine o'clock."

"And floss my teeth?"

"I was saving that detail until we joined your buddies."

"I'd kill you."

"Then stop being an ungrateful brat." Chris took hold of her skinny elbow, steadying Debra on the sinking floor of the high-speed elevator.

"Too bad your Beth is such a homebody," she cooed. "You two in Gorky Park—oh, so romantic, and off our backs." She turned sideways as a flock of silver-haired ladies invaded the cabin.

Beth Vogel. Another wave of jet lag swept over Chris, an exhausting brew of fatigue and restlessness that had kept him from getting any sleep. There was so much to see, to savor and appreciate, all meticulously selected and crammed into a seven-day trip. For the first time in weeks Beth wasn't on his mind. No, he wouldn't discuss their sudden breakup and endure Debra's tongue-in-cheek "Oh, how disappointing."

"You and Jessie Hunt," he said. "Enjoying your new friendship?" The girls had barely spoken a word to each other since the group had met at the check-in counter at Dulles International.

Debra turned away and studied the control panel, her shoulders positioned an inch higher.

The elevator slowed, stopped, and the doors slid open like symbolical curtains.

The entrance hall of the hotel reflected the same grandeur of the Soviet times as did the metro stations. Tiered chandeliers enticed a woman in a sari into snapping a quick picture as she rushed after her husband rolling his suitcase across the marble floor. Pointing fingers to the high ceiling, teenagers in matching green t-shirts tilted their heads back and giggled furtively, as if in awe of the frescoes that glorified the long-gone era.

Chris spotted Peter Moss and his standoffish girlfriend, Jessie Hunt, by the left wing of the curved staircase. Debra's childhood pal, Luke Higbee, was absent from the rendezvous point; his backpack, stuffed with camping gear, sat at Jessie's feet.

"You both decided to come," Peter said pleasantly, but his thin-lipped mouth twitched.

"I never said I wouldn't." Chris looked around. "Where's Higbee?"

Jessie rolled her eyes as Luke emerged from the gift shop. He shook a plastic bag where the red headdress of a doll peeked out. "A teakettle warmer. I'll tell my sister it's a hat." He tried to get a high five out of Jessie, but she ignored him, her pale eyes fixed on the hotel's entrance. Luke winked at Debra. "So, Deb, is Mr. Waller on board?"

"On board with what?" Chris asked.

Debra shrugged. "Guys, it was your idea. Don't put me in the middle."

"Well, somebody, it's now or never if you're going to bring this up at all," Jessie said. "Valya will be here any moment."

"Okay." Red blotches spread over Peter's cheekbones. "Mr. Waller, we want to ask you for a favor."

Chris turned his hand, palm up. "What?"

"Someone else went on this tour last summer."

"Your brother, yes. Deb told me."

"My half-brother." Peter moved a step toward Chris. "His last name is Ogden, not Moss. The guide has no way of knowing we're related, unless someone warns her."

Jessie raised her arm in front of her boyfriend as if to stop Peter's advancing. "Mr. Waller, please. We just don't want the guide to know how we found her. Maybe you could tell her the tour was your idea and Peter contacted her on your behalf."

"Why?" Chris asked.

"To confuse her." Luke extracted the souvenir doll out of the bag and pointed its pudgy hand at Chris. "You stumbled on Valya's website. Deb doesn't speak any Russian. Jessie will be my girlfriend. We've never heard about last summer's group or seen the footage they filmed."

"And I'm your kindergarten teacher," Chris said. "Why would the guide care who found her website?"

Peter studied Luke and his teakettle warmer as if debating what was more annoying, the doll or his buddy's perpetual grin. "If Valya hears that we saw my brother's film, she might change her program."

"So what?" Chris asked. "Don't you want to learn something new?"

A quick exchange of troubled glances told him that when the real story came out, he wouldn't like it.

"You won't have to lie if you skip the village," Luke said.

"I don't 'have to' anything," Chris assured him.

"Sir, do you believe in psychics?" Jessie asked. "Stuff like mind reading?"

Chris turned to Debra. "What's all this BS about?"

She pouted.

"The guide is like a performance artist, not a psychic," Luke said. "It would be interesting to see if she can read through a load of misinformation."

Chris stared at his cousin. "You told me this was a folklore tour."

"Among other things," Debra said. "Chris, really, you don't have to go. We'll be okay."

A day in a village, in the company of a "psychic" and this bunch of juveniles, seemed like a waste of time compared to the riches of Moscow museums. "See you later" would be a justified reply to Debra's suggestion.

"That's not what I promised your mother," Chris said instead. "And I won't lie about who found—"

"It's her," Jessie said.

A young woman strode across the lobby, a cell phone pressed to her ear, her eyes scanning the tourists congregated around the base of the staircase. For a second her glance met Chris's, but she looked away, searching for someone else.

"Valya Svetlova?" Peter called out.

Silence.

Dressed in beige slacks and a white blouse, with blushing cheeks and a braid streaming over her shoulder and down her chest, Valya could have been a poster girl for any Russian travel agency, except for the fact that not a hint of a smile touched her lips. Watching Valya's widening eyes, Chris thought the guide was startled by the sight of their group rather than glad her guests had arrived.

Don't stop now. Keep reading with your copy of SOUL OF THE UNBORN by City Owl Author, Natalia Brothers.

And find more from Courtney Maguire at www. courtneymaguirewrites.com

Glossary of Japanese Terms

Aho – (Kansai dialect) idiot

Amado – exterior shutters made of solid wood to protect the home from elements or for security when the house is empty

Bakayaro – vulgar; stupid bastard

Bokken – wooden practice sword

Chabudai – small, short-legged table

-chan – familiar honorific often used for women, children, and people with a close relationship

Chikushou – curse similar to "son of a bitch" or "dammit"

Daimyo – feudal lord

Damare – vulgar; shut up

Domo arigatou gozaimashita – formal; thank you

-dono – honorific roughly translating to "lord" or "master"

Eboshi – tall formal cap made from silk or paper coated in black lacquer

Edo – Former name of Tokyo; castle town centered around Edo castle and the home of the shogun

Engawa – strip of wood flooring that runs around the outside of the house, similar to a porch; can be closed in using wooden shutters during bad weather or when the house is empty for security

Futon – traditional bedding that is laid out on the floor for sleeping and then rolled up and stored in a closet during the day

Fuzakeruna – vulgar; lit. "stop messing around." In this construction, the meaning is harsher, closer to "Fuck off!"

Geisha – lit. entertainer or artist

Genkan – entryway, traditionally where shoes are left upon entering the house

Geta – flat wooden sandal elevated off the ground by wooden prongs

-gumi – group

Hakama – a type of split skirt worn over the kimono and tied at the waist

Hajimemashite – nice to meet you

-han – (Kansai dialect) honorific; same as -san

Haori – hip- or thigh-length jacket worn over the kimono

Haori-himo – cord that holds the haori closed

Hikyaku – feudal Japanese version of the pony express; system of messengers that carried packages and correspondence on foot.

Hinoki – type of cypress; hinoki oil is often used in soaps and bath oils and has a calming effect

Hisashiburi – "long time no see"

Irrashai – a call of welcome said by shop workers to patrons as they enter their shop

Isseki nichou – idiom; one stone, two birds

Itai – ouch!

Izakaya – informal bar that serves drinks and snacks

Jinbei – matching top and trousers made of light material and worn as nightwear or house clothes

Kamidana – small Shinto altar

Kamishimo – sleeveless jacket with exaggerated shoulders worn by samurai and court officials as part of their formal costume

Kanzashi – elaborate hairpins

Katana – traditional sword of the samurai

Keigo – formal Japanese

Kikentai no ichi – idiom; sword, body, and soul are one

Kisouma – small, hardy horse traditionally used by samurai

Koi – decorative carp

-kun – honorific less polite than -san, used generally among men when addressing someone younger or of lower social status

Kuso – vulgar; shit

Kusogaki – vulgar; lit. "shit brat"

Mattaku – as an exclamation, "My goodness!"

Nagajuban – simple robe worn under a kimono

Naito-Shinjuku – post town located just outside Edo, now the modern day ward of Shinjuku, Tokyo

Natto – fermented soy beans

Ne – particle asking for agreement, similar to "right?" or "isn't it?"

Nihonshu – rice wine

O- – honorific attached to the front of a name or title for increased formality

Obi – wide belt worn around the waist over a kimono

Ofuro – bath

Oiran – high-ranking courtesan

Ojamashimasu – lit. "I will disturb you." Polite greeting used when entering a house

Okaasan/Okan – mother (Kansai dialect)

Okiya – combination house and drinking establishment that houses geisha

Okyakusama – formal; customer/guest

Omedetou – congratulations

O-nee/Oneesan – sister

Otsukaresama deshita – lit. "you are tired;" used to acknowledge someone's hard work

Ponto-cho – located in Hanamachi district in Kyoto, traditional home of geiko and maiko

Ranma – carved wood details found above doors and below ceilings

Ryo – denomination of money in the form of rectangular gold plates; value based roughly on a year's supply of rice

Sakura – cherry blossom

Samurai – military nobles and retainers of daimyo

Saya – sword sheath

Seiza – lit. "proper sitting;" posture while sitting on the knees with back straight

Shakuhachi – traditional Japanese flute

Shamisen – traditional three-stringed instrument

Shimabara – Kyoto geisha district

Shinai – bamboo practice sword

Shitsurei shimasu – lit. "excuse my interrupting;" can be used when entering or leaving a room or conversation

Shogun – hereditary military leaders

Shoji – Door or window made from a lattice frame covered with paper. Used as both walls and room dividers that can be opened or removed

Suzuri – flat grinding stone used to make ink

Taikomochi – lit. "drum carriers;" filled a similar role to court jesters and acted as both entertainers and military advisers

Takagari – hawking

Takatanobaba – archaic pronunciation of Takadanobaba; neighborhood in Shinjuku

Tatami – mats made from rice straw and rush used as flooring

Tekiya – predecessors to modern Yakuza

Tokonoma – alcove used to display art or flower arrangements

Tonsu – storage cabinet

Usotsuki – liar

Wakizashi – short sword

Yoroshiku – lit. "please treat me favorably"

Yotsuya Oukido – boundary gate used as a sort of check point for inspection of goods and horses

Youkai – "mysterious calamity;" used to refer to supernatural beings in Japanese folklore

Yukata – lit. "bathing clothes;" lightweight version of a kimono

Zaisu – basically a chair with no legs used on tatami floors

Want even more dark paranormal fantasy? Try SOUL OF THE UNBORN by City Owl Author, Natalia Brothers, and find more from Courtney Maguire at www.courtneymaguirewrites.com

One woman battles her own dark secrets—and the pull of her heart—in an award-winning supernatural thriller set in a mystical Russian village.

Posing as a folklore tour guide, Valya Svetlova takes a group of American college students and their professor, Chris Waller, to her summer home in the Russian village of Vishenky for a few nights of supernatural phenomena. She plays the perfect hostess, for Valya doesn't want anyone to discover she harbors selfish motives when it comes to one participant—the only person who can refute a tale declaring her a stillborn resurrected by a paranormal entity.

Her nascent feelings toward the handsome professor inhibit her ability to control the supernatural manifestations and her inquisitive guests. When her unforeseen affection turns Chris into a target, Valya faces an excruciating reality. It's no longer in her human power to ensure her guests' safety. Yet to keep them alive, Valya must brush off her humanity and become the thing she fights so desperately to prove she is not—a soulless monster.

Please sign up for the City Owl Press newsletter for chances to win special subscriber-only contests and giveaways as well as receiving information on upcoming releases and special excerpts.

All reviews are **welcome** and **appreciated**. Please consider leaving one on your favorite social media and book buying sites.

For books in the world of romance and speculative fiction that embody Innovation, Creativity, and Affordability, check out City Owl Press at www.cityowlpress.com.

Acknowledgments

There was a time when I thought I wouldn't even get to write one of these books and now I've written two. It is overwhelming when I really think about it. I wrote a series. I am now a series writer. Holy crap!

I first and foremost have to thank the readers. If you are here because you read Bloodlaced and chose to continue exploring this world, thank you from the bottom of my soul for your continued support. I have received so many kind messages from readers like you, and each one fills my heart to bursting. I hope this continuation meets your expectations. Thank you for being on this road with me, and I hope we meet again at the next stop.

Next I have to thank my beta readers, Heather Grossart and Jennifer Worrell. You have been a never-ending source of love and support for me from the very beginning, and I can't tell you enough how much I appreciate you. Your input has been instrumental in this series achieving its final form. I couldn't do it without you.

A loud, resounding thank you to the team at City Owl Press. Thank you to the cover artist who designed the covers for both Bloodlaced and Blood Pact. I can't get over how good they look together. You really knocked it out of the park. Thank you to my editor, Heather McCorkle, who keeps me on track. I can always count on you to give great advice and push me to bring my books to the next level. And thank you to Tina Moss who is a wonderful team leader and a voice of encouragement to all City Owl authors.

Last but certainly not least, I want to thank the people who really allow people like me to do what we love and keep this crazy ship running: book bloggers and reviewers. So many do an incredible amount of work often for no pay beyond the books they receive. They are invaluable, a crucial piece of the publishing puzzle, and we don't acknowledge them enough.

About the Author

COURTNEY MAGUIRE is a University of Texas graduate from Corpus Christi, Texas. Drawn to Austin by a voracious appetite for music, she spent most of her young adult life in dark, divey venues nursing a love for the sublimely weird. A self-proclaimed fangirl with a press pass, she combined her love of music and writing as the primary contributor for Japanese music and culture blog, Project: Lixx, interviewing Japanese rock and roll icons and providing live event coverage for appearances across the country.

www.courtneymaguirewrites.com

 twitter.com/PretentiousAho

 instagram.com/courtneymaguirewrites

 facebook.com/CourtneyMaguireWrites

About the Publisher

City Owl Press is a cutting edge indie publishing company, bringing the world of romance and speculative fiction to discerning readers.

Escape Your World. Get Lost in Ours!

www.cityowlpress.com

 facebook.com/YourCityOwlPress

 twitter.com/cityowlpress

 instagram.com/cityowlbooks

 pinterest.com/cityowlpress